CLAWS OF ACTION

The Cat Lady Mystery Series by Linda Reilly

Escape Claws

Claws of Death

Claws for Celebration

Claws of Action

CLAWS OF ACTION

A Cat Lady Mystery

Linda Reilly

LYRICAL UNDERGROUND
Kensington Publishing Corp.
www.kensingtonbooks.com

LYRICAL UNDERGROUND BOOKS are published by

Kensington Publishing Corp.
119 West 40th Street
New York, NY 10018

All Kensington titles, imprints, and distributed lines are available at special quantity discounts for bulk purchases for sales promotion, premiums, fund-raising, educational, or institutional use.

Special book excerpts or customized printings can also be created to fit specific needs. For details, write or phone the office of the Kensington Sales Manager: Kensington Publishing Corp., 119 West 40th Street, New York, NY 10018. Attn. Sales Department. Phone: 1-800-221-2647.

Lyrical Underground and Lyrical Underground logo Reg. US Pat. & TM Off.

First Electronic Edition: August 2019
eISBN-13: 978-1-5161-0985-2
eISBN-10: 1-5161-0985-6

First Print Edition: August 2019
ISBN-13: 978-1-5161-0987-6
ISBN-10: 1-5161-0987-2

Printed in the United States of America

For my husband, Bernie,
for lighting my path all the way

Cast of Feline Characters

Twinkles: An aging, orange-striped tiger cat with big gold eyes, his favorite spots to snooze are in Aunt Fran's bedroom.

Munster: This easygoing, orange-striped male, the unofficial greeter of all human visitors, is a favorite of the kids on "read to a cat" Sundays.

Dolce: Long-haired, solid black, and as sweet as a bowl of strawberry shortcake, he's found his permanent cozy spot curled up in Aunt Fran's lap.

Snowball: This pure white sweetheart with one blue eye and one green has yet to find her *fur*ever home. Will her newfound bond with a temporary boarder give her a fresh outlook on life?

Pearl: An all-gray beauty with huge double paws, she's fond of getting into mischief with her brother, Orca.

Orca: A handsome black-and-white boy with a white chest and white double paws, he manages to wreak occasional havoc with his sneaky, fun-loving sister.

Smuggles: This elderly gray gent is only a temporary resident, but he's found his soul mate in the lovable Snowball. Will he end up a permanent resident at the shelter? It all depends on whether his dad is found guilty of a diabolical murder...

Blue: This fluffy Ragdoll cat that only Lara can see has an uncanny knack for pointing out clues that lead her to murderers. Now that Blue's secret has been revealed to a trusted few, will she still be there when Lara needs her most?

The Kittens: Found abandoned behind a bakery, these four darlings are the shelter's newest bundles of joy—a golden fluffball named Fritter, a black-and-white sweetheart named Aden, and two other babies whose names are up for grabs!

Chapter One

Lara Caphart could hardly believe it. The official reading room of the High Cliff Shelter for Cats was completed.

She swung the new storm door back and forth, then pushed it closed. It clicked into place with a soft snap. "Perfect," she proclaimed. "I know it sounds silly, but I am so thrilled with this door!"

One chunky hand resting on his hip, Charlie Backstrom—the contractor who'd built the cat shelter's addition—stood back and inspected his work. "Looks good," he agreed. "Now remember, when the cold weather gets here, you gotta lower the screen and—"

"You're repeating yourself, honey," Nina Backstrom said, slipping her arm through her husband's. "You've shown Lara three times now, how to lower the screen and pull up the glass pane."

"Hey, that's okay," Lara said lightly. "It never hurts to get a refresher, right?"

Charlie, handsome in a rugged sort of way, with melt-in-your-mouth brown eyes, smiled at his wife and kissed her cheek. He winked at Lara. "Wives. What would we do without them?"

Nina feigned a scowl. "Oh, I'm guessing you'd be living on frozen dinners and cardboard pizza and watching sports on TV every night."

"Instead of those scintillating mysteries you're always trying to get me to watch?" He quirked a smile at her. They both looked at Lara.

Lara held up both hands. "Don't look at me. I'm not getting in the middle of that one."

Charlie and Nina, who were both around thirty, were one of the sweetest couples Lara had ever met. They teased each other a lot, but the banter was always good-natured—at least it seemed to be. Perpetually outfitted in a gray work shirt and blue, knee-length cargo shorts, Charlie was a total contrast to his petite wife. Today Nina wore a stylish, pale-pink jersey top over white cotton shorts, a flowered bathing suit peeking out over the jersey's neckline. Beneath her strawberry-blond bob was a sharp head for numbers. She acted as financial guru—and organizational genius—for the business, while Charlie performed the labor and hired the subs. He walked with a slight limp, which he jokingly referred to as an old football injury.

"So, what do you think?" Nina said. "Are we done?"

Lara looked all around the new room and felt her smile widening. "Yes, I think we are. It's been a long haul, but now that I see the finished product, it was all worth it."

On Saturday, she and her aunt were having a grand opening for a few close friends. The following day would be the first official "read to a cat" day in the new room.

The idea for the addition had sprung from a little girl who'd tried to sneak into the shelter one day, book in hand, determined to read to a cat. After a bit of research, Lara had discovered that several other shelters in New Hampshire had "read to a cat" days.

With the help of their part-time shelter assistant, Kayla Ramirez, Lara had set up a similar program. It gained popularity more quickly than they'd anticipated, but they had only one problem: space. Aunt Fran's Folk Victorian home was the entire shelter, the small back porch having been transformed into the "meet-and-greet" room. In that room, cats and prospective adopters made permanent matches, some of which seemed almost magical.

Earlier in the year, Lara and her aunt had made the decision to add the room to the rear of the house, adjacent to the back porch. A local architect designed the plans, and Lara hired Charlie Backstrom to oversee the project. He used subcontractors when needed but did most of the work himself. A master carpenter, he'd built custom shelves with adjustable tiers for the children's books.

He'd pulled off a near miracle, completing the project by the date specified in the contract. Over the course of the construction, which had dragged on for nearly four months, one thing after another went wrong. A pipe burst in the new bathroom, the floor tiles had been damaged in shipping, and a large shrub in Aunt Fran's yard had to be uprooted because the building specs hadn't accounted for it.

To save money and to speed things up, Lara had done a lot of the painting herself. She'd even finished the bathroom ceiling—no easy task. Despite the problems, Charlie's work was impeccable. He performed every task to perfection, even if he had to do it over three times.

Lara was anxious for Aunt Fran to return from her lunch date with Jerry Whitley, Whisker Jog's chief of police. Lara wanted to surprise her aunt with the custom-made door. When the oversize box arrived two days earlier, she'd rested it against the wall and warned her aunt not to open it or try to peek.

"Lara," Nina asked, "where on earth did you ever find a storm door with a cat on it?"

The new storm door, made from sturdy aluminum, bore the shape of a cat in the center. It was a splurge, but Lara couldn't resist spending a bit extra for it. She knew Aunt Fran would love it. Thanks to a few hefty donations from generous sponsors, the cost hadn't broken the budget.

"I scoured the internet and found a manufacturer that made custom designs," Lara explained. "Luckily, they were able to make a cat."

"Do you mind giving me the company's name?" Nina asked. "I'd like to check them out and refer our customers there, if that's okay."

"Sure," Lara said, and gave her the name. "It'll come right up if you Google it," she added.

Nina pulled her phone out of her pocket. "I'll add it to my notes. Thanks, Lara." She tapped her phone a few times, then slipped it back into her pocket and rubbed her hands together. "Now, before Charlie and I head out to White Lake for an afternoon swim, may I take advantage of your hospitality and play with a few of the cats?" She wiggled her fingers. "I need a cat fix."

Charlie rolled his eyes. "Here we go."

"Oh, be good." Nina swatted his arm lightly with her fingertips.

Charlie stayed behind to fiddle further with the door as Lara led Nina through the kitchen toward the large parlor. On the way, she noticed the red message light blinking on the shelter's landline.

Nina followed her gaze. "Do you need to check that?"

"No, I'll check it later." She held out a hand toward the large parlor, where a carpeted cat tree rested in front of the picture window. Nina went ahead of her into the room.

Orca and Pearl, their newest arrivals, had planted themselves on separate levels of the cat tree. The two were siblings, each with forepaws the size of catchers' mitts. Orca was long-haired and black, with four white feet, while Pearl was silky soft and pure gray. Lara called them "double trouble" because of their feline antics. What one didn't think of, the other did. Orca had been known to distract Lara by kneading her shoulder and purring in her ear, while his sneaky sister batted all the trinkets and lip-gloss tubes off her bureau. Lara now kept her possessions tucked safely away in drawers, out of reach of their huge paws.

From his perch, Orca leaned over the edge and batted at Pearl with one gigantic paw. Pearl swiped at him with her own paw as if he were a furry toy.

"Oh my gosh, those two are so cute. And those paws—they're so big!" Nina cooed.

"They're polydactyl cats," Lara explained. "Instead of five toes on each forepaw, they have six."

Nina gazed at them, her pale-green eyes lighting up. "Do you think the gray one will let me hold him?"

"That's Pearl, and she's a girl," Lara said. "I'm sure she will. She's very lovable."

Nina stooped and held out her hands to the gray kitty. Pearl leaned into her, and Nina swept her into her arms. Pearl purred into her ear, and a wistful look crossed Nina's face. "Oh, you're so sweet. I sure wish I could take you home."

"Charlie's not big on cats, is he?" Lara asked her. She'd sensed that when he was working on the addition. Even Munster's attempts at bonding with the contractor had been soundly, if gently, rebuffed.

Nina shook her head. "Don't remind me."

She hugged Pearl for a while, and then sighed and released her to the floor. Snowball padded over and brushed against Nina's arm. Nina laughed and tickled the white fur between the kitty's ears. She straightened. "I'd better be going. I'm sure Charlie's getting—"

The jingle of the front doorbell interrupted her.

Lara shrugged and looked at Nina. "Will you excuse me a minute? I have no idea who that is. We're not expecting anyone."

Nina stepped away to one side. Lara opened the door to find a scowling, fiftysomething woman standing on the top step.

"Hello. May I help you?"

The woman, tall with stringy blond waves that brushed her shoulders, held up a clipboard thick with papers. She wore the expression of someone who'd just stepped in a wad of bubble gum and couldn't get it off her shoe—or, in this case, her bright red sneaker. Around her neck she sported a chain from which a large pendant dangled, a blackbird with a jeweled eye perched on a golden branch.

"Are you Miss Caphart or Mrs. Clarkson?" she said brusquely.

The woman's tone was so rude that for a moment, Lara had to stop and think. "I'm Lara Caphart. What can I do for you?"

"I'm Evonda Fray. I'm the health inspector."

Lara hoped her face didn't register the shock she felt. "Um, health inspector?"

The woman heaved a sigh, as if she were tired of explaining herself to dolts. "Yes, health inspector. Surely you've heard of them. They protect the public from unclean environments?"

A wave of ire rose in Lara's chest. Was she implying that the shelter wasn't clean? And why was she here in the first place?

Lara took in a calming breath. She tried to think why a health inspector would show up, unannounced, at the shelter, but nothing came to mind. Had Aunt Fran made an appointment with the woman and forgotten to tell Lara? Not likely. Aunt Fran was too efficient to let something like that slip.

"I'm sorry," Lara said, attempting to soften her tone. "I…we weren't expecting you. Did you make an appointment with my aunt?"

Evonda Fray barked out a laugh. "Health inspectors don't make appointments, Miss Caphart. You ought to know that."

Maybe she should have, but she didn't. Even in her days working part-time in a Boston bakery, she couldn't recall a health inspector making a surprise visit.

Lara suddenly remembered that Nina was there. "Ms. Fray, you'll have to excuse me for a moment. I have guests and I need to explain the interruption."

"It's *Mrs.* Fray," she snapped. "I'd appreciate you addressing me properly."

Oh, if only, Lara thought.

She nodded and turned toward Nina, but she had already ducked out. Lara strode off and went back to the new reading room. Charlie and Nina were still there, whispering in low tones. It looked as if they were preparing to leave.

"Nina, Charlie…I'm so sorry about the interruption. The health inspector showed up without warning."

Charlie absently picked a piece of lint off the arm of Nina's pink jersey. "Health inspector? Whoa. Major bummer," Charlie said. He waved a hand around the room, then his face relaxed. "Hey, look, I wouldn't worry. This whole place is spotless. You guys keep it so clean…"

"I know. We do. But—"

Nina reached over and hugged Lara. "We'll get out of your way. You've got enough to deal with right now. And give Fran our regards, okay?"

Lara swallowed. "I will," she said glumly.

"We drove Nina's car today," Charlie said, "but I'll come back tomorrow with my truck and get rid of that big box the screen door came in. I leaned it against the back of the house, so it won't be in your way. Oh, and one more thing. I noticed that the storm door has a slight gap at the bottom. When I come back, I'll add some weather-stripping."

"Thanks, Charlie. That would be great. We have a permit for the recycling station, but that humongous box will never fit in the Saturn. You're both coming to the open house on Saturday, right?"

"We wouldn't miss it," Nina assured her.

With her aunt away and the Backstroms leaving, Lara didn't look forward to being alone with General Evonda. Gideon had planned to stop over with BLT wraps from the coffee shop when he got a break, but he must have gotten tied up at the office.

She almost begged Charlie and Nina to stay, but then thought better of it. They'd driven Nina's car here instead of Charlie's truck so they could head directly to White Lake after the door was installed. They deserved a break and were looking forward to an afternoon of relaxation.

Besides, she and Aunt Fran had nothing to hide. She could handle Inspector Red Sneakers.

She'd dealt with worse.

Much worse.

Chapter Two

Stomach in her throat, Lara returned to the large parlor. The inspector scribbled furiously on her clipboard, her red-ink scratches getting larger with each entry. Outside, a car door slammed. Lara's gaze darted to the front window. Relief flooded her.

Aunt Fran was home.

The chief had just dropped her off and was already easing his car out of the driveway. Lara heard the door to the kitchen open and close. "I'm back, Lara," her aunt called out.

Seconds later, her aunt emerged into the large parlor from the kitchen. Lara prayed her aunt would pick up on her worried vibe. "Aunt Fran, this is Mrs. Fray, the health inspector," she said in a flat voice.

Aunt Fran, her cheeks rosy, her hair fluffed back from her face in soft waves, put on her brightest smile. For a woman in her late fifties, she had youthful skin and sparkling green eyes. She'd always reminded Lara of the way the actress Audrey Hepburn looked in her later years.

"Mrs. Fray, it's a pleasure to meet you," Aunt Fran said in the kindest of tones. "I'm Fran Clarkson, Lara's aunt. We operate the shelter together. Can we get you anything? A cold drink?"

Evonda smirked. "Seriously? You're already trying to bribe me?"

Every muscle in Lara's body tensed. Something told her this inspection was not going to go smoothly. Fortunately, her aunt piped in before she could utter the reply that was dancing on the tip of her tongue.

"Mrs. Fray," Aunt Fran said courteously, "I only offered you something because it's quite hot out today and I thought you might be thirsty. If that's not the case, please forgive me for being presumptuous."

For a moment, the inspector looked taken aback. Lara suspected she wasn't accustomed to being spoken to so directly. Evonda gave Aunt Fran a brisk nod, her mouth turned down in an almost cartoonish scowl. If Lara were to sketch the curve of her lips, they would look exactly like an upside-down U.

Evonda stood there and glanced around for what seemed an eternity. Finally, she jammed her pen over her clipboard. "All right. Now show me the cages. Where do you keep the cats?" She uttered the word "cats" as if it began with an "r" instead of a "c."

"Mrs. Fray," Aunt Fran said, "this is not a traditional shelter. It's a family shelter, with only a limited number of cats. We don't have cages because we don't need them. We have an open concept here. The cats have free range."

It was a spiel Aunt Fran had related to visitors many times. Nonetheless, it irritated Lara that they should have to defend their shelter at all.

Evonda opened her mouth wide enough for a bat to fly in. "You don't have cages? How many cats live here?"

"Right now, we have six," Aunt Fran said, with a surreptitious wink at Lara. "But we've had as many as twelve."

Lara smothered a smile. She knew Aunt Fran was thinking of Blue, the Ragdoll cat that only Lara could see. Technically, with Blue, they had seven.

She racked her brain, trying to picture where all the cats might be at that moment. It was close to one o'clock—catnap time for most of the resident felines. *Thank heavens*, Lara thought, murmuring a silent prayer.

Orca and Pearl had fled their perches at the sound of Evonda's grating voice. They were probably upstairs playing tumbleweed on Lara's chenille bedspread. Dolce and Twinkles, who were best buds, typically dozed atop Aunt Fran's bed during the daylight hours. Munster was a wanderer, always on alert to greet someone at the sound of a new voice. He hadn't made an appearance yet, which was odd. Had he already sensed that an enemy had barged into their midst?

Snowball was a lovebug, always wanting to chill with a human. She sat on the sofa, her tail switching with agitation as she regarded Evonda with one green eye and one blue. Her white fur stood slightly on end—a sure sign of stress. A clump of it stuck to the tapestry pillow that rested against the arm of the sofa. Lara made a note in her head to give Snowball a good brushing after the inspector had gone.

Evonda shot a look at the white cat. For a single moment, Lara thought Evonda's gaze softened. Then her voice cut through her like a hatchet. "I'll start with the kitchen," she announced.

Lara nodded. "Follow me."

Evonda trooped behind Lara into the kitchen, while Aunt Fran stayed behind, probably to ward off any feline invasions.

In the kitchen, Lara felt her mouth go dry. The inspector poked and prodded every possible corner and cranny. She even ran the faucet in the sink and opened the door to the freezer, which Lara felt was far beyond the limits of her authority. She still wasn't sure why the woman was here. Nonetheless, Lara bit her tongue, praying Evonda would leave them alone after she was through.

Evonda wrinkled her nose and frowned. "It smells in here."

Stay calm, Lara cautioned herself. She smiled at the inspector. "Yes, it does, doesn't it? It's that wonderful new lemon-scented cleaner we're using. Smells so fresh."

Evonda deadpanned her but didn't respond. After making more red scratches on her clipboard, she demanded to see the rest of the house. She swept her ruthless gaze over every room, while Lara stood by and fumed.

Orca and Pearl must have sensed that they were under some sort of uninvited scrutiny. They huddled together on Lara's bed, quieter than she'd ever seen them.

Twenty minutes later, Lara felt as if she'd been squeezed through a laundry wringer and then run through a clothes dryer. She was hot, sweaty, and more than a little annoyed. Oddly, the inspector hadn't even asked to see the meet-and-greet room—the place where people and cats were introduced to one another. What kind of an inspector was she?

They all reconvened in the large parlor.

"Miss Caphart, Mrs. Clarkson, I'll make this short and sweet—well, maybe not so sweet. I'm going to cite you both for running a cat café without a license."

"Wait a minute. *What?*" Lara sputtered. "We don't run a cat café! What gave you that idea?"

"Mrs. Fray, that is totally incorrect," Aunt Fran said tightly, coming over to stand next to Lara. "We do not sell food or drink here. We never have, and we never will. Our function is to match people with cats. Period."

Evonda sneered at her. "These people who get matched up with cats—do they *pay* for such a privilege?"

"No, they do not," Lara said. "They pay an adoption fee, but only if they apply to adopt a cat and their application is approved. We couldn't operate this shelter if we didn't have the funds to care for the cats, which includes top-quality veterinary care."

"So, you admit it, then," Evonda said, a jubilant gleam in her eye. "Money *does* change hands."

A sick feeling wended its way through Lara. It didn't matter what she said or how she responded. Evonda Fray would twist every word and use it to her own advantage.

Lara started to craft a retort, but the inspector held up a hand. "Before you both start yammering at me, be aware that I've already spoken to several people who've adopted from this shelter. They all confirmed that drinks and cookies were served to them in your so-called meet-and-greet room."

"Served, but not sold," Lara protested. "And you never even looked in that room. If you did, you'd know we keep it spotless."

Ignoring her, Evonda went on, tsking under her breath. "Very unsanitary. Giving people cookies with all that cat hair and God knows what else flying around. I'm surprised someone hasn't picked up a disease."

Lara felt as if she'd stumbled into an alternate universe. What on earth was she talking about? Every cat owner ate in the same house with their cats. Why would eating a cookie in the meet-and-greet room be any different?

Aunt Fran moved closer to the inspector. Lara noticed that her aunt's fingers had curled into fists. "Mrs. Fray, we will not stand for this. This is harassment, pure and simple. If you cite us for operating a cat café, I assure you that we will take you to court. You'll have to explain yourself to a judge, and quite frankly, you don't have a leg to stand on."

Only a giant red sneaker, Lara thought uncharitably.

Evonda grinned. "Go ahead," she said. "That would truly make my day. In the meantime, I'm giving you twenty-four-hours' notice to cease and desist. I'll be stopping by in the morning with your official order."

"You can't do that," Lara said, feeling her blood rise to the boiling point.

After a final glance at Snowball, Evonda winked at her. "Oh yeah? Watch me. I'm shutting you people down."

Chapter Three

Lara stood at the front window seething as she watched Evonda's red Camry back out of the driveway. The Camry's wheels spun far too fast for this quiet residential street. She wished the chief had been here to witness it.

"Well, that couldn't have gone any worse," she told her aunt. "Do you think she'll really shut us down? Can she do that?"

Aunt Fran's eyebrows dipped into a deep V. "I'm not sure, Lara. We're going to need some legal advice on this. I certainly didn't expect the woman to get so…combative."

"That's one word to describe her. I can think of a bunch of others."

Lara went over to the sofa and scooped Snowball into her arms. She dropped down and snugged the cat under her neck. "Know what I think? I think she knew before she even got here that she was going to issue that order. It's like she had it in for us from the get-go."

"I had that feeling, too," Aunt Fran admitted. "Still, let's try not to read too much into it. We've learned the hard way that making assumptions is never wise."

A text pinged on Lara's cell, which was tucked in the pocket of her shorts. "Oh, thank heavens. It's Gideon," she said, reading it. "He's on his way over with our lunch." She thumbed a quick response and stuck the phone back in her pocket.

Aunt Fran's face relaxed a bit. "Good. Maybe he can help us sort this out."

"Uh-oh. I just remembered. There's a message on the shelter's landline I never got a chance to play."

She also hadn't gotten a chance to surprise her aunt with the new door. The health inspector had swept in first and sent them both into a tizzy.

Propping Snowball on her shoulder, Lara went into the kitchen. She started to press the Play button on the answering machine when a familiar—and welcome—voice sounded from the doorway.

"Hey, everyone. I come bearing food." Gideon stepped into the kitchen holding a large paper bag.

"That was fast."

He grinned. "I was in the driveway when I texted."

Lara ran over, threw her arms around his neck, and hugged him. "We're so glad you're here. We've got problems, big ones, and we need your advice."

"Uh, can I put the sandwiches down first?"

"Of course." Lara chuckled. "I'm sorry. I didn't mean to lunge at you like that." She took the bag from his hand and set it on the kitchen table. "It's just…oh, we've had an awful day."

His face creased in concern. "Are you okay, honey?"

"I'm fine. I'm not sure about the shelter, though."

Aunt Fran came in, and Gideon greeted her with a kiss on the cheek. "I'll get some plates and some iced tea for you two," she said. "Sit. Eat your lunch."

Gideon pulled two paper-wrapped sandwiches from the bag, along with a large bag of kettle chips. "Two BLTs on tomato-basil wraps, one with provolone."

Lara smiled. "You remembered my cheese."

"Of course! Now tell me what's happening."

While they ate, Lara and Aunt Fran related the events of Evonda Fray's so-called inspection. Gideon listened thoughtfully, interrupting only with an occasional "hmmm" or an "oh boy."

When they were through, Lara took a deep breath. She'd barely touched her BLT. The tiny bit she'd consumed sat like lead in her stomach.

"You should have seen her face when she was leaving," Lara said, crumpling her napkin. "It was like…like she'd triumphed over some evil enemy and was getting ready to reap the spoils."

Aunt Fran looked pained. "I hate to say it, but Lara's right. The woman clearly enjoyed lording it over us. I don't think I've ever met anyone so cantankerous."

Lara looked over at Gideon. "She can't shut us down, can she? Please tell me she can't."

Gideon's face turned serious, and he leaned forward. He'd eaten his entire wrap, save a few stray pieces of lettuce. "First of all, you said she used the phrase 'cease and desist,' but she didn't say from what. That sounds to me like she was hedging. Did she mean cease and desist from operating the shelter? Or just from serving food on adoption days?"

"How can we know?" Aunt Fran said. "She didn't specify, but she did say she was going to shut us down." She looked at Lara. "After that, it got a bit…contentious, I guess you'd say. She left looking like a cat who'd swallowed a whole pint of cream."

"Please, don't compare that woman to a cat," Lara begged. "She's more like a…a…monitor lizard, or a troll."

Gideon looked pensive as he took everything in. He sat back and crossed his arms over his chest. "All right, at this point here's what I'm guessing. I think Mrs. Fray felt unsure about the limits of her authority. She had to know you already had a license to operate the shelter. I'm sure she reviewed it at the town hall before she came here. That might be the reason why her threat, for lack of a better term, was somewhat hazy."

Lara sagged in her chair. "So, what do we do now? Just wait for the other shoe to drop?"

Gideon tapped his fingers on the table. "Lara, can you bring me your iPad? I want to check something in the statutes."

"You bet."

She left the kitchen and returned a minute later with her tablet.

Gideon set it down in front of him. "Give me a few, okay?" he said, tapping his fingers over the keys.

"Sure. I'll clean up the table." Lara wrapped up her barely eaten BLT and tidied up Gideon's area.

"You hardly ate a thing," Aunt Fran said to Lara.

"I know, I'm sorry. My appetite sort of ditched me, thinking about that inspector."

"Okay, here's what I was looking for," Gideon said. "This is from Chapter 143-A, Section 3, which defines food service establishments. I won't read the whole thing, but one of the definitions of a food service establishment is 'a private or public organization or institution, whether profit or nonprofit, which routinely serves food.'"

Lara blinked. "Are you saying our shelter falls into that category?"

"Well, now, that's the question, isn't it?" Gideon said.

"Please, Gid. Don't go all lawyer-y on us. We just need to know if we've been doing anything wrong."

"Honey, I understand, but bear with me for a moment. If you analyze that definition"—he held up a hand and ticked off the points on his fingers—"the shelter *is* a private institution, and it *is* a nonprofit." He paused.

Lara felt her blood pounding in her ears. "Go on."

"The question we need to answer is, does it routinely serve food?"

Lara pondered his question. When she and Aunt Fran had first opened the shelter, they felt strongly about offering refreshments to prospective adopters. It gave people a sense of how they might interact with a cat in their own homes, especially if they were about to be first-time cat owners. It also eliminated the guilt some people felt at a traditional shelter, where furry faces stared out at them from behind the bars of steel cages. At High Cliff, the cats had the run of the house. If they were passed over for adoption, they continued to lead contented lives in an environment filled with love.

At last, Lara said, "Well, we routinely supply cookies and liquid refreshments—nonalcoholic, of course—to anyone who visits on adoption days. Only if they want it, though. Lots of people refuse refreshments. They just want to meet the cats."

Gideon nodded slowly. Lara could almost see the gears turning inside his brain.

"I'm sorry, but I'm really getting frustrated here. Are we violating the law or are we not? That's all we want to know."

He blew out a breath and folded his hands in front of him on the table. "Honey, I'm not trying to be evasive, but the law isn't black or white. Most areas of the law are like an amorphous gray blob, able to change shape with each individual interpretation. That's why we have judges—to interpret the law. As you can probably guess, no judge ever interprets the law exactly the same way."

Lara dropped her head into her hands and rubbed her eyes. Snowball chose that moment to climb onto her lap and issue a muted purr. Lara pulled the cat close, unable to suppress a smile. Cats always knew when their humans needed that special feline touch.

"Gideon," Aunt Fran said quietly, "what do you suggest we do now?"

"You said Mrs. Fray was going to drop by in the morning with her cease-and-desist order. Let's wait to see what it says. Who knows? She might even change her mind before then. Once she's had a chance to think about it, she might soften her position. Maybe she'll realize she was just being a jerk."

"I can't imagine that happening," Lara said evenly. "There is nothing about the woman that's soft. She's hard-hearted and hardheaded. One thing I'm sure of: the milk of human kindness does not flow through her veins."

"Lara, we don't really know that," Aunt Fran put in, her tone a mild rebuke. "We don't know enough about her to make that judgment."

Lara thought about that. "Then I intend to find out more about her."

As soon as she had a chance, Lara was going to Google the name Evonda Fray and find out as much as she could about the woman. Luckily, it was an uncommon name. At least she hoped it was. It shouldn't be all that hard to find the one she was looking for. What did Fray do before she was the health inspector? How was it they'd never heard of her before?

"Gideon, do you know anything about Mrs. Fray?" Aunt Fran asked.

Lara made a face. "You read my mind."

Gideon looked troubled by the question. "Not very much, but I do know that she replaced Trevor Johnson, who was fired about a month ago. He'd been the health inspector for almost six years. A buddy of mine, a fellow lawyer, was approached by Johnson in the hope that he could represent him in a suit against the town. My friend turned him down because of a conflict of interest."

"Trevor Johnson. That's a familiar name," Aunt Fran said.

"You might have read about him in the paper," Gideon said. "Apparently, a few complaints had come in about him. He wasn't doing his job, he was letting things slide, vague accusations like that. Unfortunately, he was also caught accepting a substantial gift card to a certain establishment in lieu of, shall we say, a more thorough inspection of their kitchen."

"Oh my gosh," Lara said. "What a dopey thing to do. Jeopardizing his job for a gift card."

"Yeah, but Johnson claimed the restaurant owner gave it to him as a birthday gift for his mother. He didn't see it as a bribe at all, even though, technically, it violated the rules. As for Evonda Fray…" He paused.

"What?" Lara prodded.

"Supposedly, she was the one who put the final nail in his coffin—so to speak, that is. She took a photo of him chatting privately with the owner of a certain popular eatery—this is a different one, now—right here in town. Fray claimed she caught them near the dumpster behind the restaurant, and that she saw an envelope change hands."

"She spied on him," Lara said, disgusted.

"Maybe, Lara. But if he was accepting bribes, he was breaking the law."

"Did he tell you which restaurant it was?"

Gideon looked grim. "He said to me, in so many words, 'you don't want to know.' I left it at that."

Lara thought about that. It wasn't as if Whisker Jog was chockablock with eating places. "But don't you think it's odd that after squealing on the guy, Evonda suddenly becomes the new health inspector?"

Gideon shrugged. "Hard to say. I don't know enough about it to make that call." He rose from his chair and went over to Lara. He bent over and hugged her close. "Listen, honey, if she tries to close the shelter, and I doubt she will, we'll fight it every step of the way. We'll go to court and file a cause of action. The way I see it, the most she can do is to prevent you from serving refreshments, but we'll fight that, too. She can't interfere with the work you're both doing here. You have a license for that."

Lara pressed her head against his chest, then breathed out a sigh of relief. "Thanks, and I'm sorry if I sniped at you. I'm just superfrustrated with all this."

"You didn't snipe." He pushed back a strand of her copper-colored hair and tucked it behind her ear. "You're understandably upset. I sure as heck don't blame you for being angry."

Aunt Fran excused herself. Lara sensed she wanted to allow them a private moment, but then the doorbell rang.

Lara jumped visibly, and Snowball squeaked. "Oh, no. Please tell me she didn't come back to harass us."

"Would you like me to answer the door?" Gideon offered.

Aunt Fran hesitated, but Lara nodded. "If you wouldn't mind."

Gideon squeezed Lara's shoulder, then left to answer the front doorbell. Moments later, the sound of voices drifted into the kitchen—Gideon's and another male voice. Lara perked her ears to listen, but she couldn't make out what they were saying.

When she heard the front door close, she expected Gideon to return. He didn't, so she set Snowball on her kitchen chair and went into the large parlor to peek out the front window.

Gideon was in the driveway, standing next to a dark-green SUV. A man who looked to be in his thirties stood in front of the driver's door, a pet carrier clasped in one hand. He wore Bermuda shorts and a navy tee, his high-topped sneakers rising to meet a pair of extremely hairy legs. A deep frown was etched on his full face.

Lara bounded down the front steps to check out the visitor.

The man nodded a greeting, and Gideon said, "Lara, this is Brian... Downing, is it?"

"That's right. I tried to call the shelter earlier, a couple of times, but I never got a return call."

"I'm sorry. I had visitors pretty much all morning. I never got a chance to play our messages. I'm Lara, one of the shelter's owners."

"Nice to meet you, Lara. Could we maybe talk somewhere? Someplace where it's cooler?" He glanced down at his pet carrier.

Lara hesitated to invite him into the house. She was still feeling the burn from Evonda Fray's dreadful visit, and she didn't know this man at all. Gideon obviously hadn't met him before either.

"Maybe we can sit on the back porch?" Gideon suggested.

Thank you, Gideon.

"That would be perfect." Lara peeked into the pet carrier. "I see you have a cat with you."

"Yeah," Brian said. "That's my Smuggles. I'll tell you about him when we get inside. I don't want the poor guy to overheat. It's hotter than blazes out here."

They walked around to the other side of the house, where the official door to the shelter led into the meet-and-greet room. Brian set down the carrier and they sat at the table.

"So, what's this about, Mr. Downing?" Lara said.

"It's Brian, okay? If you call me Mr. Downing I won't know who you're talking to."

Lara chuckled. "Fair enough. Would you like to give Snuggles a break and take him out of the carrier?"

"Thanks. That a good idea." Brian unzipped his pet carrier—a fancy-looking affair with a padded pillow inside—and lifted out a chubby, gray tiger cat. The kitty settled down comfortably in his lap.

"By the way, it's Smuggles, with an 'm.' When I first got him, he wasn't used to having regular meals. He'd smuggle bits of kibble from his bowl and hide them in his bed." Brian swallowed, and Lara saw that he was getting emotional. "He doesn't do it anymore. He knows I'd never let him go hungry."

Lara reached over and scratched the kitty under the chin. "Brian, what is it you called us about this morning?"

"Two things. First off, I have a favor to ask. Secondly, the reason I called was to warn you about my landlady. I overheard her on her cell phone this morning after she showed up, unannounced, at my apartment. She was talking to someone about this place—I distinctly heard her say 'High Cliff Shelter.' I wanted to warn you, in case there was something you could do to head her off at the pass."

Gideon, who normally had the patience of St. Francis of Assisi, made a time-out sign with his hands. "Brian, go back to the beginning. Why don't you start by telling us who your landlady is?"

Lara had a sinking feeling she knew the answer.

"Yeah, sorry. I'm jumping all over the place." He huffed out an exasperated sigh. "I live in Moultonborough, in a three-story apartment building. My landlady's name is Evonda Fray. She lives here in Whisker Jog."

A feeling like an icy fist clamped Lara's insides. She looked over at Gideon, who maintained a poker face. "Evonda Fray is your landlady?"

"Yeah, unfortunately. She's a real horror, meanest piece of work you ever met. My lease says I can have one cat. I even put down a pet deposit—two hundred bucks—even though Smuggles doesn't do anything but sleep all day. He's an elderly kitty. My vet thinks he's twelve or thirteen."

Lara could guess where this was going. "Is she trying to renege on her agreement?"

He nodded. "Yup, you guessed it. See, she wasn't the original landlord. She bought the apartment house a few months ago from the nice old guy who owned it. He didn't want to deal with the upkeep anymore. She got herself a heckuva deal, too. He should have held out for more, but he just wanted to unload the place. He's sick—on his way out, if you get my meaning."

"I can understand his reasoning," Lara said. "He probably didn't want to saddle his family with having to sell his property after he, you know…"

"Yeah, I got that, too. But here's the problem. Evonda is claiming that my cat is scratching the paint on the walls and wrecking the place. It's not true. Smuggles doesn't scratch much of anything anymore. He pretty much sleeps all the time."

"Brian," Gideon prompted, using his most encouraging tone. "You said you heard her talking on the phone about the shelter."

He blinked. "Yeah, I did. I heard her say something like 'I'm gonna give those cat hoarders a run for their money' and 'Wait till they get a load of Hurricane Evonda.' And then she laughed—actually cackled, like a witch! It was like she couldn't wait to inspect this place so she could give you guys a hard time."

Lara looked over at Gideon and felt her face drain of color. "But…why would she do that?"

Brian shrugged. "She's anticat, I guess. Some people don't like cats, but they're not so militant about it. But Evonda, well, she *really* doesn't like cats. That's why I called you before—to warn you."

Lara wished, now, that she'd played the messages. "Brian, did she actually call us *hoarders*?"

"She did. That part I heard loud and clear."

"Did she say anything else?" Lara was afraid to hear the answer.

Brian shrugged. "I couldn't hear much else, and then she hung up so she could turn her fury on me." He rubbed his fingers between his cat's ears.

"What did she do?" Gideon asked.

Brian's face pinched with anger. "First off, I asked her why she was there. My lease says that unless it's an emergency, the landlord has to give twenty-four-hours' notice of an inspection. But she thinks she has the right to inspect any time she feels like it. Lucky thing I'm on vacation this week. I hate to think what she might have done if I hadn't been home."

"Brian," Gideon said, "did you contact a lawyer about this? Or someone in the police department? She clearly overstepped her authority when she entered your apartment without cause."

"No, not yet. I'm trying to figure out my next move. One thing I know for sure, I'm getting out of there and finding another place to live. I've got three months left on my lease, but I don't care. I'm bailing anyway. She'll probably sue me for the rent, but I'll go to court and fight it if she does. I just want out of there, as soon as possible."

"I don't blame you," Lara said. "But…if you don't have a place to move to yet, why is Smuggles with you?" She had a sinking feeling she already knew the answer.

Brian's face flushed. "Here's the thing. I'm terrified to leave Smuggles alone in the apartment while I go hunting for some new digs. That woman scares me. I've made some calls, and I've got leads on two apartments. I just need a chance to nail something down. It should only take a few days. A week, at most."

"Brian, I want to help you, but I'm not sure what we can do."

His voice lowered. "All I want is a safe place for Smuggles to stay, just until I get an apartment. It'll only be for a short time, I promise."

Lara felt torn. "I wish…look, we simply aren't set up to be a boarding facility. Our vet, Amy Glindell, will be glad to board Smuggles for you. She has nice, clean facilities and a wonderful staff. I can give you her number and—"

Brian shook his head, his eyes watering. "You don't get it. This cat endured so much trauma before I rescued him. If I send him someplace where he'll be put in another cage, he'll think he's reliving that nightmare, no matter how clean the place is. It's still a cage." He twisted one hand over the other. "I Googled you guys. I know all about this place. It's a home for cats. No cages, no restrictions. It'll only be for a few days, I promise. I'll pay you double whatever the regular adoption fee is. I just don't want him to be frightened."

Lara felt bad for Brian, she truly did, and she definitely wanted to help Smuggles. But if she agreed to board the kitty, would she be setting a precedent?

She shook her head. *Setting a precedent.* She was picking up too much legalese from Gideon.

"Brian, give me one good reason why Smuggles can't stay with you while you look for a place."

Brian's face darkened. "I'll give you a reason. That witch Evonda said if I didn't get rid of my cat immediately, she'd come over and do it for me. One way or the other."

A cream-colored cat suddenly leaped onto the table. Her sapphire-colored eyes fastened on Lara, she nestled up against Brian's arm. Lara thought she saw Brian's hand twitch.

She stifled a smile.

Decision made.

Chapter Four

After introducing Brian to Aunt Fran and giving him a tour of the shelter, during which he greeted each cat with a smile and a scratch behind the ears, Lara and Gideon showed him the new reading room.

"I can't believe what you guys have done here," Brian said, his hands shoved in his pockets. "I'll bet there's not another shelter like this in the state...or anywhere, for that matter. No wonder I've heard such good things about it."

"Thanks," Lara said. "Aunt Fran and I are proud of what we've accomplished."

Lara and Gideon walked him out to his car. Brian noticed the oversize box the new screen door had been packed in. As a small gesture for taking in Smuggles, he offered to dispose of it for them. "It'll fit in the back of my SUV, no problem," he said. "I was heading to the recycling station anyway to look for some boxes." He rolled his eyes. "Like that's how I want to waste my vacation—packing up my apartment."

Gideon helped Brian load the box into the back of his SUV, while Lara carried Smuggles upstairs to her bedroom. A puffy cushion, big enough for a Saint Bernard, rested in one corner on the floor. Most of the cats in the house ignored it, opting instead to hang out on Lara's bed and wrestle her chenille bedspread into submission.

Lara had to hand it to Brian—he'd come to the shelter prepared. Along with Smuggles's special formula food, bowls, and favorite toys, he'd brought along a T-shirt that he'd worn but hadn't laundered. Lara pulled the tee out of the brown paper bag in which everything had been packed. She spread it over one corner of the cushion, then gave Smuggles a tickle under the chin. The kitty closed his eyes and rested his head on the tee. His muted purr told her he was settling in for a long snooze.

Gideon returned holding a large envelope. He glanced at his vintage Superman watch. "Shoot. I've got a closing in forty minutes."

"I'm sorry. I didn't expect any of this drama today."

He smiled and kissed her on the cheek. "Not a problem. I'll make it back in time. I'm glad I was here to help out."

"What did you say to him?"

"I advised him to go to the courthouse this afternoon to file for a restraining order. Evonda Fray made unacceptable threats to him. He needs to be proactive."

"Is he going to do it?" Lara twisted her hands.

"I think so. He gave me these—his cat's health records."

Lara took the envelope. "Wow. He really did come prepared. Thanks. I tucked Smuggles into a cozy corner in my room, with a litter box close by. I'll have to keep an eye on Orca and Pearl, though. I'm sure they'll try to plunder his food."

Gideon smiled with approval. "I can't think of a better temporary home for Smuggles. I'm glad you took him in."

* * * *

With her head spinning in a thousand directions, Lara didn't know what to do first.

She strolled outside onto the front porch, which was actually on the side of the house. A warm summer breeze, dry and fragrant, wafted over her. It was a welcome change from the stifling humidity they'd been enduring for the past several days. Tomorrow was going to be humid again, so she wanted to enjoy it while she could.

Aunt Fran sat outside in the yard, under the big maple, in her favorite Adirondack chair. Propped in her lap was her latest library book—a popular historical novel that was getting rave reviews. With her straw hat pulled low over her face, she didn't see Lara.

Instead of joining her, Lara went back inside and into her art studio. The small parlor had once been her childhood hangout, back in the days when she stayed with her aunt every day after school. Her mom, who now lived in Vegas with her hubby, Rod, had been more than a tad jealous of Aunt Fran back then. Lara's reunion with her mom last Christmas had set them both on a new path. It helped heal their fractured relationship so that they could both move forward.

Lara had been working on a watercolor for the new reading room—a painting of a dark-haired boy reading to a small gold cat. The child's expression needed work—she still hadn't captured the joy on his face as he read aloud to the kitty.

She set up her supplies—paints, brushes, tile for blending colors, water glass—and went to work. Or tried to anyway. Evonda invaded her thoughts like a storm trooper, waiting around every corner to taunt and annoy her. An hour later, having made little progress, she set everything aside.

Lara went upstairs to her bedroom. On the plump cushion in the corner, Smuggles was stretched out with his eyes half-closed, his head resting on Brian's T-shirt. At the sight of Lara, the cat swished his tail and issued a soft purr. Lara bent over and stroked his furry head. He looked comfy enough, so she left him to snooze in peace.

She turned her floor fan slightly, and a gentle breeze wafted toward her bed. Lara tossed her tablet onto her bedspread and plunked down beside it. She fired it up and entered Evonda Fray's name into the search engine.

No surprise—her name brought up several links right away. After all, how many Evonda Frays could there be? From the photos that popped up on the screen, it was definitely the same woman. Straggly blond hair, a hard expression, a smile that never reached her eyes.

Fray had worked at numerous jobs, which didn't surprise Lara. With her grating personality, it was unlikely she'd won any congeniality awards from coworkers. People like Fray changed jobs frequently, always on the lookout for a better gig.

One particular link caught Lara's eye—a Web site to a photography business of which Evonda was the proprietor. Lara clicked the link. A stunning array of wildlife photos filled the page. Predominant among the photos were birds of prey—snowy owls, bald eagles, turkey vultures. Lara remembered the blackbird pendant she'd seen hanging around the health inspector's neck. Did Fray have a fixation on birds?

The sale prices for the framed photos varied, but most were in the two-hundred-dollar range. Fray surely wouldn't have gotten rich from her business. She had, however, earned some glowing reviews from people who'd purchased her photos.

Lara scrolled all the way to the end. The most recent entry was back in 2014. Did Fray still sell her photography? Or had she closed down the business in pursuit of other interests?

As for social media, it didn't look as if the woman had a Facebook page, or a Twitter or an Instagram account. *Not the social type*, Lara surmised, though that certainly didn't surprise her.

A horrible thought gripped Lara. She tapped at the keyboard and went to their own Facebook page—the High Cliff Shelter for Cats. Would Fray have been so malicious as to leave a nasty comment there?

After a quick check, Lara breathed a sigh of relief. If Fray had visited their Facebook page, it wasn't obvious. The page did, however, have a recent like from Brian Downing. That made Lara smile.

She powered off her tablet and plugged it in to recharge just as Snowball hopped onto her bed. Lara grinned at the cat, then ran her hand over Snowball's pure-white fur. Several white hairs clung to her fingers. "You, young lady, need a good brushing. Look at the way you're shedding!"

For the rest of the day, Lara busied herself with cat grooming and other tasks to take her mind off the health inspection. Aunt Fran tried to be cheerful. She bustled around the kitchen, setting a small plate of brownies on the table.

Neither of them touched the brownies.

Neither of them mentioned Evonda.

By eleven, Lara tumbled into bed.

Waiting for the health inspector to show up in the morning felt like free-falling from a plane without a parachute.

Chapter Five

By Tuesday morning, Lara's nerves felt as if they'd been shredded with a cheese grater. She'd risen early, unable to sleep once the sun poked its nose through the blinds. After feeding the cats, she busied herself cleaning the kitchen and changing all the litter boxes, but every time she heard a noise, she jumped.

At her aunt's urging, she finally agreed to take a break and have a fast breakfast.

"I assume you're skipping the coffee shop this morning," Aunt Fran said. Dolce, a long-haired black kitty, was nestled in her lap. Aunt Fran spread strawberry jam over an English muffin half.

"I am." Lara poured herself a cup of coffee and grabbed a banana from the fruit bowl. "I want to be here when Evonda shows up with her cease-and-desist order."

"*If* she shows up." Aunt Fran rested her hand on the black kitty curled in her lap. "In my opinion, bullies are cowards at heart. She might well be all bluster and bark, with no bite."

"Maybe, but I can't risk it," Lara said. Nor did she believe it.

A striped orange cat ambled into the kitchen. Munster hopped onto Lara's lap, rested his chin on the table, and examined her banana peel. He started to reach for it, but she held him back. "Aren't you the pushy one today?" she teased.

Munster was one of the original cats adopted by Aunt Fran, along with Dolce and Twinkles. The three were house cats, not available for adoption. Friendly and sociable, Munster was the unofficial greeter of all human visitors.

"How did Smuggles do last night?" Aunt Fran asked.

"He did well, actually. He seems content, although I'm sure he misses Brian. He pretty much stays curled up on the cushion and sleeps. This morning I gave him fresh water and food. Most of his teeth are gone, so he can only eat soft food. He used the litter box during the night, which tells me he feels comfortable being here. Later, I'm going to give him a good, long brushing."

"Are you sure it was he who used the litter box?"

"Yes, because I saw him. I…well, I slept kind of badly last night. At one point I woke up and found Orca and Pearl wrestling over something they'd dug out of my laundry bag." She shook her head and chuckled.

They finished breakfast, and Lara made sure the sink was spotless. To keep herself from going crazy, she pulled the vacuum cleaner out of the downstairs closet and began running it over all the rooms.

By ten fifteen, Mrs. Fray still hadn't arrived. Had she changed her mind? Or was she making them sweat it out by showing up late?

"Was that the doorbell?" Lara shoved the vacuum into the hall closet.

"No. That was only my phone with a text." Aunt Fran pulled it out of the pocket of her summery green capris. "It'll be okay, Lara. Whatever happens, we'll deal with it."

"But today's an adoption day, Aunt Fran! What are we going to do?"

Her aunt steered her over to the sofa, and the two sat down.

"Aren't you going to read your text?" Lara asked her.

"In a minute. Let's talk about this. As far as we know, the inspector's only issue was the fact that we serve snacks in the meet-and-greet room."

"That we know of," Lara cautioned. "Who knows? Maybe she'll say our water wasn't hot enough, or one of the cat bowls had a speck of food in it, or something equally ridiculous."

"I hear what you're saying," Aunt Fran said calmly. "But right now, all we can do is wait. Until we receive that order, we should go ahead with adoption day as we normally would. Tuesdays are usually pretty quiet, especially during the summer. It's possible no one will show up at all."

Snowball padded over to the sofa and leaped onto Lara's knees. Lara pulled the cat close to her chest, smiling at how easily the cat's gentle purr soothed her battered nerves. "You're always so levelheaded. Me, I'm like a firecracker waiting to explode. That woman pushed all my buttons yesterday. I'm still reeling from it."

"Believe me, she pushed several of my buttons, too. But I've learned that sometimes it's best to play a waiting game. It's surprising how many problems iron themselves out without any outside interference."

My wonderful, wise aunt, Lara thought. *What would I ever do without her?*

Aunt Fran looked at her cell. Her eyes clouded. "Hmmm," she said, almost to herself. She tapped out a reply, then slipped the phone back into her pocket.

"It's something bad, isn't?" Lara said.

Aunt Fran looked troubled. "I'm not sure. That was Jerry. He's on his way over here. He said he has something to tell us, and he wanted to be sure we were both here."

Lara sank her fingers into Snowball's soft fur. The window air conditioner in the large parlor kept the room comfortable on hot summer days, but the sudden chill that skittered down her spine felt as cold as a glacier.

She rose from the sofa and propped Snowball on her shoulder, then began pacing the room. It was the cat's favorite way to cruise the house, and it gave Lara something to focus on while they waited for the chief of police.

Five minutes later, she saw the chief's car pull into the driveway. He parked directly behind the aging Saturn Lara shared with her aunt. Lara felt her heart do a high jump when his car door slammed shut.

Aunt Fran got up quickly and answered the doorbell. "That was quick," she told the chief with an anxious smile. "You must have been close by."

He gave her a peck on the cheek and strode into the large parlor. From his grim expression, Lara knew something was wrong. "Good morning, Lara."

"Hi, Chief," Lara said dully. She was in no mood to be perky.

"I'm afraid I need to talk to both of you," the chief said. "Something has happened."

Lara shifted Snowball from her shoulder to her arms, then set her down on the floor. She knew the chief wasn't a cat lover. He tolerated them only because he cared for Aunt Fran. Snowball dashed off in the direction of the kitchen, no doubt in search of a midmorning snack.

"Let's sit," Aunt Fran said, taking a seat on the sofa.

The chief nodded, then glanced around before lowering himself down next to her. Lara knew he was scoping out the room for a possible feline intrusion, especially a Munster attack. Munster had been trying to cozy up to the chief for a long time. The most he could score was a grudging pat on the head and a slight push in the opposite direction.

Lara sat in her favorite wing chair and faced the pair.

"Would you like something to drink, Jerry?" Aunt Fran asked, ever the perfect hostess.

"No, thanks. I've been up since the crack of dawn. I've already had about forty cups of coffee." He twisted the brim of his hat in his large hands. "We got a call early this morning from a newspaper delivery guy. He was doing his usual route, over on Loundon Street, when he noticed something odd. There was a car in the driveway of one of his customers, and he thought he saw someone sitting in the driver's seat."

"Why is that so odd?" Lara asked him. "A lot of people go to work early."

"True," the chief said. "But in this case, something else caught his eye. He went over to the driver's side and looked inside. He's a nosy sort to begin with, but I don't think he was prepared for what he saw."

A sinking feeling lodged in Lara's stomach. "What was it?"

"A woman was sitting behind the wheel. It was obvious she was"—he cleared his throat—"no longer breathing."

Aunt Fran paled. "Was the engine running?"

The chief shook his head. "No, she hadn't even started the car. Her cell phone was on the console beside her. It looked as if she'd started to text someone, but she didn't get very far."

"Jerry, you're being very cryptic," Aunt Fran said. "Are you going to tell us who it is? Is it someone we know?"

Jerry issued a long sigh. "The deceased is Evonda Fray. The same woman who ordered you to cease and desist."

* * * *

Every bone in Lara's body morphed into mush. She slid down off the chair, onto the floor, and pulled her legs to her chest. She rested her head on her knees, barely feeling the tears sliding down her cheeks. She was numb.

Not again. Not again.

The words rushed through her ears like a thunderous waterfall, an unwelcome reminder of the other deaths that had crossed her path since she'd returned to Whisker Jog.

Less than two years earlier, she'd stumbled upon the body of a local businessman at the edge of her aunt's property. The murder was solved, but not long after that, she spotted a body in the old cemetery on Deanna Daltry's property. Then, last Christmas, a woman was killed during a cookie competition. Somehow, Lara always happened to be close by when the bodies were discovered.

Would it never end?

Aunt Fran went silent for a moment, then, "Was her death…from natural causes?"

The chief frowned and shook his head. "I wish I could say yes, Fran. Unfortunately, it was abundantly clear that foul play was involved."

"Chief," Lara put in, "you said it looked as if Evonda had started to text someone. Do you know who it was?"

He gave her a wry look. "Yes, I do know. And before you ask, no, I can't tell you. Right now, everything we viewed at the scene is strictly confidential."

A heavy silence fell over the room.

Aunt Fran folded her hands in front of her and bowed her head. After a long moment she looked up and said, "You'll need to excuse me, Jerry. Lara and I need some hot tea, with lots of sugar."

"Be my guest," he said kindly. "Need any help?"

"I'll help," Lara said and started to rise.

Aunt Fran went over and pressed a hand to her shoulder. "No, stay right here, both of you. It'll only take me a minute."

Oh good glory, Lara thought. *Do I look so shaken that Aunt Fran thinks she has to wait on me?*

A sudden movement at one corner of her vision made Lara glance over to her left. From in front of the carpeted cat tree, a fluffy, cream-colored cat with startling blue eyes watched her.

Blue.

Lara wished desperately she could stroke the cat's gorgeous fur or tickle her under her chin. But she knew the Ragdoll cat was as ephemeral as smoke, a presence that would fade as her energy waned.

You're here to comfort me, aren't you? Lara thought.

In response, Blue lowered herself to a sphinx position. Her dark-brown tail twitched, and she blinked.

Lara felt the chief studying her. She turned to face him. "Is there anything else, Chief? Something you're not telling us?"

"Wait until Fran gets back," he said quietly.

"I'm here," Aunt Fran said, coming in with a tray.

The chief jumped to his feet and retrieved the tray from her. He set it down on a side table. Aunt Fran had brought out three mugs. "How about I pour?" he said. "Seeing as you added a third mug, I've decided to join you."

He prepared a mug for each of them, then sat down again. Blue had already vanished. Lara remained on the floor, her fingers clasped around her mug. Even on a day that would soon be sweltering, she relished the warmth seeping into her hands.

"Chief, you said the delivery guy noticed something in particular," Lara reminded him.

"He did. And the only reason I'm going to disclose it to you is because he's already blabbed about it to half the town, so we aren't going to be able to withhold it from the public. The guy's a chatterbox by nature, but when we took him in for questioning, he told everyone he bumped into what he saw."

"The poor man was probably so traumatized," Aunt Fran offered, "that telling people helped him deal with what he saw." She took a tiny sip of her tea.

The chief flashed a smile at her. "That is a very generous way to look at it."

"You're stalling, Chief," Lara said.

His expression sobered. "When the delivery person peeked into Ms. Fray's car window this morning, he saw a red sneaker sticking out of her mouth. The toe of the sneaker was jammed inside."

Lara gasped, nearly spilling her tea. Evonda had worn red sneakers the day before, when she performed her so-called inspection of the shelter. "Oh my...that is just...gruesome." She set her mug down on the tile in front of the fireplace.

Aunt Fran looked horrified. "That is truly awful. It sounds to me as if the killer was trying to make a statement." Her voice trembled.

"That's how I see it, too." The chief hesitated, looking distinctly uncomfortable. "There's something else. On the front seat, next to her cell phone, was an order relating to this shelter. In fact"—he cleared his throat again—"she was actually holding the order in one hand."

"The cease-and-desist order?" Lara asked.

"Exactly. Evidently, she was planning to deliver it to you in person this morning. Either that or she planned to bring it to the sheriff's office and have them serve you officially. She could have done it either way."

Lara slowly shook her head. "No. She would have taken great pleasure in hand-delivering it here." She swallowed. "Is the order...official?"

"Technically, yes," the chief said. "In this case, however, Ms. Fray hadn't filed a motion for summary enforcement with the district court. Presumably, she was going to do that today, but..." He broke off.

"Yeah," Lara said after a long pause. "But."

"It wasn't as bad as you think," the chief said. "Whether she liked it or not, she obviously knew you had a permit to operate the shelter. The order was only to cease and desist from serving any manner of food or drink to prospective...shoppers, I guess you'd call them."

Aunt Fran smiled. "We call them people who want to give loving homes to deserving cats."

Chief Whitley returned her smile, a slight twinkle in his eye despite the situation. "I know you do, Fran."

"Chief, today's an adoption day," Lara said. "I don't mean to sound unsympathetic, but what should we do now?"

"I'm aware," he said, his tone ominous. "Unfortunately, I'm going to need you both to come down to the station today to give statements to one of the state police investigators. This morning would be preferable, but you need to do it before the end of the day."

I know the drill, Lara thought grimly.

"Is that because of the cease-and-desist order?" Aunt Fran asked.

The chief shifted slightly on the sofa. "Pretty much. Plus, Evonda was heard bragging to people yesterday about 'putting that cat shelter in its place.' Both her son and daughter-in-law repeated it when they were being questioned at home this morning."

Lara suspected Evonda had said far worse than that. The chief was no doubt being diplomatic. "So Evonda had kids?"

"Only the one son. Her husband died several years ago."

"As far as giving statements, this morning is better for us," her aunt said.

"I agree," Lara said. "Is it all right if we go down there now, Chief?"

"That'll be perfect. I'm heading back to the station now, so when you get there, ask for me. I'll hook you up with the right people." He drank the last of his tea.

Aunt Fran looked over at Lara. "Lara, I think we should go ahead with adoption day, but refrain from serving snacks."

"I think that's wise, Fran." The chief's gaze drifted sideways. "Oh boy, here he comes again," he said dryly. "My new best friend." He held up one large hand as a barrier, but Munster had become adept at doing an end run.

Ignoring the chief's outstretched hand, Munster hopped onto the sofa and approached him from the side, tucking his golden head under the chief's elbow. His purr was loud enough to be heard outside.

"Yeah, yeah, you like me," he said to the cat. "I get it." With one finger, he scratched the fur between Munster's ears, then pushed him slightly to one side. Munster yawned, stretched out to his full length, and then leaned against the chief's thigh for a comfy snooze.

Lara couldn't help giggling. Munster's antics had broken the tension. Even the chief looked grateful for the interruption.

"Well, that's all for now, except..." He rose and gave Lara a pointed look.

"I already know what you're going to say," Lara said. "Don't get involved, don't ask any questions, let the police handle it."

"Precisely," the chief said. "I'm serious, Lara. This is not a joke. I don't want a repeat of what happened before."

"Which time?" Lara asked.

He narrowed his eyes, his jaw firm. "Every time. You've put yourself in jeopardy far too often by asking questions. This time let us do the asking. Deal?"

Lara nodded. "I hear you, Chief. Oh—one last thing. You didn't tell us the name of the man who found Evonda's body."

The chief dropped his hat on his head and smiled. "Good day, Fran, Columbo. I'll be in touch."

Chapter Six

When they got to the police station, Lara was forced to park the Saturn on the street nearly a block away. Several state police cars had taken all the available spaces in front of the station, and also in the small lot behind it.

Inside, in the tiled lobby area, a handful of people milled about. Some looked eager, but others looked bleak and depressed. Lara had never seen so many people here at one time, though she made it a point to steer clear of the police station as much as possible, given her history with finding bodies.

Were they all waiting to be interviewed? Lara wondered.

On a wooden bench adjacent to the water dispenser, a youngish couple sat with their heads bent, their hands clasped between them. The woman had short, light-brown hair and a slight build, with skinny arms that stuck out like twigs from her sleeveless yellow blouse. Her companion, who was far taller, wore tan shorts and a faded blue cotton shirt. Behind his black-rimmed glasses, his eyes were red-rimmed and swollen.

The woman looked oddly familiar. Had Lara gone to school with her, eons ago? She looked about Lara's age—twenty-nine and approaching the dreaded 3-0. If she'd been a former classmate, the last time Lara had seen her would've been in the sixth grade. Lara's family had relocated to Massachusetts just in time for her to suffer through her first year of seventh grade in a strange school with kids she'd never met before.

Lara spied a chair near the door. "Aunt Fran, why don't you take that seat? I'll let the dispatcher know we're here."

Her aunt nodded and went over to claim the chair. "Okay, but I'll text Jerry. That might be even faster."

At the reception window, which Lara assumed was made of bulletproof glass, a severe-looking fiftyish woman with dark hair pulled into a tight ponytail sat in front of a switchboard. Lara talked into the speaker embedded in the glass. "Good morning. I'm Lara Caphart, and I'm here with my aunt, Fran Clarkson. Chief Whitley asked us to come in this morning to be interviewed."

The dispatcher didn't bother to look up. "I'll let him know you're here."

"Thank you."

When Lara turned around, she was surprised to see that her aunt had already gone missing. With a courteous smile, she squeezed her way around a clot of people and glanced down the hallway that she knew, from experience, led to the only two interview rooms. She spotted Aunt Fran. A uniformed officer was escorting her into one of the rooms.

She went back into the lobby. An empty seat had opened up, right next to the familiar-looking woman. Lara sat down beside her, and the woman turned and looked at her.

Yes! I know her.

"Good morning," Lara said in a quiet voice. "I feel as if I know you from somewhere. Are you, by any chance, Jenny? Jenny...Cooper?"

The woman sniffled, then dabbed at her nose with a pink tissue. "Yes, I am. Well, it's actually Jenny Fray now."

Fray. *Oh no...*

"You look familiar, too," Jenny said, "but...I'm sorry, I can't remember your name."

"It's Lara. Lara Caphart. I think the last time we saw each other was probably in junior high."

"Oh my gosh, yes. Lara, with the beautiful red hair! How dumb of me not to remember."

"It's not dumb at all," Lara said kindly. "Sixth grade was a long time ago. Is...was Mrs. Fray your...?"

"My mother-in-law," Jenny supplied, a thread of steel in her voice. She touched the hand of the man sitting beside her. "Tim?"

At first the man didn't appear to hear her, but then she jiggled his hand. Finally, slowly, he looked at his wife, then over at Lara. With his severe spectacles and dark, curly hair, he reminded Lara of that singing icon from the old days, Buddy Holly.

"Tim," Jenny said, "this is an old classmate of mine, Lara Caphart. We went to middle school together." She looked at Lara. "Lara, this is my husband, Tim."

Lara froze, unsure what to say. "I...hello, Tim. I'm so sorry for your loss. I only heard about it a short while ago."

Tim stared at Lara with glazed eyes. "Thank you. We're...Jenny and I are still in shock. The police insisted we come down here to give official statements, even though they already talked to us for hours this morning. Separately," he added darkly.

Of course they talked to you separately. They wanted to make sure your stories jibed.

Jenny gave Lara a sheepish look. "I don't think it was hours. It only seemed that way because we were both so...horrified."

"I don't know what more Jenny and I can tell them," Tim rattled on. He locked gazes with his wife. "Neither of us has any idea who could have done this."

"I'm sure it's just standard procedure," Lara said. "They probably have to talk to everyone who was close to the, you know..."

"Victim," Tim said sharply.

"Yes." Lara's voice came out like a squeak. She cleared her throat. "That poor man who found her, I'm sure he must be traumatized."

"Are you kidding?" Tim gave her a crooked smirk. "Roy Tierney? The guy's a character for sure. He's one of those people who talks to everyone, whether he knows them or not. Don't worry about him being traumatized. He's having a field day telling everyone what he saw. He's getting his fifteen minutes of fame, as they say."

"But won't that hamper the police investigation?" Lara said, feigning surprise. "I mean, don't they try to keep some stuff out of the news so they can tell a real confession from a phony one?"

"Maybe." Tim shrugged. "Nothing they can do now. Once the horse is out of the barn..."

His tone had gone from guarded to matter-of-fact. Lara couldn't help wondering if Tim and Jenny were truly grieving for Evonda or if they were putting on an act. Their reactions seemed mechanical, almost practiced.

A uniformed officer came into the lobby from the hallway. He glanced at Tim, then homed in on Jenny. "Mrs. Fray, would you please follow me? The investigator is ready to take your statement."

Jenny's face turned ash gray. "Um, sure." She squeezed Tim's hand, then rose and followed the officer.

"Can I get you something to drink?" the officer asked, his voice fading as they both disappeared down the hallway.

Lara couldn't help feeling for Jenny. She had a pretty good idea of how the interview would go. The investigator would ask Jenny the same questions, over and over, until she was ready to jump up and scream. By the time she left, her nerves would be tangled around one another like licorice strands.

"My wife doesn't deserve this," Tim said, interrupting her musings. He twisted his long fingers in his lap. "She's been through enough."

His declaration gave Lara a great opening, but suddenly she felt tongue-tied. What had Jenny been through? Did it have anything to do with Evonda?

Lara decided to start with a safe question. "How long have you and Jenny been married?"

Tim's eyes softened, and he gave up a weak smile. "It'll be two years in September. We went to the town hall, just the two of us. Jenny looked so pretty. She wore a daisy in her hair that day. She looked almost too young to get married. My…mother didn't attend. She never approved of Jenny."

Of course she didn't.

"What about Jenny's folks?"

"Only her mom is living, and she's not doing very well. Her dad flew the coop ages ago. We don't even know where he is, nor do we care," he added harshly.

"Oh, I'm sorry to hear that. Jenny seems like a lovely woman. I remember her in school. She was shy, but she always wanted to help people."

Tim's voice cracked. "Still does."

A memory came back to Lara. A skinny little boy with shaggy hair who'd broken his leg and had to get around on crutches wearing an ungainly cast. Jenny had insisted on carrying the boy's books from class to class, struggling not to drop them as she balanced them atop her own. If another kid tried to help, Jenny would shake her head and say, "No, thank you. I've got it."

Strange, Lara thought. *What made me think of that after all these years?*

She shifted on her chair. She began to feel uneasy. The lobby was getting too warm. Had they turned off the AC? She felt her light jersey top sticking to her skin.

Lara jumped at the sound of a familiar voice.

"There you are," Aunt Fran said, coming over to stand in front of Lara.

"Wow. That was fast. You weren't in there very long."

"Long enough," Aunt Fran said, glancing at Tim.

Before Lara had a chance to introduce her aunt to Tim, the same officer who'd led Aunt Fran away came back into the lobby. "Ms. Caphart, will you please follow me?"

I feel like I'm back in school, being summoned to the principal's office.

"I'll wait for you here," Aunt Fran said. She took Lara's vacated chair.

"Bye. Take care," Lara said quietly to Tim before following the officer down the hallway.

* * * *

Lara's interview ended shortly after eleven. The state police investigator had been a humorless type, with a bland face and an even blander personality. Over and over, he asked her the same questions. Lara was careful to answer them the same way every time. Would that persuade them that she was telling the truth? Or would the investigator conclude that her account of Evonda's visit to the shelter had been a carefully rehearsed spiel?

She nearly kissed the ground—or rather, the dusty floor—when the investigator finally told her she could leave. Aunt Fran was sitting in the same chair in the lobby, reading a paperback. Tim Fray was gone.

"Only eleven fifteen and it's already in the low nineties," Lara said as they were leaving the police station. "I'm beginning to think I prefer snow."

"Perish the thought," Aunt Fran said, picking her way carefully down the granite steps. Sporting fairly new knee replacements, she was walking like her old self again. Nonetheless, she was extracareful when negotiating stairs or any uneven surface. "So, tell me. How did your interview go?"

"I don't know. Every time he asked me a question, I got the sick feeling I was suspect number one on their hit parade."

They'd almost reached the front sidewalk when a dark-green state police car pulled up in front of the station. It double-parked alongside a Whisker Jog cruiser. Seconds later, both front doors swung open simultaneously. The trooper who'd gotten out on the passenger side opened the rear door. He leaned down to talk to their passenger, and then a man got out of the back seat.

Aunt Fran grabbed Lara's wrist. "Lara. Isn't that…?"

"Oh, no! It's Brian Downing. I was going to call him as soon as we got home."

Brian's full face looked flushed. He wore a short-sleeved shirt and a pair of light-colored slacks, a pair of brown loafers on his sockless feet. He spoke briefly to the trooper who'd opened his door, and together they walked up the sidewalk toward the station.

Brian stopped short when he saw Lara. His face grew animated. "Lara, I was going to call you this morning before everything hit the fan! How's Smuggles doing? Is he okay?"

"He's fine, Brian. He's comfy and he's eating well, so don't worry about him."

Brian sagged visibly. "Thank God. You heard what happened, right?" He glared at the trooper who was breathing down his neck.

"I did. But why are you here?"

"The cops want to question me further. They think I had something to do with Evonda's death. Can you believe that? I'm a pacifist, for cripes' sake!"

The troopers were getting impatient. "Sir, we have to go inside now," the one closest to him said. "I'd advise you not to speak to anyone."

"Who are you to advise me?" Brian snapped at him. "You're trying to put me behind bars. And you haven't even read me my rights!"

The trooper, who looked barely old enough to shave, rolled his youthful eyes. "You're not under arrest, sir. We're only taking you in for further questioning."

The other trooper, who was clearly a more seasoned member of the force, locked his hand around Brian's upper arm. "Let's go, Mr. Downing. We're wasting time. The sooner you go inside, the sooner you can leave."

"I'll call you later, Lara," Brian said as the troopers propelled him toward the building. "Take good care of Smuggles!"

Lara stared after him for at least a minute, then turned back to her aunt. "This is not good. Do you think they found something they think links him to the murder?"

Aunt Fran looked troubled. "I don't know. But I hope he knows enough to call an attorney if things get dicey for him."

Lara swallowed. "Aunt Fran, do you think...he *could* have done it?" She slipped her arm through her aunt's, and they walked toward where the Saturn was parked.

"Anything is possible. We don't know him well enough to judge, do we?" Aunt Fran said. "I suggest we do as Jerry advised and let the police handle the questioning."

Lara couldn't help smiling. "Is that a hint?"

"More of a command," her aunt said quietly. "I don't want you putting yourself in danger again, Lara. Not even with a guardian cat watching over you."

Chapter Seven

Not a soul showed up for adoption hours at the shelter that afternoon, but later in the day, Charlie Backstrom's truck pulled into the driveway. Lara was rearranging books in the new reading room when she spotted him through the window. Holding up a small red box, he smiled at her as he hopped out of his truck and strode over.

"Charlie! Come on in," Lara said. "I was just putting away some books on these beautiful new shelves."

He stepped inside, pride shining on his face as he glanced over the bookshelves. "They did come out nice, didn't they? If I do say so myself." He laughed slightly.

"They're wonderful," Lara said. "I love the adjustable feature. If we get in some of the larger picture books, we can easily shift things around to accommodate them."

Charlie swung the storm door back and forth a few times, apparently to assure himself that it worked properly. "Anyway, I brought over that weather-stripping I promised you. It'll only take me a minute to put it on."

Lara had completely forgotten about the weather-stripping. Charlie had promised to return to attach it along the bottom of the storm door. "Thanks. We've had a lot of disruption today, so it totally slipped my mind."

Charlie's expression sobered. "Yeah, I can imagine. I heard about what happened with that health inspector. Everyone in town's talking about it. Totally bizarre, huh?"

"Bizarre doesn't begin to describe it," Lara said quietly. She really didn't want to discuss Evonda's murder. It was too raw, too fresh, and too close to home. Her mind was still reeling from it. "I just hope the police will find the killer soon."

"Ditto that," Charlie said. He stooped down and opened the storm door again, this time running his hand along the bottom.

"Would you like something cold to drink?" Lara asked him. "We have lemonade, and there might be a can of ginger ale."

"Thanks. I'll take a tiny bit of lemonade, just enough to wet my whistle." He held his thumb and forefinger about an inch apart.

"You got it."

Lara went into the kitchen and returned a minute later with a small glass half-filled with lemonade. Charlie was sitting on the floor with his legs outstretched, the red box resting on his thigh.

"Ah, thanks," he said and took a few gulps. He set down the glass behind him, then opened the box and pulled out a strand of what looked like gray felt. "This stuff is great. Easy to attach, and it never cracks or dries out. It'll help in the summer, but it really keeps the drafts out in the winter. If more people did this, their heating bills would be lower."

Lara sat on one of the low cushions and watched him work. She admired how deftly he performed small tasks, the attention he paid to the tiniest details.

"There you go," he said, hoisting himself off the floor. He opened and closed the door a few times, then nodded with approval. "Nice and snug," he pronounced. "You're all set."

Lara smiled. "Thanks again. Do I owe you for the weather-stripping?"

"Nah. You kidding? You're one of my best customers. Besides, I get a contractor's discount. I only paid about three bucks for it."

"I appreciate it, Charlie. Thanks for coming by."

"While I'm here, I'll take that box to the recycling station for you. I didn't see it outside. Did you move it?"

Lara thought for a moment. "Oh, you mean the box the door came in. Someone stopped by yesterday and offered to take it for us. He had to go there anyway to get some packing boxes."

"Well, then, that saves me a trip," Charlie said. He scooped the weather-stripping box off the floor, along with the lemonade glass. He drained the glass and handed it to Lara. "Thanks for the drink. It hit the spot. By the way, Nina and I are looking forward to Saturday. Is there anything we can bring?"

Saturday. The open house.

Inwardly, Lara groaned. What if the police haven't arrested Evonda's killer by then? Would she and Aunt Fran want to host the unveiling of the new reading room with an unsolved murder hanging over them?

Lara wasn't sure how to respond. "No, just yourselves, Charlie. But thanks for asking."

He nodded and opened the door, but then paused. "Okay, then, but if there's anything we can do, just give us a call, okay? We both feel really bad about what happened."

"I will," Lara promised, feeling her throat tighten.

With a final wave, he trotted back to his truck.

After putting away a few more books, Lara went into the meet-and-greet room. Something about this room gave her comfort. The reason, she suspected, was that so many cats and kittens had found their forever homes here.

Resident-wise, the shelter was in a lull right now. Only three of the cats were available for adoption—Snowball, Orca, and Pearl.

Lara meandered over to the bulletin board she'd set up on the wall when the shelter first opened. Photos of kitty moms and dads with their adopted furballs nearly covered the allotted space. Callie and Luna, two fearful kittens, were the first to be adopted. They were now enjoying happy lives with a local woman Lara had once fingered as a possible killer.

So many others had followed. Lara herself had snapped the pic of the two sweet kittens, Bogie and Bacall, who'd been taken in by retired actress Deanna Daltry.

One of Lara's favorite matchups was the one between Butterscotch and a little boy named Oliver. From the day he arrived at the shelter, the marmalade male had shunned humans. But shortly before the holidays, Oliver had come in and read to the cat from his favorite alphabet book. The child's voice was so soothing and loving that it melted Butterscotch's heart. When Oliver returned after Christmas, the cat nearly had to be pried out of the boy's lap to get him into the carrier for the ride to his new home.

The reading program worked, Lara was convinced of it.

"I can almost read your mind," Aunt Fran said, popping into the room. "You're thinking about all the cats we've placed in wonderful homes."

Lara smiled. She ran a finger over the photo of Valenteena, a petite, black-and-white girl with a vocal personality who'd been a favorite of Lara's. Teena now lived with an active family in a rambling country home. With plenty of room to explore, and a food dish that was always full, she was leading a life of bliss with people who adored her.

"I was thinking about what a little imp Valenteena was. Remember the day she opened my Christmas presents and added a few claw marks to the nightie my mom gave me?"

Aunt Fran laughed. "Oh my, yes. She gave us a giggle that day, didn't she?" Her face turned somber. "I know it's hard, Lara, but try not to dwell on Evonda. We did nothing wrong, and we had nothing to do with her... demise. The police will sort it out. We just have to be patient."

The police will sort it out.

Lara knew from experience that it wasn't likely to be that easy. The path to a killer was narrow and winding, fraught with traps and deception.

"I know," she said, waving a hand at the air. "Don't mind me. I'm feeling a little gloomy today." She turned and stared out the window, into the yard. The leaves of the solitary maple were a lush green, and a slight breeze sifted through them. About ten feet above the ground, a birdhouse hung from a sturdy branch. A tiny chipmunk skittered around the trunk of the tree, then disappeared into a secret hole in the ground.

Her aunt moved closer into the room. "Lara," she said in a near whisper, "have you had any...*sightings* lately?"

After Lara's most recent brush with a killer, she'd revealed her secret about Blue to both Gideon and Aunt Fran. A cat no one else could see wasn't the easiest thing to talk about. She was relieved that neither of them had told her she was insane or doubted her for a moment. At least she hoped they hadn't.

"This morning, only for a few moments when the chief was here. I think she was trying to comfort me with her presence." Lara felt herself choking up.

Aunt Fran squeezed her niece's shoulder. "Come on in the kitchen. I just made a pitcher of iced tea. Let's—"

A knock at the door made them both turn. Brian Downing's face peered through the glass.

"Brian!" Lara said, unlocking the door. "Come on in. What's going on?"

Brian stepped inside and nodded to Aunt Fran. "Hey, I hope I'm not bugging you folks. I thought this might be a good time to check on Smuggles. Is it okay if I see him for a few minutes?"

"You're not picking him up?" Lara asked. "Not that we mind having him. He's a sweetheart. But I thought..."

He shook his head. "Unfortunately, I'm not out of the woods yet. The police grilled me today like I was the Boston Strangler." His expression clouded. "It's possible I'll be arrested for Evonda's murder."

"Are you kidding me?" Lara squawked.

"Brian," Aunt Fran said calmly, "why don't you sit? I'll bring out some iced tea and you can tell us what happened."

Lara gawked at her aunt. Did she realize she might be entertaining a killer?

"Um, yes. Sure. Have a seat."

A few minutes later, the three of them sat at the table, glasses of chilled iced tea resting in front of them.

Brian took a long gulp from his glass. "Man, that's good. Thank you." He swiped the back of his hand over his lips. "Listen, I want to be right up front with you. You guys have been good to me, and I won't forget it."

Lara knotted her fingers together in her lap. Was he going to confess to murder?

"I didn't exactly tell you everything about what happened yesterday. After Evonda told me to get rid of Smuggles, I...I kind of chased her outside to her car. I couldn't stop myself—I saw every shade of red in the spectrum when she said that."

"It was an awful thing to say," Aunt Fran said.

Brian huffed out a noisy breath. "When she got to her car, she jumped inside real fast, closed the door, and started the engine. I heard the locks click, so I figured I'd scared her. I started pounding on her window with my fist, screaming at her like a crazy person. At that point, I think I *was* crazy." He took another sip from his glass. "Anyway, I'm afraid I used some pretty rough language. She started pulling out of the parking lot to get away from me, but the back window on the driver's side was open a few inches. I grabbed it with both hands and pulled at it to stop her from driving off before I was finished yelling at her."

Lara squeezed her fingers over her brow. This was not good.

"Do you think anyone saw you?"

"Yeah, I know they did. When the police showed up this morning to question me, they also talked to my neighbors. Just my luck, the gal downstairs from me saw—and heard—the whole thing from her window. She related it pretty much as it happened. I don't blame her for squealing on me—she had to report what she saw, right? I just—" He pounded the side of his fist on the table. "I just wish I hadn't let my temper get out of control. It's all coming back now to bite me in the butt."

Aunt Fran looked pensive. "Not to sound like someone out of a crime drama, but that all sounds like a lot of circumstantial evidence."

That made Brian smile, briefly, then his expression morphed into one of sheer misery. "Yeah, but the problem is, whoever killed her did it from the back seat, and my fingerprints are all over that back window on the driver's side. Who's to say I didn't show up at her house early this morning, jump into her back seat, and strangle her from behind?"

Aunt Fran tapped a finger to her lips. "But in a way, the fact that your neighbor told the police what she witnessed works in your favor."

Brian frowned. "How do you figure?"

"Because it explains why your fingerprints were on that window," Aunt Fran said. "Otherwise, they'd have only your word for it."

"I get what you're saying." Brian sighed. "I don't know if it matters, though. The cops are still eyeing me a little too close for comfort."

"Brian," Lara said, her stomach in a knot, "did you say Evonda was… strangled?"

He nodded. "Yeah, but the cops aren't revealing what the killer used to do it. They tried to make *me* tell *them*, but of course I couldn't because I didn't kill her."

Somehow, Lara believed him. Brian's outburst of temper had been the result of a threat to his cat. If anyone could understand that, Lara could.

"You know what's weird, though?" Brian drummed his fingers on the table. "That thing about the sneaker. It's downright bizarre, if you ask me."

"How did you hear about that?" Lara asked him.

His laugh was mirthless. "You kidding? That nimrod Roy Tierney has been blabbing all over town about how he found Evonda dead in her car with her red sneaker stuffed in her mouth. The way he's telling it, you'd think he discovered the Holy Grail, for cripes' sake."

For another minute or so, they sipped their iced tea in silence. The sound of a new human voice had attracted the shelter's official greeter—Munster.

"Aw, I love this cat," Brian said brightly, grinning at the orange-striped kitty strutting toward him.

Munster didn't stand on ceremony. He leaped onto Brian's knee and rubbed his furry head against his chest. Brian scratched him under the chin, eliciting a monster-size purr.

Not to be outdone, Snowball padded into the room. She looked up at Brian, who smiled and patted his knee. "Come on, there's room for both of you. No one ever accused me of being skinny."

Snowball climbed onto his knee and leaned into him. Brian laughed. "This place is great. I knew bringing Smuggles here was the right thing to do." His smile faded. "Is it—I mean, can I visit with Smuggles for a few minutes? I bet he's fast asleep somewhere, right?"

"Of course you can. He's probably still in my bedroom. I'll go get him." Lara rose and collected the empty glasses, then paused. "Brian, I take it that you want him to stay with us for a while?"

"Yeah, I do. If it's okay, that is. At least until I know what's going to happen to me. And will you promise me something?"

Lara looked at her aunt. "I guess that depends on what it is," she said cautiously.

"If…I get sent to the pokey, will you keep him here and take care of him? You're the only ones I'd trust with him."

Aunt Fran exchanged a look with Lara, then was first to speak. "You can rest easy, Brian. If it gives you any comfort, know that Smuggles will stay here with us until you're ready to take him home. However long that takes."

"Thank you." Brian's eyes turned glassy.

Lara delivered the glasses to the kitchen sink, then headed upstairs. Smuggles was curled up in the big corner bed. He opened one eye when Lara reached down to lift him. "Come on, baby, your dad wants to visit with you."

Lara carried the cat downstairs, and Brian spent about twenty minutes with him in the meet-and-greet room. The elderly cat was content to lounge in his owner's lap and snooze. It was obvious that the two were close buds.

With a promise to keep them updated, Brian left shortly thereafter. Lara followed Aunt Fran into the kitchen and immediately called Sherry. She'd received several texts from her bestie over the course of the day but hadn't had a chance to respond.

"Hey, you got time to join me for an ice cream cone?" Lara asked her.

Sherry almost growled into the phone. "You bet I do, girl. We've both got lots to talk about. We might need three ice cream cones *apiece* by the time we're done."

Lara laughed. Her friend's no-nonsense tone had a magical quality. It lifted her spirits even on her worst days, regardless of the circumstances. She couldn't imagine what she'd ever do without her.

They agreed to meet at four thirty at Queen's Dairy Bar, a popular ice cream spot on Main Street.

Lara made a quick call to Gideon. They made tentative plans for later that evening and she promised to let him know when she got back from her date with Sherry.

Aunt Fran chuckled. "I couldn't help overhearing. You're going to have ice cream with Sherry, and then dinner with Gideon?"

"Sounds decadent, doesn't it?"

"Not really. Sometimes food really is the best medicine."

"Actually," Lara explained, "Gideon and I are planning a light supper. Salad with a loaf of rosemary bread and a glass of wine at The Irish Stew."

"Mmm. Now you're making me hungry."

"Why don't you come with us? Gideon would be thrilled to have you!"

Aunt Fran shook her head. "Thanks, but not tonight. My brain is worn out from everything that's happened today. I think I'll stretch out on the sofa with a bowl of Cheerios and my book and read to my heart's content."

Lara shoved her hands into the pockets of her pink capris. She leaned against the counter. "Aunt Fran, is it awful, my thinking about stuffing my face when a woman we knew was horribly murdered?"

"No," Aunt Fran said gently. "It's not horrible. The one meeting you and I had with Evonda was an unpleasant one, but that was all on her, not on us. She didn't deserve to die, but neither of us had anything to do with what happened to her. I feel sad for her family, and of course I'll attend the memorial service, if they have one. Aside from that, all I really want is for her killer to be brought to justice."

Lara was shocked. "You'd go to her memorial service?"

"Certainly. Wouldn't you?" Aunt Fran carried the newspaper from the counter to the table and sat down.

"Honestly, I don't know," Lara said, trailing after her. "I guess I hadn't thought that far ahead. Wouldn't it seem, you know, hypocritical if we attended?"

"Not at all. It's simply a sign of respect to the family. That's the least they deserve, isn't it?"

"Yeah, I guess you're right." Lara smiled. "Why are you so smart?"

Aunt Fran gave a dramatic shrug. "It's a trait I inherited from my favorite niece."

Chapter Eight

"I was tweezing my eyebrows this morning when I heard about the murder," Sherry told Lara. "I almost plucked out an eyeball!"

They sat at one of the wooden picnic tables behind Queen's Dairy Bar. All around them kids squealed while moms and dads and older siblings scolded and fussed. Tiny sparrows picked at the ground for stray crumbs. A young woman shared a vanilla cone with her eager black Lab.

Lara licked the edge of her soft-serve chocolate cone. She normally attacked ice cream cones with the zeal of a polar bear, but her attempt at finishing this one had been half-hearted at best. Most of it had already dripped onto the grass, and that was right before a sprinkle-coated blob had plopped onto her knee.

She took one last bite, wrapped a napkin around it, and tossed the whole thing into a nearby waste can.

"Good shot," Sherry said, studying her friend. "Although I never thought I'd see the day you'd throw one of those things away."

"I was starving before I got here," Lara said, "but once I started to eat, I lost my appetite." She wiped her mouth with a fistful of flimsy napkins. "Aunt Fran and I didn't find out about…the murder until the chief came over this morning to give us the bad news."

Sherry examined the remains of her dwindling cone. "Word got around fast. That ditzy Roy Tierney came into the coffee shop this morning right after the police let him go. Oh my gosh, you should've heard him. He was blathering to everyone about the red snea—"

The anguish registered on Lara's face stopped her midsentence.

"Hey, I'm sorry," Sherry said. "I didn't mean to get graphic. What's that saying? *Mea culpa?*"

"You don't have to apologize." Lara turned over what she knew in her mind. "In fact, the more I learn, the more I—" Averting her gaze from Sherry's, she rubbed her thumb over an old stain on the picnic table.

"The more you *what*? The more you can go snooping around?"

Lara lifted her chin. "No. I didn't mean that. Not exactly. I only meant that the more we know, the sooner Evonda's killer can be caught."

"I love the way you slipped the royal 'we' in there. Like you're part of the investigative team." Sherry bit off another chunk of her cone.

"Don't worry. I know I'm not part of the team, as you put it." She shot her friend what she hoped was a disarming smile. "No more about Evonda, okay? New subject. What's happening with you and David? Any definite plans yet? Should we be shopping for frilly gowns?"

It was almost a year ago that David and Sherry had met. He'd gone into Bowker's Coffee Stop for breakfast one morning, and the two had felt an instant attraction for each other. Though David had wanted to give Sherry a diamond ring seven months earlier, at Christmas, Sherry knew it was too soon for her. The few relationships she'd had ended badly. She had no intention of rushing into this one. They'd agreed that if they still felt the same about each other on the anniversary of the day they met, they would officially become engaged.

Sherry's cheeks pinked. "Frilly? Never. But I think we're going to do it, Lara. I think we're actually going to do it."

Lara squealed.

"Don't count your chickens yet," Sherry cautioned. "We still have a lot to talk about. Where to live. What kind of wedding. Where to have it…"

"Minor details," Lara scoffed. "The main thing is how you and David feel about each other. Is this right for you, Sher? Is this truly your heart's desire?"

"Oh my God. You sound like a character from a romance novel." Sherry hesitated only for a moment. "But…yeah, I think it is. I mean, after a year together we should know, right?"

"Then go for it," Lara said, feeling a pang. Would she and Gideon ever get to that point? "And whatever I can do to help, just let me know, okay? I'll even hand-paint your wedding invitations, if you'd like. Assuming you don't invite four hundred people."

Sherry's eyes glistened, and her mouth opened slightly. "Oh, Lara, that would be awesome. I'll bet no one else has ever done that. And don't worry about the guest list—no way are we inviting four hundred people. Forty at the most, and even that's a stretch."

Lara started to get excited now, thinking about the wedding and all the planning. "So, you think you'll wear something traditional?"

Sherry grinned. "Who knows? I haven't thought that far ahead." She popped the last bite of her cone into her mouth.

"Uh, yeah. I don't believe that for a minute. I saw that bridal magazine in your back seat a couple of days ago."

Sherry laughed, choked on her bite of cone, then finally swallowed it. "Leave it to the town detective to notice that." Her face softened. "I'm so glad you moved back here, Lara. If you were still in Boston, I don't know how I'd get through this."

"You'd get through it just fine. You'd have your mom, Loretta—"

"Yeah, but there's no one like you. As for Loretta," she said flatly, "the minute we make the announcement, I have a bad feeling she'll want to take over the reins and start planning it all on her own. Without any input from me and David, of course."

"You can handle her. I've seen you do it."

"Yeah, I guess I can. Hey, keep it under your hat for now, okay? I haven't really said much to Mom yet."

"Don't worry," Lara assured her. "Your secret is safe…for now. Hey, I meant to ask you. New subject, by the way. Do you remember Jenny Cooper from middle school?"

Sherry wiped her hands with a napkin. "Jenny? I think so, yeah. Quiet, kept to herself. Not much of a joiner. Not that I was, but Jenny was different. What makes you ask about her?"

"Turns out she's Evonda Fray's daughter-in-law," Lara said.

"Whoa. Seriously?"

"Yup. I met her, and her hubby, at the police station this morning."

Narrowing her eyes, Sherry gazed off into the distance. "I'm trying to remember her better. I know she went to Whisker Jog High, but for some reason I don't think she graduated with my class. I can't remember why, though, whether she moved, or…" She shook her head. "Maybe it'll come to me."

"Don't worry about it. I was just wondering." Lara looked at the time on her phone. "Good glory, is it almost six? I'm meeting Gideon at his place at seven. We're having a light supper tonight at the pub."

"Then let's get a move on," Sherry said.

A family of three—a pregnant mom and two young girls—strolled past them, glancing all around for a free table.

"We were just leaving," Lara said, smiling at them. "Take this one."

The mom looked relieved. "Oh, thank you," she said, tilting her chin at the table. "Janey, April, go sit over there. April, no! Don't set the cone down on the—Here…wait." She scuttled over and grabbed the cone from the younger girl while the child swung her legs around and settled in at the table.

"They're adorable." Sherry grinned and hoisted her purse onto her shoulder.

"Thanks," the mom said, blowing a strand of hair out of her eye. "Some days it's a juggling act."

"Think we'll ever be doing that?" Sherry said to Lara on their way to the parking lot.

Lara dug into her tote for her keys. "Doing what? Shuttling our kids around to get ice cream cones?"

"Yeah, you know. The whole mom thing. Think we'd be good at that?"

The idea made Lara smile. "Probably, but let's not jump three steps ahead. I'm definitely not ready for diapers yet. Changing them, that is."

Sherry snorted. "I'll never be ready for diapers."

"Goes with the territory," Lara warned.

By the time Lara and Sherry got to their cars, Lara's spirits had revived a bit. Once Sherry and David made it official, she could occupy herself with the wedding plans. Ideas for painting the watercolor invitations were already skipping through her head.

It was the one thing she could contribute to making Sherry's wedding unique. It would also be a welcome distraction from the unpleasantness of murder.

Chapter Nine

The Irish Stew was quieter than usual, mainly because it was early in the week. Several tables were empty, but nearly every booth was filled. Their favorite booth—the one in the far corner—was occupied, but the hostess had seated them at a cozy booth for two near the bar. On the dark-paneled wall next to them, the photo of a long-retired Red Sox player who'd dined at the pub ages ago hung from a sturdy nail. The scent of onions and herbs drifted from the kitchen, sending aromatic tendrils curling into every nook and cranny.

"I always forget how good this rosemary bread is until I get here," Gideon said. He slathered butter over a small piece and popped it into his mouth.

"It's one of the things the pub is known for," Lara reminded him. She jabbed a fork into her iceberg wedge.

As they ate their dinner, a silence settled over them. Lara liked to think it was a comfortable silence, the kind enjoyed by two people who've been together for a long time. Tonight, however, the tension felt as thick as the gravy in the pub's famed beef stew.

Gideon dabbed his mouth with his napkin and pushed aside his plate. He smiled over at Lara, but his eyes held a look of deep concern. "You've been awfully quiet," he said. "Did anything else happen today, other than meeting the Frays at the police station and Brian visiting his cat?"

Lara shook her head. The bubble of joy she'd felt after all the wedding talk with Sherry had burst the minute she got home. "No, it's just me. I'm in gloomy land today. Doesn't it strike you as totally weird that five people, counting Evonda, have been murdered since I moved back to town?"

For a long moment he studied her, and then his gaze softened. "Maybe a little," he confessed. "Hey, listen, coincidences happen all the time. You know that. Whisker Jog is just having a bad run, that's all."

Lara knew he was trying to make her feel better, and she loved him for it. Lately, though, she couldn't shake the feeling that murder followed her around like a baby duck waddling behind its mother.

"When you think about it," Gideon went on, "if it hadn't been for you, more than one of those killers might have gone free."

Lara sat back and folded her napkin. "I guess you have a point. So, what you're saying is, the universe brought me back here for a reason? Like, to solve murders?"

He chuckled. "Not exactly. But if the universe had anything to do with your moving back home, then hats off to the universe for a job well done." He reached over and took both her hands in his. "Seriously, Lara, we already know that the world holds all kinds of magic. You've proven that to me many times over."

Lara knew he was referring to Blue. It still warmed her heart to remember how accepting Gideon had been when she revealed her secret about a cat no one else could see. Blue had pulled her out of a bad spot more than once. Not only had Gideon never doubted her for a moment, but he'd embraced the idea of her having a spiritual guardian, and a feline one at that.

"Hey, I meant to ask you. Do you know Roy Tierney?"

"The guy who found Evonda this morning? Not really, but he used to deliver Uncle Amico's paper when he still lived at home."

Gideon's uncle, a sweet old man who'd just reached his ninetieth birthday, had moved into an assisted living facility a little over a year ago.

"Any reason you're asking?"

"Not really. I just wondered if you knew anything about him. I mean… maybe *he's* the killer. Maybe he only pretended to find Evonda's body—"

Gideon shook his head and smiled. "Nice try, honey."

Lara groaned. "I know, I know. I'm grasping, aren't I?"

"Lara." Gideon frowned. "You're already starting to worry me. I don't mean to beat up on the past, but remember what happened in December?"

Remember? How could she forget that terrifying confrontation with a desperate killer? Even now, Lara shuddered to think how it might have ended if it hadn't been for Blue.

"You don't have to worry." Lara squeezed his hands. "Lessons learned. I promise."

Gideon looked doubtful, but his face relaxed slightly. He paid the bill—it was his turn—and Lara swung her legs out of the booth.

A man who'd been sitting at one of the tables suddenly rose from his chair. He swept past their booth so quickly that his legs brushed Lara's sandals.

Lara pulled her legs back.

"Sorry," he muttered. "My fault."

"That's okay," Lara said. "No harm done."

Red-cheeked with a square, sturdy build, the fortysomething man stared at her for an uncomfortable moment. "Hey, I know you. I've seen your picture in the paper. You're Lara Caphart, aren't you?"

"Um…" She couldn't actually deny it. "Yes, I am."

"I thought so."

Lara glanced over at Gideon. From his expression, she knew he was slipping into protective mode but was trying to be discreet about it.

Gideon slid out of the booth and held out his hand. "Gideon Halley."

The man's flabby hand pumped Gideon's for a nanosecond. "Yeah, um…hi. Trevor Johnson." He switched his gaze back to Lara, his small, dark eyes boring into her. "I heard you got embroiled in this Evonda Fray mess. What a freakin' nightmare, huh?"

Lara went mute. Who was this guy? And how did he know about Evonda's visit to the shelter?

Wait a minute. Trevor Johnson. Now Lara remembered the name. He'd been the health inspector before Evonda—the one who supposedly got fired for accepting a bribe.

"If you mean her tragic death," Lara said crisply, "then yes, I'm sure it's a nightmare for her loved ones."

Johnson barked out a harsh laugh that grated in Lara's ears. "Loved ones? Like, are you kidding me? If she has loved ones, they've got horns sprouting from their heads and pitchforks in their hands."

As much as Lara had disliked Evonda, she was disgusted by the man's disrespect for the dead—and for the dead's family.

"Mr. Johnson, would you excuse us, please?" Lara said. "We were just leaving."

"Um, yeah. Sure." Johnson took a step backward, bumping the table behind him. "But I got one more thing to say, Miss Caphart. I heard about what happened at your shelter yesterday. Yeah, don't look so shocked. There are no secrets in this town." He pointed a stubby finger about an inch from her face. "Listen, I don't like cats. Never did. Never will. But I had that job before that witch got me fired, and I know a café when I see one. Bottom line—you guys ain't a café. Just sayin'. I'd have never done to you people what she did."

His lips tight, Gideon closed his hand around Johnson's finger. "I think we're done here, Mr. Johnson. Do you need me to escort you out to your car?"

Johnson's face paled. He snatched his finger out of Gideon's grasp. "No," he said with a curt nod at Lara. "Have a good evening."

In the next instant, Johnson turned on his heel and strode toward the exit.

Lara slumped back into the booth. Her hands were shaking. "Oh my God. That was awful. Can you believe that guy?"

Gideon looked furious. "Now I know why he got fired. On top of all his other issues, he's got the manners of a goat."

Lara looked around. Several people sitting nearby gawked at them. "I'm ready to leave," she said softly.

Gideon slipped his arm through hers and they went out to his car. She'd never seen herself as the damsel-in-distress type, but at that moment she was sorely tempted to melt into his arms. Instead, she got into the front seat and pulled on her seat belt. She stared through the windshield.

How could this be happening? It's like a recurring dream. A recurring bad *dream.*

She made an instant decision. This time, she was not going to get involved. Let the police do their own investigating. Let the police find the killer.

Lara never wanted to hear the name Evonda Fray again.

Chapter Ten

Her sunglasses covering half her face, Lara walked to the coffee shop the next morning with her head down. She didn't want to see anyone or be forced to engage in polite chatter with any passersby.

She was in a mood.

Aunt Fran had tactfully suggested that morning that they postpone both the grand opening celebration on Saturday, as well as the first official "read-to-a-cat" day on Sunday. Reluctantly, Lara had agreed. Until Evonda's killer was caught, the shelter remained under a dark cloud. Her heart heavy in her chest, she'd made all the announcements on their social media pages.

The outside temps hovered in the eighties and it wasn't even ten o'clock. The sun beamed in the eastern sky with the promise of another broiler.

Without so much as a glance through the window, Lara walked past Kurl-me-Klassy, the salon where Kellie Byrd trimmed her hair once a month. Kellie's window boxes, overflowing with pink pansies, looked in need of a cool drink.

Lara went into Bowker's Coffee Stop. Sherry and her mom, Daisy, had run the café by themselves for years—a schedule that left almost no time for a social life. At the end of last year, Daisy had landed a side gig baking her scrumptious sugar cookies for a specialty gift basket company. The extra income was a godsend. Instead of Daisy having to juggle cooking with serving, they were able to hire a helper.

Jill, with her short, dark hair and jeweled eyebrow rings, bustled around the tables like an energetic steam engine. Initially she'd worked at the coffee shop only on weekends to bolster the income from her day job. After the holidays, however, her day job went south. She'd gotten so attached to the coffee shop that she'd agreed to come on board full time.

Lara headed directly to her favorite stool at the counter. Sherry was missing. Probably in the kitchen. The tables were nearly all filled. The enticing scent of cinnamon and apples wafted over the café.

"Hey, girl." Jill, holding a steaming coffeepot aloft, slipped her free arm around Lara in a hug.

"Hey, Jill." Lara hugged her back.

"You need a pick-me-up, I can tell. Apple muffin and coffee coming right up."

"Thanks. That'll hit the spot. Where's Mr. Patello today?" Lara dipped her chin at the empty stool beside her.

"Been sick, I think. Who knows, with him?"

The elderly gent was cranky and fussy, but he was a fixture at the coffee shop. He always took up two stools—his own and his friend Herbie's. Herbie had died a few years earlier, but Mr. Patello saw to it every day that no one could occupy his friend's spot by plopping his hat on it.

Jill returned with her coffee, muffin, and Sherry, then scooted off into the dining area.

"Hey, I wondered if you were coming in this morning." Sherry grinned and slid the bowl of creamers over to Lara. With her fingers, she made a twisting motion over her lips in a be-careful-what-you-say gesture. "See that old dude over there with the red cap?" she whispered.

Lara turned her head toward the dining area. A slight man with deeply wrinkled skin was hunched over a table at which three men were eating. His cardinal-red hat was at least three sizes too big for his head. "I see him," she said.

"Roy Tierney," Sherry said quietly. "He doesn't usually come in here mornings. But ever since he found the, you know, *body* yesterday, he discovered he's got quite the audience here. He's been blabbing for half an hour about it to everyone. You'd think he'd have gotten it out of his system yesterday, but *noooo…*" She sighed. "I guess he's going to milk the story for all it's worth. His fifteen minutes of fame, right?"

Fifteen minutes of fame—the same expression Brian Downing had used.

Lara absently buttered her muffin. "It's getting out of control, Sherry. Last night at the pub, a guy named Trevor Johnson confronted me. Do you know him, by the way?"

Sherry's expression changed, and she looked away. "Um, you mean the guy who used to be the health inspector?" She bent to find something underneath the counter.

"The very same." Lara told Sherry about her encounter with the man at The Irish Stew.

"Next time just ignore him," Sherry said, her voice muffled from under the counter. "He's bitter over getting fired."

"I hope there isn't a next time," Lara said, then chuckled. "For one scary minute, I thought Gideon was going to punch his lights out. Not that he would, but he didn't like the way Johnson was sticking his finger right in my face."

Sherry stood up and smiled, a package of napkins in her hand. "Found 'em."

"Johnson really gave me the creeps. Have you ever met him?" She swallowed another chunk of her muffin.

"Um…" Sherry looked away. "Once, maybe, I think."

Hmmm, why was her friend being so evasive? Did she know something about Johnson she didn't want to reveal?

A cluster of four men shuffled toward the front door, the red-hatted Tierney in the lead. "Hoo boy, lemme tell ya, when I saw that plastic band wrapped around that lady's neck, why my liver about dropped!" Tierney pushed open the door and headed outside, his rapt audience trailing in his wake.

Sherry crossed her eyes. "See what I mean? The guy's a nut. Even the cops haven't been able to keep his lips buttoned."

Lara shook her head. Tierney might be a nut, but she couldn't picture him as the killer. He was too much of a blabbermouth—he'd have wanted to tell everyone about it. If he'd murdered Evonda, by now he'd have probably confessed.

No, it was Trevor Johnson Lara wanted to know more about. Had the police interviewed him? According to Gideon, Johnson's feelings about Evonda had been well-documented. Shouldn't he be at the top of the suspect list?

She finished her coffee and muffin, then paid the tab. "Hey, I'd better run. Kayla's coming over later. We're going to work on setting up the new reading room today."

"Isn't your book club meeting today?"

Lara and her aunt belonged to a classics book club that met at the coffee shop every Wednesday afternoon. Brooke Weston, a high school student, and Mary Newman, a local business owner, were the other two members. Mary was on vacation this week with her husband in Montreal.

"It was," Lara said, "but Mary's away, so Aunt Fran called Brooke and canceled it. Besides, she figured with everything else that's going on…"

"Say no more." Sherry scooted around the side of the counter and gave Lara an impulsive hug. "You didn't do anything wrong, Lara, so try not to dwell on it. I know it's hard, especially because you're, well, you, but—"

Lara laughed. "Yeah, I'm me. Sometimes I wish I were someone else."

"Don't you ever say that," Sherry scolded. "Now go home and be the cat lady and stop thinking about the murder. Okay?"

If only, Lara thought dolefully.

She gave her friend a half-hearted promise to do as instructed.

Walking home, she reminded herself of her vow to let the police, and only the police, find Evonda's killer.

Not my job. Not my department.

So why did she have the irresistible urge to hurry home and Google the daylights out of Trevor Johnson?

* * * *

Kayla Ramirez showed up around eleven thirty, earlier than usual for her. Lara was more than happy to see her.

A vet tech student at a local college, Kayla had impressed Lara and Aunt Fran the previous summer when they were looking for a part-time helper. While she loved all animals fiercely, Kayla had a strong preference for cats. She treasured her job at the shelter and knew every feline resident's quirks and preferences. With her classes out for the summer, she had far more flexibility in her schedule.

"Hey, I left a container of books in the reading room," Kayla said when Lara came into the kitchen. She was having a glass of lemonade with Aunt Fran, who had Dolce curled in her lap.

"Excellent," Lara said.

"Wait till you see them, Lara," Kayla gushed. "Practically new. All good stuff, too." She pushed her glasses higher on her nose.

Kayla's enthusiasm would normally ignite Lara's spirits. Today she had to force herself to paste on a smile.

"That's great. Where did you get them?"

"From my gram's neighbor. Good thing I'm friends with her, because my gram never tells her anything about my work," Kayla added, a slight edge to her tone. "Anyway, the neighbor used to buy books for her grandkids, but she made them leave them at her house so they could read them only when they visited. Kind of like a bribe, you know? Once they got older, she packed them away in a plastic tub. I told her about our reading room, and she was thrilled to donate them."

"I was telling Kayla what happened with Mrs. Fray," Aunt Fran said quietly.

"Yeah, major bummer." Kayla frowned. "I've known people who didn't like cats, but it sounds like she was way over the top. God rest her soul." She crossed herself.

"I know, and I don't think it's because she was afraid of them. I didn't get that sense at all." Her mind skittered back to that single moment when she'd have sworn Evonda had gazed tenderly at Snowball.

Lara and Kayla went into the reading room and began putting books on the shelves. "I love the new door, by the way," Kayla said. "How did you ever find a screen door with a cat?"

Same question Nina had asked. Lara shrugged. "The usual way. Trolling the internet."

Kayla stooped in front of the box of books. "Should we shelve them alphabetically by author?"

"Good question." Lara fished through the books. She was pleased by the wide selection of volumes, all with beautifully illustrated covers. Most looked brand-new. "Most kids don't really think in terms of authors. They want books for their age group that interest them. Oh, look at this one. The cover shows a caterpillar reading to an ant." Lara smiled and held it up for Kayla.

"Aw, isn't that the sweetest? The caterpillar's wearing glasses!" Kayla closed her hands over her heart.

They decided to shelve the books by approximate age group. When they were done, there were still several shelves free for more books.

"There, that's done for now," Lara said. "As we go along, I'm sure we'll have to do some shifting."

"And some kids will bring their own books," Kayla noted. With sympathy in her gaze, she touched Lara's arm. "Are you bummed about postponing the opening day?"

"Don't remind me." Lara forced a smile. "Hey, it's okay. It'll all work out eventually, right?"

Kayla nodded, but she looked crestfallen. She'd been looking forward to their first "read-to-a-cat" day more than anyone.

As for everything working out, Lara wasn't sure she believed it anymore. Once again, an ugly murder had gripped their little town in a vise. She hadn't heard of any progress being made in the police investigation. Did they even have a single suspect in mind?

"Lara?" Aunt Fran came into the room. She looked around and smiled. "Oh, my. It already looks cozy and inviting in here, doesn't it?" Her smile faded. "Jerry just called. He wanted us to know there's going to be a memorial service for Evonda on Friday morning."

"So soon?"

"Yes. Apparently, the medical examiner has released her...body. The police are still analyzing evidence from the crime scene, but at least the poor woman can be laid to rest. Her son wants the service held as soon as possible."

"I don't blame him. He wants closure."

"You'll attend, won't you, Lara?"

Lara hugged her aunt. "You know I will. It's the right thing to do."

Lara thought of another, more important question.

Will the killer attend as well?

Chapter Eleven

Googling the former health inspector's name proved to be a frustrating task.

Lara bit down on her lip as she searched, once again, for a Facebook page for Trevor Johnson.

Nothing. At least not for *her* Trevor Johnson. He also didn't have an Instagram or a Twitter page. The man didn't appear to have a social media presence whatsoever.

One thing she did land on was the news clip Gideon had referred to, about Johnson getting fired. A vague reference to a suspected bribe was described in only a few sentences. It made Lara wonder if the case against Johnson had any real validity. Had Evonda set him up? Had she fudged the story about him accepting a bribe?

As much as Lara had been turned off by Johnson's uncouth behavior, she hated the idea that his career might have been unfairly sabotaged. Gossip was a vicious thing. It had been known to destroy careers and tear lives apart.

I can't do this anymore. It's not my job.

Switching gears, Lara pulled up one of her favorite Web sites. The world's most famous artists were listed alphabetically by name. A simple click of the mouse revealed images of their paintings, along with background info.

She clicked the link to Renoir, one of the early Impressionists. It was the works of Renoir that Lara had first imagined when she offered to paint watercolor invitations for Sherry's wedding.

Renoir had painted a series of dance scenes, but the one Lara remembered best was *Dance in the Country*. In the painting, a dark-haired man and red-haired woman sway in each other's arms, while the background fades into soft brushstrokes. The woman's joy is evident in her warm smile. The model for the woman was, in fact, the woman Renoir would later marry.

Although Lara worked with a different medium—watercolors—it was the concept she wanted to capture. She knew it was too soon to get excited about the project. Sherry hadn't even announced her engagement. Still, it would be fun to toy with a few ideas—and it might help take her mind off the murder.

The small parlor—aka her art studio—was warm but not unbearable. Keeping the shade down during the day blocked the sun and kept the space comfortable. Lara switched on her floor fan. She tied her curly red hair high off her neck with a scrunchie, set up her supplies, and went to work.

Around five thirty, after she'd experimented with a few whimsical scenes of Sherry and David dancing in each other's arms, she heard voices drifting from the kitchen. It was time to think about throwing something together for supper for her and Aunt Fran. She began cleaning up her work area.

Without warning, Aunt Fran opened the door. "Lara." Her face was the color of ash, and she clasped the doorknob for support.

Lara rushed over to her. "Aunt Fran, what's wrong? What happened?"

Chief Jerry Whitley appeared behind her aunt, his expression somber. Another man was with him, but from where Lara stood, she couldn't see his face.

"What's going on?" Lara asked.

"They…need to talk to us," Aunt Fran said, her voice softer than a child's.

Alarms went off in Lara's head. Whatever this was about, it wasn't good.

She looped her arm through her aunt's, and they all went into the large parlor. Orca and Pearl occupied separate perches on the cat tree. Their ears perked at the visitors, but they didn't venture down. Snowball was curled up on the sofa, her nose resting on her paws.

The chief stared at his shoes and twirled his hat, then his brow furrowed. His casually dressed, fortysomething companion, whoever he was, set down a briefcase on an end table.

At the sound of the chief's voice, Munster had trotted downstairs and rubbed against his trouser leg. The chief's face remained impassive, as if he hadn't noticed. He cleared his throat. "I'll try to make this as painless as possible. Earlier today, the state police got a call from the crime lab. Unfortunately, I didn't hear about it until about a half hour ago. Bottom line, they have Evonda Fray's car impounded. As you would expect, they've been going over it with a fine-tooth comb."

A ribbon of fear wound its way through Lara. "And?" Her voice sounded distant in her ears.

"I'm afraid they found cat hair in the back seat."

Cat hair? In Evonda's car? The woman hated cats.

Lara's body felt numb. Where was Chief Whitley going with this? "I don't understand. What are you talking about?"

The chief went on. "The state police investigators believe that the cat hair came from the killer."

Every nerve in Lara's body tingled. She swallowed. "S–so? The killer probably owns a cat. Lots of people have cats."

The chief's voice was low. "The cat hair was gray, from a short-haired cat. Most of it anyway." With a pained expression, he eyed the cat tree, then looked over at the sofa. "I'm afraid we're going to need hair, I mean, fur samples from two of your cats. The gray one up there, and…Snowball."

Lara's knees wobbled. She looked over at the crime lab guy, whose cheeks were flaming. He looked as if he'd rather be anywhere else on the planet than where he was.

"This is a joke, right? Because you *cannot* be serious about this."

The chief sighed. "I'm sorry, but I'm afraid we are. Obviously, the cats will not be harmed. It's only fur."

Aunt Fran looked ready to snap. "Jerry," she said with carefully controlled fury, "are you saying you want to snip sections of their fur to take to the lab?"

"I don't want to," he answered flatly. "Unfortunately, it's part of my job." He looked over at the other man and nodded. "This gentleman is from the crime lab. He's here to take the…samples. It's a simple procedure. It will only take a minute or two of your—"

"No," Lara said hotly. "He is *not* going to take a sample of either Pearl's fur or Snowball's. What is the matter with you people? How can you even think anyone in this household was involved in that murder?" She had a sudden urge to stomp her foot, but it would only make her look like a spoiled child.

The tech guy shot a look at the chief, then pulled a sheet of paper out of the briefcase and handed it to him.

The chief held it out to Lara. "This is a warrant, giving us the authority. It was obtained earlier this afternoon."

Tears poked at Lara's eyes. She swiped them off, then snatched the warrant out of his hand. Her vision blurred at the words.

"Miss." The tech spoke up, his voice softer than she anticipated. "Chief Whitley actually misspoke. There's no snipping involved. I only need to brush each of them a few times. I promise. That way I have a better chance of getting the follicles." He attempted to smile, but it was more like a grimace. "I have a clean, new brush for each of them." The tech pulled two brushes, each in a sealed bag, out of his briefcase.

This can't be happening. This must be one of those nightmares that goes from scene to scene with no end in sight.

After a long moment, Lara gave the man a brisk nod. She held Pearl in her arms while the tech ran a soft brush over her coat. After several sweeps, he dropped the brush into a bag, sealed it, and labeled it. They repeated the process with Snowball, who looked pleased as ever at the attention from a stranger.

Munster pawed at the tech's leg, as if begging for his turn. The tech smiled. "I'd pat him, but I can't risk contamination of the evidence." He dropped the two bags into his briefcase and snapped it shut. "By the way, I think your cats are very cute."

"Thank you, Fran, Lara," the chief said, his face red. A vein throbbed over his left eye. He looked almost angry. He plunked his hat on his head and proceeded behind the tech guy through the kitchen. He paused at the door. "I just want to say one thing, Fran. I made the decision to deliver the bad news myself, because I thought it would be better coming from me rather than from one of the state police investigators. I guess I was wrong."

He was almost outside on the porch when Aunt Fran grasped his sleeve. "You know what hurts the most, Jerry?" Her voice trembled.

"I'm afraid to ask."

"You didn't even remember Pearl's name."

Chapter Twelve

"What's happening, Aunt Fran?" Lara asked, her stomach in a knot. She tried to swallow a bite of her potato salad, but it stuck in her mouth like a boulder. She had to wash it back with a sip of lemonade to make it slide down her throat. "What did we do to deserve this? Our shelter is being attacked—*we're* being attacked—and we don't even know why."

Aunt Fran still looked pale. Better than she had an hour earlier, but definitely not herself.

In fact, Lara hadn't seen her looking this bad since that fateful October day, nearly two years earlier, when Lara first arrived in Whisker Jog. After receiving word from Sherry that her aunt hadn't been doing well, Lara left her studio apartment in Boston, rented a car, and drove to the Folk Victorian home that her aunt had lived in for as long as she could remember. Frail and weak, her aunt had answered the door clutching a kitten in one hand and a cane in the other. With two badly arthritic knees, Aunt Fran hadn't been able to care for all the strays she'd taken in. The house was in dire need of a good scrubbing, and her aunt was in desperate need of help.

"I can't eat either," Aunt Fran finally said, pushing her plate aside. "As to your question, I don't know why this is happening."

"I'm sorry about the chief." Lara reached over and squeezed her aunt's hand.

"Don't be." Aunt Fran lifted her chin stoically, but Lara saw the hurt in her eyes. "Whatever is meant to be, will be. I still don't get this thing with the cat hair. What would make the police suspect it was Pearl's or Snowball's?"

The more Lara thought about it, the angrier she got. "The chief knows we have a white cat and a gray cat. I suppose the information could've come directly from him." The idea that the chief would tattle that way made her immensely sad.

Aunt Fran released a sigh. She was thinking the same thing.

"Oh, no," Lara said. "I just thought of something. Smuggles—Brian's cat." She looked at her aunt.

"Has gray fur," Aunt Fran said slowly. "Slightly darker than Pearl's because he's a tiger cat, but definitely gray. But here's the problem with that theory. Brian didn't bring Smuggles here until *after* Evonda had left on Monday."

"You're right," Lara said. "But Evonda had been in Brian's apartment at least one time. She could've picked up a few cat hairs that way, without realizing it, and somehow it got left in her car." Her head throbbing with conflicting thoughts, Lara collected their dishes and brought them over to the sink. "It kills me to say this," she said, coming back to the table, "but this might all go back to Brian Downing. I like the guy—he's a real cat lover—but he didn't hide the fact that he loathed Evonda. Maybe all his drama yesterday was just a cover-up to disguise his guilt."

"Could be. Didn't he admit, though, that he grabbed Evonda's car window when she was trying to leave the parking lot at his apartment? Maybe some of his cat's hair got inside her car that way."

"That's a thought," Lara said. "Darn. I wonder if the gray cat hair they found belongs to Smuggles and not Pearl."

The ping of a text sounded from Aunt Fran's pocket. She looked at Lara, then pulled out her cell and read it. Almost imperceptibly, she shook her head, then slipped the phone back in her pocket.

Lara stared at her aunt.

"I won't keep you in suspense," Aunt Fran said with a wry smile. "That was Jerry. All it said was 'can we talk later.'"

"You didn't answer him," Lara said wickedly.

"I'll answer him when I'm ready to answer him." Her aunt stared at the table, as if mulling everything in her mind. "Lara, I almost hate to ask this, but…have you had any clues lately? From a certain guardian cat?"

Lara smiled. Her spirit cat, Blue, hadn't made an appearance since Tuesday morning, when the chief showed up to break the bad news about Evonda's murder. "Oddly, no. But maybe there's not enough yet to go on."

"Is it possible…" Aunt Fran began, then shook her head. "No, never mind."

"Tell me," Lara coaxed.

"I just wondered, could Evonda have touched Pearl or Snowball when we weren't looking? Maybe gotten a few cat hairs on her clothing?"

"Touched? You mean like, patted her?" Lara looked at her aunt, aghast.

Aunt Fran nodded. "Stranger things have happened. Maybe she wasn't the cat hater she claimed to be."

"Wow. That's something to think about, I guess. Still, I can't picture it." A memory tickled her brain. "Although…"

"Although?" her aunt prodded, after a long moment.

"That day she was here, before we went into the kitchen, I'd have sworn, for a split second, that she looked at Snowball with something like…I don't know, tenderness? Affection? But it went away so quickly that I figured I imagined it."

"Maybe not." Aunt Fran said. "Maybe that's the answer."

Chapter Thirteen

Early Thursday morning, a call came into the shelter. A woman who worked at a bakery in Tamworth, the adjacent town, had found an abandoned litter of kittens at the bakery's back door when she arrived to begin her shift.

"We'll be there as soon as we can," Lara said, and immediately called Kayla.

"I'll be at your place in twenty," Kayla said. "We can go from there."

Lara had spent the better part of the night tossing in her bed, agonizing over the results of the cat-hair analysis. The whole incident with the crime scene tech had seemed surreal, as if it had happened to someone else. When she awakened, she rubbed her eyes and wondered if she'd dreamed the whole thing. Then reality kicked in with the force of a steel-toe boot. A fresh wave of worry washed over her.

Lara debated whether or not to tell Kayla about the warrant the police had served the day before. She decided not to mention it, at least for now. The incident might well blow over. In the meantime, it would only give Kayla something else to worry about. Lately Kayla had seemed distracted. Lara didn't want to press her on it, but she suspected the young woman was having issues at home.

Forty minutes later, they pulled into a small parking lot behind the bakery—a clapboard affair painted a startling shade of lilac. Two covered trash cans squatted near the back door, which flew open the moment they stepped out of the Saturn.

"Oh, thank heavens you're here!" A slender, thirtyish woman with huge brown eyes and fluffy pink hair rushed toward them. "I'm Meg Carmel, by the way. Sorry to call you guys so early, but…I've got a situation."

"It's never too early to call the shelter," Lara assured her. "I'm Lara, and this is Kayla."

"Great to meet you both. I'm hoping you're going to be my saviors," she said with a concerned look. "Come on in. I did the best I could getting them settled in a comfy spot, but these guys need help—and soon."

They followed Meg through the bakery's rear entrance. The room was obviously a storage room, with metal shelves extending along one wall. The shelves were stacked with boxes of foodstuffs—flour, sugar, canned goods, and other supplies. At the far end was the door to a walk-in fridge. In front of that, on the floor, was a deep, cardboard bakery box.

"Take a peek." Meg pointed at the box, a pear-shaped diamond winking off her left ring finger.

Kayla had already spotted them. "Oh my God, look at them," she squeaked, dropping down in front of the box.

Lara took in a breath at the sight. Four tiny kittens, about five or six weeks old, were nestled on a bed of towels inside the box. Two were black-and-white, one was solid black, and the fourth was the tiniest ball of golden fur Lara had ever seen.

"Look at those little faces," Lara said, bending to stroke each of the kittens with a gentle finger. "You said someone left them in front of the door?"

"Exactly. See, I always come in around four in the morning to start baking," Meg explained, "so it's always dark out. Anyway, when I got here, I saw this huge wicker basket"—she spread her arms about a yard apart—"just sitting there on the pavement in front of the door. In the dark, I nearly tripped over the darn thing! A sheet had been tucked around the inside of it, which was way weird. My heart tripped for a second. I thought maybe someone had left me an unpleasant surprise or something, you know? All kinds of creeps out there these days." She shook her head. "But then I heard a teeny, tiny cry, so I pulled back the sheet. This is what I found." She gazed at the kittens. "Imagine someone dumping these little darlings like they were trash?" She sniffed.

Unfortunately, as Lara well knew, it happened far too often. She peered more closely at the kittens. They definitely had fleas, and the tiniest one—the golden fluffball—struggled to cozy up to his siblings.

"I'm sure they're hungry," Meg said worriedly. "I made a formula from powdered milk and tried giving each one drops from my finger, but I don't think they were sure what to do. The little gold one turned his face away. He was having none of it. Poor little things are probably starving."

"Is this a bakery box?" Kayla asked her. "It's huge."

"It is, but it's the kind we use for commercial deliveries," Meg explained. "I wanted to be sure the little cuties couldn't escape. 'Course, if the health inspector were to pop in right now, my bakery would be toast, wouldn't it?" She laughed.

"We'll definitely take them," Lara assured Meg. "They need immediate veterinary care. Our vet in Whisker Jog, Amy Glindell, is terrific. She'll give them a thorough exam, treat them for fleas, worms, etc. Doesn't look as if anyone cared about them enough to have gotten them their first shots. Amy'll take care of that, too."

Looking disgusted, Meg crossed her arms over her shapely chest. "Sometimes I like cats better than people. Actually, I *do* like cats better than people."

"I'm with you there," Kayla said sharply. "People suck, don't they?"

Lara kept her expression neutral, but the bitterness of Kayla's response surprised her.

"Meg," Lara said, "do you have any idea who dumped the kittens here?"

Meg shook her head. "No, but—well, I'm sort of known around here as a cat nut. I have four of my own. Someone might have figured, you know, because I love cats, that I'd take them all in. Or at least find them homes."

Kayla frowned and shook her head. "We should get going, Lara. These babies need to get to the vet ASAP."

Lara gave Meg one of the shelter's business cards. "Feel free to call and check on them any time," Lara said. "And don't worry, they're in excellent hands. In a few weeks, I bet you won't even recognize them." She pointed at Meg's diamond ring and smiled. "Are you engaged?"

Meg looked at her hand. "Oh, yeah." She giggled. "Happened about two months ago. I lucked out and found a guy who isn't a complete jerk. Hard to do these days, right?"

"You sound kind of jaded."

"Nah. Just that I went through more than my share of frogs. It was about time I met a prince. Well, an almost prince. These days, the good ones are few and far between."

"Well, congratulations," Lara said. "I wish you both the best."

"Thanks." Releasing a sigh, Meg cast a final glance at the kittens. "You'll make sure they all find good homes, right? You won't—" She swallowed, and her brow creased.

"At the High Cliff Shelter, every cat remains with us until we find them the right home. And we're darned fussy, too. We never adopt out a cat or kitten unless we're sure it's a perfect match."

Meg sagged. "Oh God, that's such a relief. Sorry, but I don't know anything about your shelter. I just Googled animal shelters on my phone and called the closest one."

"When you get a chance," Lara said, "take a peek at our Web site. I think you'll be pleasantly surprised."

Meg hugged them both, tears forming in her eyes. "You gals have already made my day. Hold on a second, okay?" She dashed through a swinging door toward the front of the bakery. She returned holding a square pink box. "Apple fritters. Fresh out of the fryer. To die for, if I do say so myself."

"Oh, I can't wait to try them," Lara said, though she certainly didn't intend to die for one. "Thank you, Meg."

"Thanks," Kayla said without much enthusiasm. "They sound great." Turning away, she gently picked up the cardboard box containing the kittens. Her face softened into a smile as she gazed down at their tiny faces.

After another round of goodbyes, Lara and Kayla went out to the car. Kayla tucked the box with the kittens safely onto the back seat. "They should be fine till we get to Amy's," Kayla said. "No way they can climb out of there—it's too deep. Better get the AC cranking, though. It's already getting too warm for them in the car."

Lara nodded and climbed into the driver's seat. She flicked the AC on High. "We'll have air in a minute."

"I'm glad she contacted us," Lara said, on the way home. "Several people have already called the shelter asking if we had any kittens. I know we'll be able to find great homes for them. But we're going to be superparticular."

"Mmm-hmm."

Lara tried again. "I can't wait to taste one of those apple fritters, can you? And Aunt Fran's going to love them."

"Yep," Kayla said.

Something was definitely up with Kayla. On the way to the bakery, all she'd been able to talk about was rescuing those kittens. Now she seemed irritated about something. She'd been understandably angry at someone abandoning four helpless kittens, but Lara sensed something else was going on.

Kayla had recently made a permanent move to her grandmother's home in Tuftonboro. It helped her save money, which she needed for tuition, and from there, it was only a short ride to the shelter. Plus, her gram occasionally needed help with groceries and appointments, so the arrangement worked well for both.

Lately, however, whenever Kayla mentioned her grandmother, it was always with an edge to her voice. Something was amiss in the household. Lara would bet on it.

For now, Lara decided to let it go. Kayla was moody at times. Besides, everyone had the right to a bad day, didn't they? For sure, Lara'd had her share.

They were pulling into the parking lot of the veterinary hospital when Kayla swiveled her head toward Lara. "I have a great name for the gold one," she said, animated now. "Fritter."

Lara smiled. "I love it. Fritter it is."

"And the black-and-white one, the one with the black patch under his chin? Can we name him Aden, A-D-E-N? It was my maternal grandfather's name. He had a goatee just like that."

"I like the name, but are we sure it's a him?" Lara asked. "When Snowball first came into the shelter, I thought she was a male."

Kayla shrugged. "I guess we'll know soon enough. But the name could work for either a male or a female, so what's the dif?"

In no mood to argue, Lara swiftly agreed. But once they got back to the shelter, she intended to have a chat with Kayla.

The young woman was hurting, that much was clear. If there was any way Lara could help, she would.

Chapter Fourteen

With the kittens safely delivered to the veterinary hospital, Lara and Kayla headed back to the shelter.

Aunt Fran was in the kitchen, throwing together a macaroni salad. "I thought I'd do this early, before the day gets any warmer. How about burgers on the grill with macaroni salad?" she asked Lara.

Lara smiled. "Are you kidding? Count me in." She peeked into the glass bowl in which Aunt Fran was blending the salad ingredients. "You're adding peas?"

"Of course. You and I both like them, right?"

"Uh, yeah, we do." But Chief Whitley didn't. The man hated peas. Did that mean he wasn't invited? Usually, when they grilled outside, it was a given that Aunt Fran asked the chief to join them.

"You need me to pick up anything?" Lara asked.

"No, but thank you for the offer. I still have some of the beefsteak tomatoes I bought at the farm stand last week. We can use those on the burgers. Kayla, some pink lemonade?" Aunt Fran wiped her hands on a towel and pulled a pitcher out of the fridge.

"Sure, sounds good. Thanks."

Lara set the pink box on the kitchen table. She grabbed some plates and napkins, and then opened the box. Six apple fritters nestled inside, golden brown and coated in a sugary glaze. The sight of them made her taste buds dance for joy. She reached into the box for a fritter and set it on Aunt Fran's plate.

"Oh, they look delicious," Aunt Fran said, sitting at the table with them. "Split this one with me?"

"Sure," Lara agreed, although she'd hoped to scarf down a whole one on her own.

Kayla removed one from the box and set it on her plate.

"How are you today, Kayla?" Aunt Fran asked, gazing kindly at her. Had she gleaned that Kayla wasn't in the best of spirits?

"I'm okay," Kayla said and took a small bite of the fritter.

Lara exchanged a glance with her aunt, and then she and Kayla gave Aunt Fran a recap of what had happened with the kittens.

"So, we're going to have four tiny new residents," Aunt Fran said. "I can't wait to see them."

"They're going to need a lot of care for a while," Lara cautioned. "I'll make up the cot in the isolation room and sleep in there until they're okay to be on their own at night."

Dolce sidled in from the large parlor and leaped silently onto Aunt Fran's lap. She laughed and placed a hand on the kitty's back. "My constant companion."

"We've already named two of the kittens," Kayla piped in. "Fritter and Aden. The other two names are up for grabs."

"Well, you gals can name them," Aunt Fran said.

Munster and Snowball trotted into the kitchen, each one sizing up the room for a free lap. Kayla scooped up Snowball and kissed her head, which left Munster to seek out the last available lap—Lara's.

"Everyone has a cat," Lara said with a laugh.

"Everyone *should* have a cat," Kayla snapped, hugging Snowball to her chest.

Oh boy, Lara thought, *that touched a nerve.*

Was Kayla angry because her grandmother didn't allow cats in the house? Was that the reason she'd been a bit testy lately?

The sight of Snowball's sweet face reminded Lara of the afternoon before, when that crime scene tech had shown up with the chief to take a sample of her fur. She'd been so distracted with their kitten mission that it had temporarily slipped her mind.

Kayla looked embarrassed at her outburst. "If it's okay, I'll head home. I wasn't supposed to put in any hours today anyway. I'll be back tomorrow for adoption day."

"Of course, Kayla," Aunt Fran said in a soothing voice. "Whatever works for you. Lara and I will be attending the service for Mrs. Fray, but we should be home by noon."

Lara set Munster on her chair and cleaned up the table. Kayla hadn't finished her fritter, so Lara wrapped it in foil for her to take home. "Would you like one for your gram?"

Kayla shook her head. "No. She can have a bite of mine."

Lara wished she'd had a chance to talk further to Kayla, but she seemed anxious to leave. She probably needed some time alone to sort out her thoughts.

Lara was shoving the wrapped fritter into a paper bag when the front doorbell rang. She jumped. More bad news on the way?

When Lara didn't move, Kayla shot her a strange look. "I think that was your doorbell."

Her heart hammering in her chest, Lara went to the front door on legs that felt like cooked noodles. *Deep breaths*, she reminded herself. *Deep breaths*.

A state police investigator—the same one who'd interviewed her on Tuesday—stood stiffly on the doorstep.

"Miss Caphart, I'm sorry to trouble you." His clipped tone told her he wasn't sorry at all. "We're going to need you to come down to the station for a few more questions. If you need a minute to get ready, that's fine. We'll go in my car."

Lara peered into the driveway. An unmarked state police car idled behind the Saturn. "But...why?" Lara swallowed. "Can't you ask the questions here?"

"It's just a formality," he said. "We'll see that you get a ride home."

Aunt Fran moved up beside her. "What's going on?"

"It's nothing." She didn't want her aunt to stress over it, even though she herself was scared witless. "The police just want to ask me a few more questions. I'll be back soon. Nothing to worry about."

Aunt Fran looked stricken. "Should I call Gideon?" she asked under her breath.

"Not yet. I can call from there if I need to." She gave her aunt a fast hug and, over her shoulder, caught a glimpse of Kayla.

Still clutching Snowball, Kayla stared at her, openmouthed.

"It'll be okay, Kayla," Lara said, sensing her distress. "I'll be back before you know it."

Kayla nodded. Then she hugged Snowball even harder and ran back into the kitchen.

Chapter Fifteen

For the umpteenth time, Lara looked at the photo. She'd been grinding her teeth for so long, it was a wonder she hadn't worn them to nubs.

Once again, she examined the enlarged pic of a length of plastic strapping. This time, it blurred and wiggled in her vision. What was she supposed to see? An image of the murderer?

Lara pushed the photo aside. "As I already explained, Lieutenant, it looks like the kind of clear plastic strap used for shipping. Other than that, I have no way of identifying that *particular* plastic strap. It's not as if our shelter does any shipping. And unless I'm mistaken, this type of strap looks like it needs to be put on by machine, not by hand."

State Police Lieutenant Conrad Cutler, thin and fit and ridiculously handsome, ran a hand over his military brush cut. He wasn't the same man who'd driven her to the station. They'd pulled a "switcheroo" on her and changed interrogators.

Cutler nodded sagely. "I understand that. But your shelter does receive packages on a regular basis. Isn't that what you said earlier? Or did I misunderstand?" He pretended to flip through a dog-eared notebook until he found the correct page.

Lara closed her eyes and pulled in a calming breath. "Yes, pet supplies and litter. Once a week on average. In a multicat household, we go through a lot of cat litter."

But something poked at her brain. Something she'd heard in passing. What was it?

"Let's talk about cat hair," he said. "Would it surprise you to know that the hair sample taken from your shelter's gray cat matched the ones found in the back seat of the victim's car?"

An intentionally tricky question. He wasn't confirming that it *was* a match—only asking if it would surprise her.

"In fact, Lieutenant," Lara said evenly, "it would surprise me. I have to add, though, that while Evonda made it clear to us that she was not a fan of cats, she could have picked up a stray cat hair on her shoe, or even on her clothing, when she was inspecting our shelter. In a home with cats, the hair is pretty much everywhere. Since neither my aunt nor I have ever been in Mrs. Fray's car, that would be the only way I could imagine hair from one of our cats being found there."

He fixed her with a look. "That was a neat little speech, Ms. Caphart. Did you practice it?"

Her voice rose, and she speared him with a glare. "Why would I practice it? I had no idea you were going to bring me in for questioning. Besides, why would I need to rehearse the truth?"

His eyes narrowed, and his thin lips quirked. He reached for the manila envelope he'd set on the edge of the table and pulled out another photo. "This is another picture of the plastic strap, Ms. Caphart. Which, by the way, is called Polypropylene, not plastic." He dropped it on the table in front of her.

Lara gasped, and her stomach revolted. She covered her mouth with her hands. "Oh, my good glory, is that…?" She swallowed back the lump of bile she felt rising in her throat.

Hoo boy, lemme tell ya, when I saw that plastic band wrapped around that lady's neck, why my liver about dropped…

That's it. That's what she'd been trying to remember! Roy Tierney had said that to his gaggle of groupies when he was leaving the coffee shop.

The photo was a close-up of a plastic—Polypropylene, apparently—band secured tightly around the neck of someone who, if Lara had to guess, was Evonda Fray. A purple bruise, ugly and swollen, ringed her neck beneath the path of the band.

After a long pause, during which her interrogator studied her face, Lara pushed the photo away. "If you were trying to get a reaction from me, you've succeeded. So now, why don't you enlighten me? Why are you showing me this?"

He sauntered around the table, hands on his slim hips, as if sizing her up for some orange finery.

I should have called Gideon first, Lara chided herself. *Why, why, why, wasn't I thinking?*

"Ms. Caphart"—he played with the pages of his notebook again—"did you recently accept delivery of a custom-made door?"

Lara's pulse pounded. Why would he ask about the door? "Yes. I ordered a storm door for the shelter's new addition." That nagging voice poked at her again.

"Did it arrive in a cardboard box? A large cardboard box?"

"Um, well, yes, it did. It was also packed in bubble wrap to protect it. Why would you ask about our door?"

"Was the box secured with anything else? Maybe some Polypropylene straps like the one in the photo?" He jabbed a finger at the gruesome picture of Evonda, pushing it closer to Lara.

Lara shivered. He was taunting her with the hideous photo. If she'd been nervous before, she was terrified now.

She thought back to the day the box was delivered. Yes, she did recall seeing some of those bands wrapped around it. Even though she'd been anxious to look at the custom door, the box was so unwieldy that she'd left it for Charlie Backstrom to open. She didn't want to risk damaging the door by dumping it out of the box.

"I…what was the question again?" She was getting more rattled with each one.

"Was the box containing the door secured with Polypropylene straps?"

"To the best of my memory, yes," Lara said. "Two, maybe three bands. It wasn't something I paid a lot of attention to."

Lara took a long sip from the bottle of water they'd given her, then instantly regretted it. To the police, gulping back water was probably a sign of guilt.

On the wall opposite Lara was a length of mirror, six or seven feet long. She'd seen enough crime shows to know that it was probably two-way glass. *I see you, but you can't see me!* Was another investigator on the other side, studying her? Documenting every nuance of her body language?

"Who opened the box, Ms. Caphart?" Cutler said.

An easy question. "My contractor did. His name is Charles Backstrom. But I suspect you already know that."

His smug look said it all. "How did your contractor remove the bands, Ms. Caphart?"

Lara shrugged. "I honestly wasn't paying attention. I think he had a box cutter, but I'm not sure."

"So, after your contractor removed the bands, where did he put them?"

"Again," she said, "I wasn't paying attention. He probably stuffed them inside the box. That's what I would've done. As I said, I was anxious to see the custom-made door, so I wasn't—"

"Can you tell me, Ms. Caphart, where that box is now?"

The box was huge. Charlie had propped it against the house outside. He'd promised to come back Tuesday to dispose of it, but—

Brian.

Brian had offered to take the box to the recycling station. He was headed there to look for packing boxes for moving.

But the police had already questioned Brian. More than once, in fact. Had *he* told them about the box?

"You look befuddled, Ms. Caphart. Should I rephrase?"

Lara felt like kicking him in the butt and watching him sail across the room. "I'm not befuddled, Lieutenant. As far as I know, the box is at the recycling station. If I'd known in advance about this pop quiz, I'd have studied the box a little harder."

Cutler loomed over her, his lips pressed into a grim line. "Apparently, you think this is a joke, Ms. Caphart. I assure you, it is not."

"I don't think it's a joke at all," Lara said, and lowered her voice. "There's nothing funny about murder."

Cutler's eyes glittered, and his mouth curved into a taunting smile. "Yes, I'd almost forgotten. You're quite familiar with murder, aren't you? Is it a hobby of yours?"

It took every ounce of restraint Lara had not to fly out of her chair. "I'm sure you think that's amusing, Lieutenant, but I don't. Any contact I've had with killers was not pleasant, and it was not by choice."

"So I've heard."

This is bad, Lara realized. *Very, very bad.*

"Ms. Caphart, how did the box in which the door was delivered get to the recycling station?"

She tried not to squirm in her chair, which was about as comfortable as a slab of concrete. "We had a visitor to the shelter that day. He was on his way there anyway, so he offered to take the box for us."

"Ah. How convenient for you. Did this visitor have a name?"

Lara's insides twisted. "Brian. Brian Downing."

"Brian Downing. And did Mr. Downing happen to tour the shelter? Maybe play with a few of the cats?"

Like a flash of lightning, Lara suddenly got it.

That was what this was all about—why they'd brought her here. They were trying to pin the murder on Brian Downing. And they wanted to use her as the pin.

"He—Yes. We agreed to keep his cat while he looked for a new apartment, so I showed him around. It was a very brief visit. Only a few minutes."

Or more.

"Thank you, Ms. Caphart."

Trying to keep her voice from quavering, Lara said, "Lieutenant, before I answer any more questions, I will need to call my attorney."

"No need for an attorney, Ms. Caphart. You've been very helpful and very cooperative. You may leave now. We'll see that you get a ride home." He opened the door and made a sweeping gesture with his arm.

Lara rose off her chair and fixed him with a look. "You never told me, Lieutenant. Did the hair samples from our cats match the ones at the crime scene?"

"Right now, they're inconclusive. That'll be all, Ms. Caphart. I'll let someone at the front desk know you need a ride."

Lara pushed past him. "Thanks anyway, but I'll walk."

The lobby of the police station was chilly, air-conditioned to the nth degree. Lara rubbed her arms to ward off a shiver, then stepped outside into the glaring sunshine.

The first thing she wanted to do was text her aunt, to let her know she was okay. Then it struck her—she didn't even have her cell with her. She was ushered off to the police station so quickly, she didn't have a chance to grab her tote.

A bright yellow bus chugged by on the main drag, spewing gray exhaust. Emblazoned along its side was the name of a local summer camp. Kids' heads bobbed in the windows.

Ironic, Lara thought, *because I've just thrown Brian Downing under the bus.*

Chapter Sixteen

Bowker's Coffee Stop was only a block from the police station. Lara made it there in record time. Feeling beads of sweat populating her forehead, she pushed open the door and stormed inside.

"Oh my God, you look like a bear chased you in here." Sherry plunked down a mug of coffee in front of her. "You want a muffin? Cranberry walnut today, if there's any left."

Lara slid onto her usual stool, then shook her head. "No, thanks. I already had half an apple fritter." She told Sherry about her trip to the purple bakery to rescue a batch of kittens.

"Aw, they must be so cute. I can't wait to see them. One of these days…" She shrugged and smiled.

"Any plans to make an announcement yet?" Lara said in a loud whisper.

"Yeah, like no one can hear you, Lara. As to your question, no. Not yet. Maybe on Saturday, after the—" Her face reddened. "Oh shoot, never mind."

"You were going to say after the open house, weren't you?" Lara absently stirred her coffee.

"I'm sorry. I totally forgot you postponed it." Sherry studied Lara's face. "You look really bummed today. I wondered why you didn't come in this morning. Did something else happen?"

Lara related the highlights of her trip to the police station.

"Oh, ugh. That's awful," Sherry said. "So, you think the cops are zeroing in on Brian Downing?"

"I think they want desperately to nail him for Evonda's…death," Lara said. "Either that or they think I killed her. That's always a possibility."

"If they question you again, be careful what you say, okay?" Sherry's forehead creased with worry. "They might've been trying to put you off guard by letting you think they're after Brian and not you. I saw that on a TV show once."

"I know, Sher, but this isn't TV. As for Brian being the bad guy, I'm just not seeing it. I know I'm biased because he's a cat lover, but I honestly can't picture him as the killer."

Sherry spoke quietly. "But we've been fooled in the past, Lara. Remember—"

"I know. Don't even go there."

The first killer Lara had encountered after her return to Whisker Jog had been a total shock—one that rocked the entire town. Lara had tried to erase it from her memory, but all too often it sneaked back in and haunted her dreams.

It was Sherry's turn to look troubled.

"Something's bothering you, too," Lara said. "Come on, Sher. Spill it. Don't make me bring out the hot lights."

Sherry looked all around the coffee shop, then reached underneath the counter. She slid a white envelope over to Lara. "Hold it in your lap. Don't let anyone see it."

Lara humored her friend. "It can't be that bad."

"Oh yeah?" Sherry's eyes dimmed.

Resting the unsealed envelope on her knees, Lara opened the flap and pulled out a color photo. Two figures—a man and a woman—stood before a building, adjacent to a blue dumpster. The woman was middle-aged and blond, the man short and somewhat stout. Lara's breath caught in her throat.

Oh...no. It can't be.

But it was.

The duo in the photo were Daisy Bowker and Trevor Johnson.

Lara tried to peer more closely at the pic, but Sherry pushed her hand down. "Don't let anyone see!"

In the pic, Daisy appeared to be handing Johnson an envelope. The photo, though taken from quite a distance, was very clear. Lara suspected the photographer had used a telescopic lens.

Evonda had once owned a photography business. Put two and two together...

Lara suddenly remembered what Gideon had said to her and Aunt Fran. His buddy, a fellow lawyer, had told him that Trevor Johnson had been caught accepting a bribe from a local restaurant.

Fray claimed she caught them near the dumpster behind the restaurant, and that she saw an envelope change hands...

Lara swallowed hard. She refused to believe it. Despite the glaring evidence, there was no way Daisy would bribe, or even attempt to bribe, the health inspector. Why would she?

"Sher, where did you get this?" Lara asked quietly, returning the envelope to her friend.

"I found it under my windshield wiper when I went out back to take a bag of trash to the dumpster."

"When? Recently?"

Looking distinctly uncomfortable, Sherry shrugged. "No, I–I don't know. It was like, some time back in June, I think."

"Does your mom know?"

"I had to show her." Sherry winced. "I mean, I couldn't not tell her about it, right?" She topped off Lara's mug.

"Right." Lara absently took a sip of coffee. "Um, so…what did she say when you showed her the picture?"

"She smiled—actually smiled—and said it wasn't what it looked like. I pressed her on it, but she basically told me to leave it alone. And when Mom gets that tone…" Sherry made a slicing motion across her throat.

Oh boy.

"The day you found the envelope under your windshield wiper, was it right after Johnson inspected the coffee shop?"

"It's hard to remember, but I think it was. Maybe a day or two later. Honest to God, I wasn't keeping track."

Lara couldn't believe Bowker's Coffee Stop had violated any health codes. Even if they had, it had to be something minor. The coffee shop was always spotless. Lara had seen the kitchen. It was clean enough for someone to eat off the countertop.

"Did Johnson find anything bad when he inspected? Like…I don't know. I'm not even sure what health inspectors look for."

"There was one thing. A stupid thing. Trash bags are supposed to be taken out as soon as they're filled. And normally, that's not a problem. We're always running trash out to the dumpster. But wouldn't you know, the day Johnson showed up, Jill was running late, and then a van from some retirement home showed up with about a hundred old people all wanting to order lunch at the same time. It was crazy, you know?"

"I think I remember you telling me about it."

"Yeah, well, we were so busy, we didn't have time to take the trash bags out to the dumpster. There were three bags, chock full of trash, sitting open in the kitchen. That's a major no-no. I swear, it was a fluke, but…" She raised her shoulders in a shrug.

"Doesn't sound very serious," Lara said. "Was that the only thing?"

Sherry groaned. "Some supply boxes were sitting on the floor, waiting to be shelved. Food is supposed to be stored at least six inches off the floor, so technically, that was a violation. Like I said, it was nuts around here that day. If there was ever a perfect storm of everything going wrong at once, that was it."

Lara shook her head. None of it made sense. "Did Johnson issue a citation or anything? What do they do when they find violations?"

"He gave us a form with a couple of check marks on it and told us to remedy the problems. He didn't look too concerned about anything, that's for sure. When I think back, it was so...dumb. I mean, trash bags in the kitchen? It's not like we had ants crawling in the sugar!" She threw up her arms.

Lara shivered at that thought, but she couldn't help wondering if there had been bad blood between Johnson and Daisy Bowker.

"Know what's even weirder?" Sherry glanced around and then leaned forward. "Jill's off today, so I can talk. Johnson asked Jill out on a date a few months ago. She refused, said he's not her type. I hate to say it, but Jill likes the bad boys."

"Huh. Isn't that a kicker? Did she tell you about it or did you overhear him ask her out?"

"She told me about it. Jill can be a little abrupt sometimes. I got the impression she wasn't all that tactful when she blew him off."

Even so, it still didn't explain the photograph. That's the part Lara couldn't wrap her brain around.

"Hey, I'd better go," Lara said. "If it's okay, I'll pay you tomorrow for the coffee. The police took me away so fast, I didn't have a chance to grab my tote. Can you float me?"

"Don't worry. I know where you live."

Lara laughed. If anyone could yank her out of the doldrums, it was Sherry. She glanced toward the tables in the dining area. "Someone's waving at you over there. I think they want more coffee."

"Don't they always?" Sherry said with her usual eye roll. "Either that or my firstborn child." She stretched her lips into a smile and held the coffeepot aloft. "Be right there!" she trilled. "Hey, don't mention that pic to anyone, okay?"

"I won't. No worries there," Lara promised.

By the time Lara left the coffee shop, it was nearly noon, although it seemed as if it should be closer to four. Walking home, she couldn't get the photo of Daisy and Trevor Johnson out of her head. Whatever was in that envelope, it was something Daisy hadn't wanted to share—even with her own daughter.

If it wasn't a bribe—and Lara was sure it wasn't—then what was it?

Chapter Seventeen

"I've been worried about you," Aunt Fran said anxiously, greeting her at the kitchen door with Snowball in her arms. "Is everything okay?"

Lara rubbed Snowball's head, then dropped into a chair. She didn't want to cause any more angst for her aunt, but she didn't want to lie either. Besides, Aunt Fran always knew when she was sugarcoating the truth.

"In the beginning, it was pretty rough, I'll admit," Lara told her. "But I think the police are focusing more on Brian Downing than on anyone else. I was going to text you when I got out of there, but I realized I didn't even have my phone with me."

"I figured as much when I saw your tote bag in your studio."

"I stopped at the coffee shop, too. Sorry, Aunt Fran. I didn't mean to worry you. I was just so…bummed when I got out of there." She gave her a brief rundown of the "interview" at the police station.

"What did they say about the cat hair?" her aunt asked.

"Inconclusive. That's the exact word they used."

Aunt Fran's lips tightened. She sat down and rested Snowball in her lap. "Isn't that interesting," she said. "After all that nonsense about taking the samples yesterday."

Lara suspected she was thinking about Chief Whitley's role in collecting the cat hair. In a way, Lara felt bad for the guy. As he'd said, he was only doing his job. A warrant was a warrant. It wasn't as if he could've ignored it.

"Speaking of yesterday," Lara said, "have you heard anything from a certain chief of police?"

"I've gotten four texts and two voice-mail messages." Aunt Fran lifted her chin. "I've responded to none."

Whoa. Aunt Fran was seriously ticked at the chief. Lara wondered when it would blow over. If it ever did. Was this the beginning of the end for the two?

"On a different subject," Aunt Fran said. "Kayla seemed really out of sorts to me this morning. Is she having problems at home?"

Lara shrugged. "I'm not sure. I was hoping for a chance to talk to her, but then I got blindsided by that cop showing up. I have a feeling it's something to do with her grandmother."

"I think so, too. I only wish I knew what it was about."

"You know, it's funny," Lara went on, "Kayla's mood was fine this morning until I noticed that our kitten rescuer, Meg Carmel, was wearing a diamond ring. I asked Meg if she was engaged, and she said she was—that she'd finally found a prince after all the frogs she'd dated."

Aunt Fran nodded thoughtfully. "Interesting. Kayla never talks about dating or having a boyfriend, does she?"

Munster came into the kitchen and padded in Lara's direction. He gazed up at her and licked his lips. Then he jumped onto her lap, kneaded her knees, and settled in for a nap.

Lara bent and kissed his head, then said, "You're right. She's never mentioned dating anyone as far as I remember. But look, I wasn't much different at her age. I lived in a city, so I met a lot more people, but most of the time I was unattached. The few boyfriends I had—" She crossed her eyes playfully and made a face.

"That's because the right man was here all the time, waiting for you," Aunt Fran said with a wink. "Maybe you sensed it without even realizing it."

"Anything's possible, I guess." Lara laughed.

"Oh, gracious, I almost forgot." Aunt Fran moved Snowball to her shoulder and rose from her chair. "After we saw Jenny Cooper—Jenny Fray—in the police station the other day, for some reason I got to thinking about her. I dug through some old pictures and found one of your sixth-grade class."

Aunt Fran left to go over to her desk in the large parlor. She returned with an eight-by-ten color photo.

Lara eagerly took it from her. In the pic, the kids had been lined up along the blackboard, taller ones in the rear and shorter ones in the front. She grimaced when she spotted her own image in the back row. "Oh, come on, did I really look like that? My hair looks like it got stuck in a wind machine."

Aunt Fran laughed. "Your mom was always at you about your hair, but you never wanted to get it cut."

Lara examined the photo, trying to put names to all the preteen faces. She spotted Sherry somewhere in the middle of the pack, her raven-colored hair cut in a bob and framing a smiling face. Sherry had always despised having her photo taken. When told to smile, she'd stretch her lips into a clownish grin that collapsed the moment the pic was snapped.

Running her finger along the faces, Lara searched for Jenny. She found her slumped in the front row, hands crossed in front of her, her gaze focused off to one side. The sadness in her expression made Lara's heart wrench. Had Jenny always looked so unhappy? She couldn't recall.

"I found Jenny. Poor kid, she looks so gloomy in this picture. Like the weight of the world was on her shoulders."

"I noticed that, too," her aunt said. "As I recall, her mom struggled with all sorts of issues. I suspect Jenny had a troubled childhood."

"Did you know the family?" Lara asked. "Was there a dad?"

"There was, but he lived out-of-state. Maine, I think. And no, I didn't know the family, but people talked." She raised her eyebrows.

Lara struggled to remember. Had Jenny been in her class when she entered first grade? She didn't think so. If her memory was on target, Jenny didn't attend school in Whisker Jog until fourth or fifth grade.

She peered at the photo again. Most of the other kids looked like strangers to Lara. She hadn't attended high school with them, so she never saw them as they grew to young adulthood—Sherry being the exception, of course.

And Gideon.

Gideon!

She looked again at the photo. How could she have missed him? He stood straight as a pencil in the back row, a lock of dark hair falling over his forehead. His expression was pensive, as if he were already mapping out his future. Lara touched a finger to her lips, then to his face.

"You spotted Gideon," Aunt Fran teased.

Lara felt a blush creep up her neck. "He was always adorable, wasn't he?"

Aunt Fran patted her arm. "Can't argue with that. Keep the picture. You can show it to him later."

"Thanks. I'd love to have this." She set the photo on the table.

"Would you like some lunch? I can whip up some tuna sandwiches."

Lara pressed a hand to her stomach. "Normally that would sound good, but right now I'm going to pass. Maybe later I'll have another apple fritter. Speaking of Fritter, I wonder how the kittens are doing. I think I'll give Amy a call."

She kissed Munster and set him down, then went into her studio. A phone call to Amy Glindell's veterinary clinic confirmed that the kittens had already been treated for fleas and worms—plus, they'd had their first vaccinations. Development wise, the tiniest one, Fritter, was a bit behind the others. The vet wanted to keep a close eye on her for at least another twenty-four hours.

In her studio—her favorite room in the house—Lara set up her watercolors and sketch pencils. She wanted to spend some time toying with ideas for Sherry's wedding invitations.

The Renoir painting *Dance in the Country* evoked the feelings Lara wanted to express. In Renoir's painting, the man had dark hair, while the woman was a redhead. With Sherry and David, it was the opposite—Sherry's hair was raven black, while David's hair and neatly trimmed beard were a light shade of ginger.

Lara didn't intend to copy the painting, only to extract ideas from it. She guessed that Sherry would choose a simple gown, maybe ivory or even pale blue. Her friend certainly wouldn't be holding a fan in her right hand, but her nails would be gorgeously manicured. Renoir depicted his lady sporting a golden glove on her left hand. That would never do for Sherry. Maybe a cluster of dahlias instead?

After noodling around with sketches for a solid two hours, Lara stretched her arms and yawned. The room was overly warm, and her hair was sticking to her neck. She put everything away and went into the kitchen. Her stomach grumbled, a sure sign she'd skipped lunch.

Aunt Fran was outside, sitting in her favorite Adirondack chair with a book. They'd agreed that supper would be a bit later than usual, maybe around six thirty, so Lara snagged an apple fritter out of the pink bakery box. The sugary glaze and tender apple filling practically melted in her mouth.

The next day, Friday, was an adoption day—but it was also the day she and Aunt Fran planned to attend Evonda's memorial service. Mentally, Lara wanted to be prepared. Did Evonda have friends who would attend? Or had the woman's caustic personality been a turnoff to everyone she ever encountered?

Tim Fray would be there, naturally, as would Jenny. She toyed with the idea of bringing along the class picture to show Jenny, then immediately nixed the idea. Some people didn't like to be reminded of their childhood days. Lara didn't want to risk embarrassing her.

She fed the cats a snack and replenished their water, then called Gideon. "Hey, stranger," he said sweetly. "I've missed you. Busy day?"

She told him everything, including the details of her so-called interview at the police station and her rescue mission with Kayla.

"Lara, if the police ever do that again, I want you to call me right away. I'm not a criminal lawyer, but I do know the basics. I wouldn't have let the interview get that far."

"I know, but I thought of that too late. By the time I told them I wanted to call my attorney, they told me I was free to go. I still think they're trying to nail Brian for the murder."

"I hate to say it, honey, but they might be right about Brian. I like the guy, too, but he seriously hated Evonda. He could easily have picked up a cat hair or two from Pearl or Snowball when you gave him a tour of the house."

"I know. I thought that, too." ·

"How's Smuggles? He's still there, right?"

"He is," Lara said, smiling at the thought of the chubby gray tiger kitty. "He sleeps most of the time, but he seems comfy with his surroundings. Pearl snitched one of his toys, but he didn't seem to care. He flicked his tail and blinked at her, like he was saying 'go ahead, take it.'"

Gideon chuckled. "Cute. Listen, we haven't been to our favorite clam shack in a while. You up for a date tomorrow night? We can stuff our faces with fried claims and onions rings and have a beer while we're at it."

"That, Mr. Halley, is the best offer I've had all week. You're on. Pick me up at six?"

"You got it."

Chapter Eighteen

A light rain carried by a mild wind swept in on Friday morning.

Despite the dreary skies hovering overhead, Lara was grateful for the cooler temps. The blazing heat of earlier in the week had become close to unbearable.

After agonizing over what constituted proper funeral attire, she dug her navy pantsuit and a white blouse out of her closet. After a quick scan, she deemed the outfit acceptable. It was somber enough, simple, and sedate. Instead of her usual tote, she carried the navy clutch she'd bought on consignment eons ago. She stuffed her phone inside, along with a few other essentials.

The parking lot of the funeral home was more crowded than Lara expected. She couldn't help wondering if some of the cars belonged to cops posing as mourners. Did most killers really attend their victims' funerals? Or was that only a myth perpetuated by television crime shows?

Parked in front of the one-story white building was a shiny black hearse. People trickled inside—mostly women, Lara noticed. Her arm looped through Aunt Fran's, she climbed the wide granite steps that led into the outer lobby. From there, they entered the foyer, where plush green carpeting softened their treads. White marble tables stood along the wall in several places, interspersed with velvet-covered chairs. On each table was a large vase filled with white lilies.

A thin, fortysomething man clad completely in black nodded as they entered. "Are you here for the Fray service?" he asked in a muted tone.

"We are," Aunt Fran said.

Another nod. "First parlor on the left," he directed with an outstretched arm. "On your way in, please sign the guest book for the family."

A sudden shiver ran along Lara's arms. In her entire life, she'd only been to two funerals. Would the casket be open? Would she be forced to look at Evonda's face, frozen in death?

They both signed the guest book and went into the parlor. A classical piece drifted softly from discreet overhead speakers. Facing the coffin were several rows of chairs. The casket, made from highly polished wood that looked like ebony, sat on a high platform. Lara was grateful for the closed coffin. Finding no place to kneel for a quick prayer, she murmured a silent one, then moved along to greet the family.

Tim and Jenny Fray sat at the far side of the coffin, their fingers linked, their heads bowed. It was pretty much the way they'd looked the day Lara had seen them at the police station. Jenny wore a plain black dress and ballerina flats, her only jewelry the diamond wedding band that encircled her left ring finger.

"Tim, Jenny, I am deeply sorry for your loss," Aunt Fran said quietly. She held out her hand, but only Tim acknowledged it. He gave her fingers a quick squeeze, then removed his glasses and blotted his eyes. He stuck his glasses back on his face.

"Thank you for coming," he said.

Jenny nodded, her expression passive. Was she mourning? Or was she grateful that the mother-in-law who detested her was finally out of her life?

Stop it, Lara scolded herself. She had no right to judge Jenny. Even if she had been a former classmate, Lara barely knew the woman.

It was Lara's turn to offer condolences. "I'm truly sorry about your mom," she said to Tim, looking at both him and his wife.

Jenny nodded, tight-lipped. Her eyes looked puffy, which surprised Lara. "Thank you" was all she said.

Again, Lara shivered. The parlor was cool—almost freezing. Rubbing her arms, Lara followed her aunt past rows of chairs. They chose seats near the back.

Mourners began to file in, and again Lara noticed that they were mostly women. Three women arrived together. They sported similar black hats from which shiny, raven-colored feathers protruded.

A murder of crows, Lara thought with a shudder.

The women huddled around Tim for a few moments, then took seats in the front row, as if they knew those spots had been reserved for them.

It was almost ten, time for the service to begin, when a fresh face caught Lara's eye.

Chief Whitley.

Looking solemn in a dark suit and tie, he walked in and leveled his gaze immediately on Aunt Fran. He frowned when she didn't acknowledge him. The chief took a seat at one end, a few rows from the front. Once again, Lara felt for the guy. Aunt Fran was really giving him the icy shoulder.

Lara glanced around. Something about the room bothered her. Something was missing. What was it? She couldn't quite put a name to it.

Another familiar face entered the parlor. It was Roy Tierney, the deliveryman who'd been gossiping all over town about the murder scene. Wearing a shiny black suit that had to be forty years old, he looked all around before he signed the guest book. Spotting him, Tim Fray dropped his gaze as he approached. Tierney hesitated, but then seemed to get the message. He went off to find a chair without offering any condolences.

At the stroke of ten, the thin man who'd directed them into the parlor strode in quietly. He stood before the casket and waited for the chatter to cease. When the room finally went silent, he said, "I want to thank you all for joining us here today to celebrate the life of Evonda Fray. As most of you know, her passing was abrupt and unexpected. She was in the prime of her life when it was sadly cut short. One thing we know for certain—she loved her family fiercely and adored her friends, as well as the wild birds she cared for in her yard. And now, her son Timothy would like to say a few words."

Tim Fray nodded, cleared his throat, then rose and exchanged places with the man. "Thank you all for coming here today," he began. "I know none of you wants to be here, so I'm going to be very brief." After a wave of low murmurs, he continued.

"Evonda Fray was many things to me. Worshipful mom. Passionate protector. Staunch defender. At times her personality overwhelmed me. Most times it gave me tremendous comfort. She had her causes, which I fully supported. She had her biases, which I do not defend. With all that said, I will miss her deeply." His voice caught on the last word, and his eyes became glassy. "Fly high, Mom, wherever you are."

Lara saw Jenny shift in her seat, her small face pinched.

Tim pulled in a deep breath, then blew it out slowly. "Before you leave, I hope you'll take a few moments to view the screen display set up in the back of the room. Her life in pictures, I guess you'd call it. Mom herself was an avid photographer, and she loved her birds. Crows and ravens were her favorites, but she was crazy about all birds." He offered a sad smile. "If any of you wishes to make a donation in her memory, the names of several wild bird societies are printed below the display. Thank you."

Aunt Fran reached for her purse. "I have to say, that was the shortest and most unusual memorial service I've ever been to."

"I've only been to two others," Lara said. "But this was certainly the oddest. I can't put my finger on it, but..."

Her aunt smiled. "It was nonreligious, Lara."

Light dawned. "You're right. That's it!"

No prayers.

No pastor.

No pleas to a merciful God to lift Evonda's immortal soul to the heavens.

In the next moment, a song sifted through the speakers. Lara had heard it before, on the radio.

Murmurs, growing louder now, filled the room. People tittered to one another, as if they couldn't believe what they were hearing.

Lara clutched her aunt's arm. "That song," she whispered. "It's 'Fly Like an Eagle.' Why would they play that at a funeral?"

Chapter Nineteen

"I want to see the photo gallery," Lara whispered to her aunt.

"You read my mind."

Several other people had had the same idea. They began forming a line toward the back of the room.

The three women wearing the black-feathered hats scooted in line in front of Lara and Aunt Fran. "I feel so bad for Tim," Lara heard one of them murmur.

"Poor thing, he looked so crushed, didn't he?" another one said.

"His wife certainly didn't look too broken up," the first one said crustily. "I have no doubt the little gold digger is already counting Evonda's money."

"Her share, you mean," the third one said. "If Evonda was right, that marriage is on the skids. I'm sure the little weasel is already rubbing her hands together, figuring out how she can get a chunk of Evonda's money in the divorce."

"Which she'll spend on her lover, no doubt," the second one said.

"Disgraceful," the third one put in.

The woman standing in front of Aunt Fran cast a glance around the room, then turned to see who was behind her. Her eyes were bright blue. Wisps of titian hair peeked out from under her black hat. "Oh, hello," she said. "I'm Letitia Barlow. Were you a friend of Evonda's?"

"Fran Clarkson," Aunt Fran said, "and this is my niece, Lara Caphart. And no, we weren't friends. In fact, we only met Evonda a few days ago, but we still wanted to pay our respects."

The other two woman swiveled their heads and offered hesitant smiles. They introduced themselves as Katie Fleming and Vera Baskin. Lara noticed that all three women wore the same pendant—a blackbird perched on a golden branch—that Evonda had worn during her so-called inspection of the shelter.

"I noticed you're all wearing the same pendant," Lara commented. "Is it from a club you all belong to?"

Vera gave her a sad smile. "A club? No, not a formal one anyway." She sniffled. "We, the three of us and Evonda, always called ourselves the four old crows. We joked about it all the time. Then one day I saw these blackbird pendants in a gift shop. I decided right then and there that we all needed to have one. Aren't they perfect?"

"They're so unusual," Lara said. "I like them."

"All of us love birds," Katie put in, then smiled. "Hence the hats." She pointed to her own. "But Evonda was the most militant about it. She'd do anything to save a bird. Anything."

And nothing to save a cat, Lara guessed. She wondered if Evonda's avian obsession had anything to do with her dislike of cats. Had a cat plundered her birdhouse, or killed a bird in her yard?

The line moved, and the three "old crows" shimmied up to the photo gallery. On a large screen built into the wall, enlarged pictures of Evonda had been arranged in groups. Lara peeked over Letitia's shoulder.

In her younger days, Evonda had been an attractive woman, if not classically pretty. Smooth skin, firm cheekbones, loose blond waves brushing a set of wide shoulders. Her wedding photo showed her in a plain white dress posing beside a skinny, balding man. Her smile seemed genuine. His looked adoring.

Photos of Evonda with little Timothy were abundant, from his infancy right through college. There was one of Tim as a toddler jumping into his mother's arms from the edge of a swimming pool. Another of Evonda beaming proudly at him during a graduation ceremony.

An entire section was devoted to photos Evonda had taken of various bird species. In one photo she'd captured a huge blackbird in midflight, a baby snake dangling from its beak.

Lara had to admit—Evonda had been a talented photographer.

Letitia suddenly burst into tears. "Oh my, I still can't believe she's gone." She pulled a tissue from her purse and pressed it to her lashes.

"Oh, honey, I know. I know." Katie reached her arm over and gave her friend a sideways hug. "It's all so horrible. But we have to carry on, don't we? It's what Evonda would want us to do."

"And remember," Vera reminded, "she's with her dear Douglas now."

"Yes. Yes, you're right, both of you." Letitia's cheeks turned pink. "That rumor, about Douglas and me," she sputtered out. "You know it was never true, right?"

"Of course we know," Vera said quietly, slipping her arm through Letitia's. "Neither of us ever believed it. Evonda never believed it either. She knew it was just a lot of silliness."

After another short sob session in which all three joined, the women went off toward the exit.

Lara gaped at her aunt. "Well, wasn't that interesting?"

Aunt Fran nodded, and they both moved closer to the screen to get a better view of the photos.

Lara had seen most of the photos over Letitia's shoulder, but now she moved in for a closer examination. Crows and blackbirds dominated the bird section. The detail in some of the close-ups was stunning.

Near the bottom of the screen, a small cluster of photos showed Evonda as a child. They'd been taken with a Polaroid camera—the kind that took instant pictures. Lara scanned the photos, a sense of sadness welling inside her. Evonda had been a sweet-looking child in pigtails, with a wide smile and a curious expression.

Lara started to move aside so her aunt could have a better look when a photo near the bottom of the screen made her breath halt in her throat.

An old Polaroid picture, faded and discolored with age, showed a smiling Evonda sitting on the grass in front of a well-kept, two-story home. In the folds of her skirt was a tiny white kitten.

The caption scribbled in ink beneath the photo read: *Evonda, age 6, with Casper.*

* * * *

"That was an earful, wasn't it?" Lara murmured to her aunt as they were leaving through the front lobby. "Those women seemed to know a lot about Jenny."

"They *gossiped* a lot about Jenny," Aunt Fran corrected. "We don't know if any of it was true."

Aunt Fran was right. It was easy to distort the truth, to twist it into your own unique version. Evonda's three devoted friends had no love lost for Jenny. That much was painfully obvious.

They were almost at the door to the outer waiting area when Lara spied Jenny Fray streaking across the lobby. Lara watched as Jenny made a beeline for the doorway at the rear, above which was a discreet sign that read RESTROOMS.

"Excuse me," Lara said to her aunt. "I need a quick bathroom break. I'll be right back."

Lara followed Jenny through the doorway and down a short corridor. She pushed through the door that bore the silhouette of a woman's head.

Jenny was standing over the bathroom's sole sink, crying into a paper towel. She turned sharply when she saw Lara, and then sobbed even harder.

"Oh, Jenny, I'm so sorry," Lara said, rubbing her shoulder. "This must be so hard for you." She wanted to give her a comforting hug, but Jenny's stiff demeanor told her it might not be welcomed.

Jenny sucked in a long sob. "Thank you, and yeah, it is hard," she said with a snivel. "Harder than you can imagine. Especially when everyone's making nasty remarks about you like you're some…some hussy." Tears streamed down her thin cheeks. "How dare they judge me. How dare they!"

Lara felt terrible for her. No doubt she'd overheard Evonda's three cohorts making snide comments about her.

"What matters is how you feel," Lara said, trying to sound soothing. "What everyone else says doesn't matter."

"You're right." Jenny grabbed a fresh paper towel and blotted her cheeks. She blinked at herself in the mirror. "Nobody knows how I feel. *Nobody*. Those old crow friends of Evonda's? They don't know a thing about me, or what's in my heart." Jenny turned and looked Lara straight in the eye, her own eyes shrinking to the size of peas. "Those three old bags have no idea what it's like to be in love."

That probably wasn't true, but Lara nodded in sympathy. "Jenny, can I get you anything? Do you want me to find Tim for you?"

Jenny's face went taut. "No. I'll be fine. But…unless you have business in here, I'd appreciate being alone."

Okay, I get the message.

"Sure," Lara said. "And again, I'm sorry for your loss."

Jenny gave her a pointed look in the mirror, her expression full of pain. "Thanks, Lara. I am, too."

Chapter Twenty

Lara and her aunt had been home about twenty minutes when Kayla arrived. Aunt Fran made tea and set out what was left of the fritters.

With Snowball snugged in her lap, Kayla looked a tad more relaxed than she had when she and Lara rescued the kittens on Thursday. Still, Lara sensed something was up with her. If there was any way she could help, she wanted to know what it was.

She started by relating the story of Evonda's strange memorial service.

"That song they played—'Fly Like an Eagle'?" Kayla said. "It's one of my dad's favorites. It has a mellow, bluesy sort of beat. Weird that they'd play it at her funeral, but then, maybe it was her favorite song."

"Yeah, maybe." Lara took a sip from her mug. She thought about the blackbird pendant worn by Evonda and her "old crow" friends.

"What do you make of that picture of her with the kitten?" Kayla said. "Didn't you say she hated cats?" She bent and kissed Snowball's head.

"Yeah, that was so weird," Lara said, but then remembered the odd look on Evonda's face when she saw Snowball curled up on the sofa. In that single moment, her expression had softened. Lara was sure she hadn't imagined it.

Did Snowball remind her of Casper, the little white kitten in the photo?

"We'll never really know," Aunt Fran said, stirring her tea absently. "But something must have happened later in life to turn her against cats."

"Speaking of fritters," Kayla said, "aren't we supposed to pick up the kittens today?"

"Originally, yes," Lara said. "But I got a text from Amy during the memorial service—I didn't read it till I got out to the car. She wants to keep them for another few days. Fritter is progressing a little more slowly than the others. Amy wants to keep a close eye on him, at least through the weekend."

"Oh. Okay." Kayla slumped in her chair. "Shoot. I was really looking forward to having them here today. It's all I could think about on the way over here."

Aunt Fran glanced at Lara, then looked over at Kayla. "Kayla, I've sensed something has been troubling you. Lara and I care about you very much. To us, you're family. Is there something we can help you with?"

Kayla shrugged. "No. Not really. It's just…sometimes I feel like such a loser, you know? Every weekend, my cousins descend on my gram's house. The adults do their own thing while I end up entertaining my nieces and nephews. Don't get me wrong—I adore all of them. It's just that everyone treats me like the automatic babysitter."

Lara wondered if that was true, or if that was only Kayla's perception. "While you're with the kids, what do your cousins do?"

"Oh, you know, they sit around and talk about recipes and kids and schools. Sometimes they set up the badminton net, but I'm terrible at it so I always bow out. By the time they leave"—she swallowed—"I feel more alone than ever. Does that sound crazy?"

"Not at all," Aunt Fran soothed. "Have you tried talking to your grandmother about your feelings?"

"Yeah, but she only made me feel worse. She didn't mean to—she thought she was helping—but she really doesn't get it."

"Your gram loves you very much," Aunt Fran said. "But sometimes it helps to talk to someone closer to your own generation. Not that I'm a spring chicken by any means, but Lara still has a few good years left in her." She winked and smiled at Lara.

Lara gave her a look of mock outrage. "Hey."

"Bottom line—we're both pretty good listeners," Aunt Fran said gently.

"Thanks. I know you're both trying to make me feel better. It's just that…everyone I see is hooked up with someone, you know? Lara has Gideon. Sherry has David. Mrs. C., you have the chief—and he's not even that crazy about cats."

Lara watched her aunt for a reaction, but Aunt Fran remained poker-faced.

"Kayla, when I was your age, I was living above a bakery in Boston, trying to make ends meet selling my watercolors. I worked in the bakery to earn some extra cash, mostly washing dishes. I almost never dated. When I did, they were always one or two timers. I never had anyone special enough that I could actually call him a boyfriend."

Kayla looked at her. "Are you serious or are you just humoring me?"

"I'm serious. Totally."

"Did you ever worry that you were never going to meet the right guy?"

Lara laughed. "A lot of the time, I did. But I was so focused on becoming a great artist that I told myself I was meant for other things."

"You *are* a great artist," Kayla said. She frowned and pushed at her glasses. "My gram says that I spend too much time with cats, and that's why I never meet a nice boy."

Lara's heart ached for her. She knew exactly how she felt.

When Lara and Gideon first knew they were serious about each other, she worried that Gideon might wake up one day and decide she was too involved with cats. After a heartfelt conversation with him, she realized she hadn't given him enough credit. He loved Lara for who she was, and that included being a cat lady.

"Grandmothers see things a little differently," Lara said. "I don't remember either of mine, so I can't speak from experience. But your gram is speaking from her own experience, when times were so much simpler. The downside of technology is that we've all become a little too removed from the real world. In my opinion anyway."

Kayla picked at a fritter crumb. "She thinks I should go to church more and meet someone there." She rolled her eyes. "I wanted to say, what is this, the nineteen forties? When I told her I knew of at least three happy couples who met online, she nearly dropped her false teeth. She thinks meeting guys online is the equivalent of walking into Satan's den."

Lara smiled. "Are you thinking of trying online dating?"

"I've been thinking about it, yeah," Kayla said with a shrug. "But every time I think I'm ready to take the plunge, something stops me from clicking the mouse. I guess I'm a scaredy-cat."

"Kayla," Aunt Fran said, "I truly believe that when you least expect it, and *if* you want it to happen, the right person will come into your life. That's how Lara's friend Sherry met David."

"That's right! David had never been in the coffee shop before, but that morning his boss sent him on the road to scout out a new account. He was running early, so he stopped in for breakfast." Lara grinned. "And the rest, as they say…"

"…is history." Kayla perked up a little and smiled. "Sort of like fate, right?"

"Kind of," Lara said.

"I hear you both, honestly I do. It's just…most of the students I take classes with are girls. I don't go to parties or bars like a lot of people my age. Frankly, I'd rather be with animals. If the right guy is going to drop into my life when I least expect it, he's going to have to float out of the sky."

Lara wanted so badly to tell Kayla that there was no shame in not being "hooked up," as she put it. But she sensed that wasn't what Kayla wanted to hear.

Without warning, a fluffy, cream-colored cat leaped onto the chair next to Kayla. Her turquoise eyes beaming, Blue gazed up at Kayla and reached out to her with one chocolate-colored paw.

Lara nearly gasped. She'd never seen Blue make a gesture quite like that. "Kayla," she said softly. "There's a friend with you right now—a furry friend, directly to your right."

Kayla's eyes popped open and she squeezed Snowball tighter. "Blue?" she whispered.

Lara nodded. "She reached out a paw to you. I've never seen her do that before."

Kayla's face relaxed, as if her anxiety had fled. "Oh, I wish I could touch her."

Lara had wished the same thing, many times.

A quiet fell over the kitchen, a sudden sense of peace. Blue looked over at Lara, then leaped down. Lara peeked under the table, but she was gone.

"She's gone, now," Lara said.

Kayla let out a breath. "You know what's weird?" she said quietly. "I'd have sworn I felt something brush my leg."

That didn't surprise Lara. She'd felt the same thing numerous times. Kayla was so in tune with cats and their moods, it seemed natural for Blue to want to comfort her.

"Hey, today's an adoption day, right?" Kayla said, placing her hands on the table. "We'd better make sure the meet-and-greet room is ready."

Lara grinned. Kayla was right. "What do you think, Aunt Fran? If anyone shows up, should we offer snacks or not?"

"I'll let you make the final decision," her aunt said. "But as far as I'm concerned, we are not under any cease-and-desist order. It never arrived, and we never saw it. I'm more convinced than ever that the whole thing was bogus."

"My thoughts exactly!"

All week, Evonda's horrible death had hung over them like a thundercloud, waiting to burst open with more bad news. But the shelter hadn't done anything wrong or broken any rules.

They'd do what they always did. They'd make the shelter welcoming for anyone who came there to adopt.

As they cleaned up the table and set the dishes in the sink, the doorbell to the shelter rang. Kayla looked at her watch. "Twenty minutes early. Don't people pay attention to the hours?"

"I'll see who it is," Lara said.

She went through the large parlor and out to the back porch. A face was peeking through the door pane.

Lara unlocked the door, her heart racing.

Was she letting a killer inside?

"Hi, Brian. I wasn't expecting you."

He came in and shut the door behind him, his face redder than usual. "Yeah, sorry. I probably should have called first. I just wanted to update you guys on a few things. But first, how's my Smuggles doing?"

"He's great," Lara said. "Quiet, of course. But he's eating and using the litter box, which is a good sign. I'm sure he misses you, though. Want me to bring him down for you?"

"Yeah, in a few minutes," he said. "Mind if I sit for a few?"

Lara's nerves jangled. Had he found out that she'd told the police about him taking the box to the recycling station?

"Sure. Have a seat," she said.

He pulled out a chair and plunked himself down. His face was still flushed, whether from the heat or from something else Lara couldn't tell.

"Would you like some lemonade?" she asked him, hoping he'd decline.

"Nah, I'm good," he said, waving a hand.

Lara sat down and faced him. "You said you had something to tell us? Do you want me to get Aunt Fran?"

"No, I can tell you," he said. "Two things. First, I found an apartment. Can't start moving my stuff in till Monday, but at least I have a place. It's roomy and has a great little nook in the front window where Smuggles can curl up in the sun. The landlord's having it cleaned over the weekend, so it will be in move-in condition."

"Sounds great. You lucked out," Lara said.

"Maybe." His face darkened. "Depends on the cops. That's the second thing. For some stupid, freakin' reason, they think I took one of those straps from the box I took to the recycling station for you. I didn't even see any Polypropylene straps. Anyway, bottom line is—they think I strangled Evonda with one of them!"

Lara shook her head. "Brian. I am so sorry. I shouldn't have let you take that box." She didn't see the need to tell him that the police had already questioned her about it.

"Hey, it's not your fault. You helped me. I wanted to return the favor. Anyway, if I end up being taken into custody, I just want to be sure you'll keep your promise to give Smuggles a permanent home here."

Lara folded her hands on the table and looked at him. Was she staring into the eyes of a killer? Did his anger for Evonda spill over into a rage-filled murder?

Anything was possible. She'd learned that the hard way.

"Brian, I wouldn't have promised if I didn't mean it. Smuggles has a home here for as long as he needs us. This is a shelter. This is what we do. Besides, he's sweet and not a bit of trouble."

"Like I said before, you guys, I mean gals, are the best." His face flushed. "Anyway, you know what I mean." He laughed nervously, and his cheeks reddened. "I bet you think I'm some kind of weirdo, getting all choked up about my cat, right?"

Lara smiled. "You're asking the wrong person. I never think it's weird to get emotional over a cat. We do it here all the time."

"The thing is," Brian went on, "Smuggles saved my sanity after my wife and I got divorced three years ago. I never saw it coming. We'd had problems, sure, but she always acted like she wanted to work them out. Next thing I know, she's packing her things and taking off for parts unknown." He blinked back tears.

"Brian, I'm so sorry," Lara said. "Is that when you adopted Smuggles?"

"Yeah. A woman where I work told me I should get a pet. I looked at her like, *are you nuts?* Then she told me about this older cat at the shelter where she volunteered. The cat came from a really bad sitch and needed a good home. I humored her by agreeing to meet Smuggles. One look into those sad eyes and it was all over. No way I'd let anyone else have that cat."

"I like that story," Lara said, choking back a lump. "It's a good example of the healing power of pets."

"Yeah, you said it." Brian swiped at his face.

"Where do you work?" Lara asked him.

"I work for a company north of Concord that makes precision weather instruments. I'm a quality-control engineer. It's a detail-oriented job, but that's what I do best."

Lara smiled and pushed away from the table. "I'll go get Smuggles. Be back in a sec."

She went upstairs to her bedroom, her thoughts spinning off in every direction. Smuggles snoozed peacefully on his oversize bed. Lara lifted him carefully and cuddled him to her chest. He purred and closed his eyes. Her own eyes filled with tears.

Please don't let Brian be a murderer, she prayed silently.

She headed downstairs. Kayla was in the large parlor grooming Snowball, who badly needed the brushing. She seemed to shed more every day. "Hey, what's happening?" Kayla asked. "You need any help?"

Lara held up a finger. "Be back in a minute." She went into the meet-and-greet room, where Brian sat waiting.

The moment he saw Smuggles, he lost it. He took the cat into his arms and sobbed into his fur.

Lara knew exactly what he was thinking.

This might be the last time he ever saw his cat.

Chapter Twenty-One

Adoption day had been a bust, which didn't really surprise Lara. News of the shelter's troubles with Evonda had been making the rounds.

As much as she could, Lara put it out of her mind. Until Evonda's killer was in police custody, things would probably remain in limbo for the shelter. So long as it didn't affect the cats' care, which it wouldn't, Lara could deal with the uncertainty.

Her date with Gideon gave her something to look forward to. She put on her favorite pair of shorts—blazing pink—and a lacy cotton top. With her dangly kitty earrings and a swish of blush over her cheekbones, she was ready to roll.

The no-name clam shack sat slightly off the beaten track in Tamworth. Gideon swung into the parking lot and slowed to a crawl to hunt for an empty space.

"Yikes," Lara said, angling her gaze all around. "The place is jam-packed."

"Typical Friday night…ah, look at that. Someone just pulled out. How's that for luck?" He pulled his car into the vacated space and shut off the engine.

"Good job, Gid. I'm starving, too. I hope the lines aren't too long."

In its prior life, the clam shack had been a ramshackle equipment shed that housed farming tools. An enterprising neighbor bought the land and transformed the shed into a seasonal eatery. The scent of deep-fried goodies wafted over them as they scooted up to stand in the shortest "Order" line.

Lara inhaled deeply. "I can already smell the onion rings. Sometimes I think I like those more than the clams."

"Not me. Give me those deep-fried, whole-belly clams any day," Gideon said, kissing her lightly on the temple. He slid his arm around Lara's waist. "I always hate it when this place closes in September. Let's make the most of it this year and eat here every Friday night, okay?"

Lara grinned. "You won't hear me arguing," she said, a ripple of happiness zinging through her. She loved it when Gideon talked about their future, even if it was something as trivial as eating at the clam shack.

She glanced all around. People still streamed out of their cars. Kids hopped ahead of their moms and dads, anxious to get to a window where food orders were taken. Lara spotted a familiar vehicle in the parking lot. "Isn't that Charlie Backstrom's truck?" She dipped her head toward the lot. "Next to that gorgeous red Vette?"

"Yeah, I think it is." Gideon squinted at the vehicle. "You know what? That rear tire doesn't look right to me. What do you think?"

Lara cupped her hand over her eyes. "I think it's flat," she said. "Strange he didn't notice it getting low on the way over here."

"If we see him, I'll mention it," Gideon said. "Maybe I can help him change it."

They reached the window and ordered their food, then slid over to the pickup window and collected it a few minutes later. For such a busy place, the clam shack managed to prepare and dole out orders quickly and efficiently.

Behind the shack, picnic tables dotted a large clearing surrounded by towering firs. Lara looked for a free table but came up empty. They passed a table where two women and five kids sat munching on clams and fries. Lara grinned when the littlest tyke tossed a french fry to a waiting chipmunk. The animal scooted away, fry in its mouth, and headed into the woods.

"Yoo hoo! Over here!"

Lara turned to her right and saw someone waving at them. It was Nina Backstrom, sitting opposite her husband. "Lara, over here!"

Feeling a slight flicker of disappointment, Lara waved back. She'd hoped to enjoy a quiet meal alone with Gideon so they could chat. She had so many things to tell him. So many things she wanted his input on.

Maybe it was just as well. With all the surrounding chatter and laughter, it wasn't the best place for a talk.

"Shall we sit with Nina and Charlie?" she said. "Otherwise we'll have to eat in the hot car. Either that or wait for a table."

"Sure, why not," Gideon said, good-natured as ever. "We can tell Charlie about his tire."

They wended their way around a half dozen tables until they reached Charlie and Nina's. A large brown bag rested on the table between the couple, and their meals were spread out before them.

Lara sat on the bench next to Nina, and Gideon did the same beside Charlie.

"You sure you don't mind us horning in on your date?" Lara teased, setting down their drinks.

"We don't mind at all," Nina said. "Do we, Charlie?" There was a sharp edge to her voice that surprised Lara.

Clad in his usual gray work shirt and cargo shorts, Charlie swallowed a bite of an onion ring with a loud gulp. "'Course not. Happy to have you guys." He grinned at Lara. "After all, Lara and Fran are two of my best customers. Aren't they, sweetie?"

Something in Charlie's tone set off Lara's radar. Were he and Nina smack in the middle of a tiff?

"They sure are," Nina replied in a saccharine voice.

Lara glanced at Gideon, who was trying valiantly not to notice anything amiss. He opened the greasy brown bag that held their food and set everything on the table, then deftly changed the subject. "By the way, Charlie, we saw your truck in the lot. The rear tire looks flat."

Charlie's face flushed. "Well that's darned odd. Nina's car had a flat tire yesterday." He looked over at his wife. "Did you notice my tire getting low?"

Nina's finely shaped eyebrows dipped toward her nose. "If I'd noticed it, Charlie, I'd have said something, wouldn't I?" She took a swig of the light-colored beer she was drinking.

Lara saw Gideon squirm slightly. She wasn't the only one feeling suddenly uncomfortable. What was up with these two? She regretted, now, that she and Gideon hadn't taken their food to eat in the car—or, even better, back to Aunt Fran's, where they could sit under the maple tree and enjoy it in peace.

She was relieved when Gideon switched to a lighter topic. Before long, he and Charlie were engaged in a rousing discussion of the Red Sox and the team's newest pitcher.

Nina leaned toward Lara, her expression somber. "Hey, I've been hearing about your latest troubles," she said in a lowered voice. "I'm so sorry for everything you're going through."

"Thanks," Lara said. "We're doing okay, though. Once the police sort it all out, everything will fall into place."

"You're actually going to leave it to the police?" Nina tilted her head and gave Lara an odd smile.

For the first time, Lara felt annoyed with Nina. If she was trying to be funny, she'd failed dismally. Nothing about the events of the past week had been the slightest bit amusing.

"Naturally we're going to leave it to the police," Lara said coolly. "What else would we do?"

"Oh, gosh, I'm sorry," Nina said instantly. "I didn't mean that the way it sounded. It's just...well, I heard about some of the other murders you were involved with. You know how it is. People talk."

"That's okay," Lara said, but she still felt a little miffed. "But for the record, I was never involved with murders. I just happened to get into situations where killers kind of...fell into my lap."

When she put it that way, it *did* sound suspect. Did Nina think she carried murder around like a virus?

"Charlie and I were looking forward to your grand opening tomorrow." Nina aimed a french fry toward her mouth. "I'm sorry you had to cancel it." She popped in the fry and chewed it slowly.

Why did Nina have to remind her of that? Lara felt bad enough that they'd postponed the unveiling of the new reading room. "Yeah, I am, too," she said, nabbing an onion ring off her paper plate. "But it was for the best. We'll still have it, after things settle down."

"You'll still invite us, right?" Nina asked.

Lara laughed. "Believe me, you and Charlie are at the top of the guest list."

Nina smiled, but she looked troubled. She glanced off toward the parking lot. Was she trying to spot Charlie's truck? She'd seemed irked when he asked her about the tire.

With Charlie sitting right there, Lara didn't want to ask her if anything was wrong. Clearly, something was. Lara concentrated on eating her meal, but her appetite had fizzled. Even the onion rings, which she normally inhaled, didn't have the same appeal.

Lara slid a look over at Gideon, who seemed to be eating faster than usual. He swallowed his last crispy-fried clam and wiped his mouth with a paper napkin. "Charlie, what do you say we take a look at that tire?"

"Sounds like a plan, man." Charlie clapped him lightly on the shoulder. He stared hard at Nina, who averted her eyes.

The men went off to the parking lot. Lara felt as if she could finally breathe.

Nina looked down at her barely touched food, her delicate features pinched. She took a long pull on her beer.

A sudden wave of compassion washed over Lara. Despite Nina's earlier digs about Lara's involvement with murders, she didn't want to see Nina suffer. She'd come to think of her as a friend, even if she wasn't a close one.

"We probably spoiled your evening," Nina said in a choked voice.

Lara reached over and touched her arm. "You didn't. Not at all, Nina. But something is obviously bothering you."

Nina nodded.

"Did you and Charlie have an argument?"

"Argument?" Her laugh was harsh. "I guess you could call it that. The fact is, we argue all the time. About everything."

Lara was stunned. She'd always had the impression that Nina and Charlie's banter with each other had been coquettish, the barbs tossed with an undercurrent of love. Had she totally misjudged their relationship?

Nina rested her elbow on the picnic table and leaned her chin on her hand. "I'm beginning to wonder if my folks were right about him. They never liked him, you know. They told me I had stars in my eyes. That under those rugged good looks he was just another sleazy contractor who couldn't make a living any other way."

"Nina," Lara said quietly, "you know that's not true. Aunt Fran and I are totally thrilled with the work Charlie did on the reading room. It's exactly what we'd hoped for, and more."

"Yeah, well, tell that to Henry and Izzie Brookdale."

"Your mom and dad?"

Nina nodded. "This might surprise you, but right before I met Charlie, I was *kinda sorta* engaged to one of the doctors at my dad's dermatology practice. We'd done everything but make it official. My folks couldn't have been happier."

After a long silence, Lara asked, "What happened?"

"What happened? I met Charlie, that's what happened. It was country music night at a popular tavern in Ossipee. Not the type of place I'd normally go, but one of my gal pals dragged me there. She'd met the bartender at a concert and had a mad crush on him. Anyway, we're sitting at the bar nursing our drinks when this guy comes up behind me and taps me on the shoulder."

"Charlie?" Lara smiled.

"Yup. He said our next round of drinks was on him. *Round?* I'm thinking. I just wanted to finish my watered-down martini and get the heck out of there. My friend wasn't having any luck with the bartender, and I wasn't feeling comfortable at all. It's just…it wasn't the kind of place I was used to." She paused and rubbed her eyes.

"So, what happened next?" Lara coaxed.

"So I thanked him but told him no, that we were leaving soon anyway. All of a sudden, some jazzy country number starts playing. Charlie reaches for my hand and pulls me onto this ridiculously small dance floor. I tried to refuse, but one look into those gorgeous brown eyes and everything inside me melted. Charlie—I didn't even know his name then—pulled me close to his chest. Lara, I don't know what came over me. My hormones started bouncing all over the place, if you know what I mean."

Lara knew. She'd felt the same with Gideon.

"That's how it started," Nina said, her voice shaky. "Fast and furious, as the saying goes. Long story short, I broke my engagement. My folks were crushed."

"Oh, Nina. I'm so sorry. That must have been so hard, on both you and Charlie."

She sniffled. "It was. My dad even had Charlie investigated. He figured if he could dig up enough dirt on him, I'd see the light and change my mind. He got fooled, though."

"He couldn't find anything bad, right?"

Nina's laugh was achingly sad. "Only that Charlie didn't come from the types of people my folks were used to. His mom married three times, the first two times to total losers. Luckily, the third time was the charm. Charlie finally got a dad who cared about him and who straightened him out, in more ways than one. But that didn't matter to my folks."

"What do you mean, straightened him out?" Lara asked.

"Oh, nothing, just that Charlie'd never been much of a student. He had a mouthful of horribly crooked teeth, and he struggled with schoolwork. That last stepdad was a supergood guy, though. Charlie took his surname, even though there was never an official adoption. The stepdad got Charlie's teeth fixed, got him a tutor. Encouraged him to get into sports instead of trouble." She laughed slightly. "Once Charlie got his grades up, he was able to get on the football team. By that time, they'd moved to Vermont, where his stepdad had family. After his stepdad died, Charlie and his mom came back to New Hampshire. They never really liked Vermont."

"Wow," Lara said. "I never knew any of that."

"As far as any criminal record, he had a few speeding tickets, but that was about it. I think my dad was hoping he'd pulled off an armored car robbery, or something equally awful. For all of Dad's efforts, he turned up a lot of nothing." She began stuffing the remains of her meal into the crinkled brown bag.

"I'm guessing that didn't sway your folks," Lara said.

"You guessed correctly. Charlie has tried so hard to bond with them, Lara. He really has. They just won't warm up to him. They tolerate him, but that's about it."

Lara sighed. This was a tough story to listen to. To judge someone by his perceived social status—Lara naïvely thought that was a thing of the past. She couldn't imagine why Nina's parents were being so stubbornly snobbish.

She pulled her hands into her lap and linked her fingers together. "How long have you and Charlie been married?"

"It'll be two years next April, if we make it that far." Nina sighed. "I gave up everything for him, Lara. I was the medical manager for six doctors at my dad's dermatology practice. Made good money, got engaged to a great guy making even better money. Now I'm running a one-man contracting business that we're barely holding together."

"But you fell in love with Charlie," Lara said softly.

Nina nodded. She blinked back tears.

"Did your parents go to your wedding?" Lara thought of Tim and Jenny Fray, how Tim mentioned that his mom had refused to attend their wedding.

"Oh, they went, only it wasn't held at Dad's country club. We rented space at the American Legion hall. Only about fifty were invited. As opposed to the *two hundred* fifty it would have been if I'd married my dermatologist."

Lara shook her head. What a sad state of affairs for the two. She wished she could offer Nina some sound advice, but everything that popped into her head sounded cliché or trite.

Fresh tears pooled on Nina's pale lashes. "But all of that, *all of that*, I could deal with, if it weren't for"—Nina pulled in a shaky breath—"if it weren't for the way Charlie's been acting lately."

"What do you mean?"

"He's been strange. Secretive. When I ask if something's wrong, he insists everything's fine. He gets mad if I press him too much."

Lara was stunned. They'd always seemed like the perfect couple. "How long has he been like this?"

Nina pressed her lips together. "Since right after he started working on your shelter."

This was all a shock. Lara never would've guessed that the two were having marital problems. Evidently, they'd been putting on quite a good act.

But, as Lara always reminded herself, she'd been fooled before.

Was Charlie seeing someone else? Cheating on Nina? Is that why he couldn't tell her where he was?

"One day he wouldn't answer my calls," Nina said in a shaky voice. "I couldn't stand it anymore. I went out and drove around to look for him. I found his truck parked in the far corner of the lot at the place where he buys his building supplies. At first, I felt sheer relief, until I realized no one was in the truck. It was locked up tight, nothing on the front seat. Two more times that day I went back to see if it was there, which it was. No sign of Charlie, though. He got home around six thirty, acting like nothing was wrong."

"Did you press him about where he was?"

"You bet I did. He gave me some convoluted excuse about doing a quick side job with one of the subs he used, an electrician. He said the electrician met him there and they went in his truck instead. It sounded like so much bull, but I couldn't prove that he was lying."

"Why didn't he return your calls?" Lara said.

"He claimed he left his phone in his glove box. Charlie's kind of… technologically challenged. He's hopeless with a smartphone. He still uses an old flip phone, and he gets mad if anyone teases him about it."

"Nina, think back. Did something happen right around the time you noticed the changes in Charlie? I mean, did he have a doctor appointment or something? Maybe he got some bad news he was afraid to share with you?"

"I thought of that," Nina said. "But no, nothing, except…well, you know that tavern where I told you I first met him?"

Lara nodded.

"One day I was doing laundry, and I found a crumpled napkin from there in his pocket. Which doesn't really mean anything. I know he goes there with his buds once in a while to have a few beers. But when I teased him about the napkin, he nearly bit my head off. I think that was the beginning…"

Lara's gaze drifted to the wooded area beyond the picnic tables. The forest looked so deceivingly peaceful. She couldn't help wondering if the woodland animals had their own little dramas. Fighting over a mate, trying to find enough food, sheltering for the upcoming winter.

She shifted on the picnic bench and turned toward Nina, and for a moment they sat in silence.

"I'm so embarrassed about our troubles," Nina finally said miserably. "I've tried to hide it from my family, but they know something's wrong. I've begged Charlie to tell me what's bothering him, but all he does is tell me to chill. He says I blow everything out of proportion."

Lara felt so bad for Nina. "Do you think counseling might help you and Charlie?"

Nina folded her arms on the table and looked down. "I don't know. The way things are now, I'd be afraid to ask him. You're the only person I've told this to, Lara. The friends I used to hang with kind of backed away from me after I married Charlie. They couldn't understand what I saw in him."

Some friends, Lara thought.

"My mom and dad"—she shook her head—"I can't talk to them at all anymore."

Lara wondered what she'd do in Nina's shoes. Probably give Charlie an ultimatum. *Either talk to me, agree to counseling, or say goodbye to the marriage.* Maybe that would light a fire under him.

But it wasn't her place to offer that kind of advice.

"Lara, I think he's seeing someone." Nina's voice trembled.

"Oh, Nina…"

Nina squashed a tear with her thumb. "If he is, she certainly isn't making him very happy. He's grumpy all the time. At home he snaps at everything."

"Nina, this is all a surprise to me. I never got those kinds of vibes from you two."

"I know. We know how to play the part, don't we?" A tear rolled down her cheek. She looked over toward the clam shack and gave a start. "They're coming back. Please don't say anything to Charlie, okay? He'd die if he thought I shared this with anyone."

"Not to worry," Lara said just as Gideon and Charlie trooped toward them.

"So, was it a flat?" Lara asked in what she hoped was a chipper voice.

"It was," Gideon replied, reclaiming his seat opposite Lara. "But we couldn't find a nail or anything like that. Charlie had a spare, so we changed it. Then we had to go in the men's room and wash our hands." He turned his hands over and examined them.

"It's probably just a slow leak," Charlie said, sounding subdued. "No biggie. I'll get it checked tomorrow." Instead of sitting down, he stood facing Nina with an anxious look.

Was he worried that Nina had confided in Lara? That she'd revealed their deep, dark secrets?

"You ready to go, hon?" Charlie said, moving closer to his wife. His expression had softened. His tone was suddenly loving and contrite, without the sharp edge he'd displayed earlier. He squeezed Nina's shoulder gently. She reached up and took his hand.

"Sure," Nina said, smiling up at him.

He loves her, Lara thought. She felt it in her bones.

After a round of awkward hugs and goodbyes, the two couples made their way toward the parking lot, Nina and Charlie leading the way. They didn't hold hands, Lara noticed, but they walked close enough together that their shoulders were nearly touching.

"Trouble in paradise?" Gideon asked Lara quietly.

"I'm not sure," Lara said. "I think they have things to work out."

It was the second time that week someone had confided in Lara and asked her not to share. Sherry had begged Lara not to tell anyone about the incriminating photo of her mom with Trevor Johnson.

Now Nina had asked Lara to keep her marital problems a secret.

She wanted to share all of it with Gideon—badly. He had good instincts. And he always had a way of homing in on the problem and offering a fresh perspective.

No, she had to keep their secrets to herself. It was the right thing to do, both for Sherry and for Nina. Eventually, their issues would work themselves out, without any interference from Lara.

Besides, nothing could stay a secret forever.

Could it?

Chapter Twenty-Two

"You've been awfully quiet since we left the shack," Gideon said on the way home.

Lara looked over and gave him a weak smile. "I know. Lots of stuff on my mind, I guess. This past week has been kind of a horror. And then running into Charlie and Nina—that was just the frosting on the cake. It was so uncomfortable, wasn't it?"

"Yup. I'd rather have sat on a bed of nails," he joked. "Not really, but they did kind of put a dent in our meal. You and I never got a chance to talk. So much has happened this past week, especially with you."

"I know, but we'll catch up."

"You…want to spend the night at my place?" Gideon suggested. "I don't have cats, but I do have ice cream."

The idea of spending the night at Gideon's was immensely appealing. With both their schedules so crazy, and Lara constantly having shelter duties, they didn't often get the chance to spend a long evening together to unwind.

Tonight would be a perfect one to spend at Gideon's. Once she picked up the kittens from the veterinary clinic and brought them back to the shelter, she'd be spending several nights bunking with them in the isolation room. They were going to need special care, and she wanted to keep a close watch on them.

"My, you really know how to entice a gal," Lara said. "But before I say yes, what kind of ice cream? I'll need to consider all the facts, counselor."

"I have peanut butter and fudge ripple. I ate all the vanilla." He gave her a contrite look.

"Hmmm. Can you stop at the house first so I can do a few cat things? That way it won't all get dumped on Aunt Fran. I want to be sure Smuggles is all set for the night."

"I can do whatever you want. I'll even help. Speaking of Fran, how's she been doing through all this craziness?"

Lara felt her stomach drop. She still felt bad about the rift between her aunt and Chief Whitley. "She's hanging in there, but she's really mad at the chief. Since the day he showed up with the crime scene tech to take fur samples from Pearl and Snowball, she's been snubbing him, to put it mildly. So far, she's refused to talk to him."

Gideon frowned over the steering wheel. "But she knows he didn't have a choice, right? He can't refuse to comply with a warrant."

"No, but he could have insisted that one of the state police detectives go in his place. The way he saw it, he figured we'd feel better if he showed up instead of a cop we didn't know. Unfortunately, in Aunt Fran's case, he was wrong. To make things worse, he sank his own ship when he didn't remember Pearl's name."

"Boy, you've both had a lousy week." Gideon blew out a breath. "I feel terrible that I haven't been there for you enough."

"Are you kidding?" Lara reached over and squeezed his arm. "You were there when we needed you most. That's what counts. Besides, you can't just abandon your clients because we're having a crisis."

Gideon swung into Lara's driveway and she unhooked her seat belt. So many things were going on at once. All the loose ends seemed entangled in one another. Instead of forming a cohesive pattern, they muddied the picture—making it one big, unsolvable blob. If only she could separate the threads, pull them out, and examine them, one by one...

"I don't know what to think anymore," she said, lifting her tote onto her shoulder. She glanced over at him, her heart thrumming at the way he looked at her.

They shared a long kiss, then Gideon shut off the engine.

When they went into the house, Aunt Fran was in the large parlor sitting in Lara's favorite chair, a book—a historical saga—and a cat—Dolce— propped in her lap. She looked up and smiled when they walked in.

"Did you two have a good meal?" she asked. She stuck a bookmark in her book and tucked it beneath her chair.

Lara plopped onto the sofa. Pearl immediately leaped off the cat tree and made herself at home in her lap. The gray cat reached up with one huge paw to touch Lara's face. Lara cupped her face and kissed her on the snout.

"We did, but we ran into Charlie and Nina there. It ended up being kind of a strange evening." She refrained from telling her what Nina had revealed about her troubles with Charlie.

Gideon had wandered over to the cat tree and was tickling Orca under the chin. "We sat with them, but they were both acting odd, like they were mad at each other. Charlie ended up having a flat tire, so I helped him change it."

"I meant to ask you," Lara said. "Did Charlie say anything to you about Nina?"

"No, but he had kind of a mini meltdown when he saw that tire. He slapped his hand against the truck and let out a few choice words. He said there's no way that could have happened on its own, that he'd have noticed a slow leak."

"So, what does he think happened?" Lara asked him.

Gideon rubbed Orca between the ears. "He thinks someone let the air out."

Lara sat up straight. "What?"

"Why would anyone do that?" Aunt Fran asked. "Is there something going on that we don't know about?"

Lara exchanged a look with Gideon. If only she could tell them what she'd learned from Nina about her and Charlie's strained relationship.

No. That wouldn't be fair. Unless there was a danger of someone being harmed, she wouldn't betray Nina's confidence.

"It's hard to say," Lara finally said. "But Charlie can be a bit temperamental. I learned that over the four months he worked on the addition. By the way, where are the other cats?"

"Twinkles was on my bed, last I saw him," Aunt Fran said. "And I think Munster's on the cat tree in your room. Snowball...I'm not sure. She's usually in here, chilling with us humans."

Lara let Aunt Fran know about their plans for the remainder of the evening, then went about scooping the litter boxes and replenishing the cats' water bowls. Gideon offered to help, but she knew she could work faster without him. Besides, she loved the idea of leaving him to bond with Orca.

Upstairs, Lara walked into her bedroom, and her heart twisted in her chest. Smuggles was curled up on the oversize bed, one paw resting on his purring companion—Snowball. Snowball looked blissful, stretched out with her head tucked into the elder cat's neck. Lara had to force back a lump. "Aw, look at you guys."

Leaving the two alone to snuggle, she made sure Smuggles was set for the night with water, snacks, and clean litter.

Munster was on the cat tree, looking oddly alert. Had he seen something outside in the yard? Lara rubbed his furry head and kissed him good night. "You be a good watch cat, okay? I'm leaving you in charge."

Lara stuffed a change of clothes and a few other essentials into an overnight bag. Downstairs, Gideon was still playing with Orca. He flushed when Lara came over to him. "You ready?" he said.

Lara slipped her arm through his and gave him a sly smile. "You're getting attached to Orca, aren't you?"

Gideon blushed again. "Oh, well, he's a supercute cat. I love those catchers' mitts of his. By the way, look at this. I taught him to high five." He held up the flat of his hand in front of the cat. Orca sniffed it, then rubbed his head against it. "Okay, he didn't do it that time. But he did it before, didn't he, Fran?"

Aunt Fran chuckled. "Yes, he did it once," she said tactfully.

Lara bent over her aunt and kissed her lightly on the cheek. "Be back in the morning. Sure you'll be okay?"

"Don't be silly," Aunt Fran said. "I have a house full of felines to keep me company."

Lara still felt bad leaving her aunt alone. Friday night would typically be "date night" for Aunt Fran and the chief. They usually stayed in to watch old movies, but occasionally they went out to a movie or a local concert. Her aunt always had a fragrant pan of brownies or blondies waiting for him, but it was obvious she hadn't baked anything today.

If Aunt Fran and the chief didn't work things out soon, it might spell the end of their caring relationship. Lara hated the thought. The chief was a good man. He'd always been there when Lara was in dire need. Maybe she'd have to remind her aunt of that.

Lara gazed over at the man she loved.

For tonight, she would concentrate on spending quality time with him.

Chapter Twenty-Three

Before Lara left Saturday morning, Gideon said he wanted to check something in his office. Lara trailed along with him. She loved seeing all his law books, lined up on the shelves along with some of his favorite novels. The watercolor Lara had painted of a much-younger Gideon and his dad hung on the wall opposite the front window. She'd given it to him last Christmas, and he cherished it.

"I just want to check my messages," Gideon said. "I ordered a cartridge for my printer and it was supposed to be here Wednesday. I still haven't gotten it, and I'm getting a little desperate."

"Did you call the people you ordered it from?" Lara asked.

"I did. They were supposed to let me know yesterday if they could do a Saturday delivery, but as of last night I hadn't heard from them. If it doesn't come today, it means a trip to the store for me later." He made a face.

It was more than a ten-mile ride, Lara knew, to the nearest office supply store. "I'd offer to ride along with you later, but today's an adoption day."

Gideon glanced over at his desk and saw a light blinking on his phone. "Oh good. They must've called early this morning." He pressed the button.

"Uh...yeah, hi, Mr. Halley. This is Trevor Johnson. I, um, don't know if you remember me, but I really need to talk to you. I want to make an appoint—"

Gideon grabbed the phone and listened to the rest of the message. After a half minute or so, he hung up.

He looked agitated. "Lara, I apologize for that. I wouldn't have played that if I knew it was from a potential client."

Lara frowned at him. "Potential client?"

"I have no idea what that was about, but any communication that comes into my office that way is confidential. I never should have assumed it was about my cartridge."

"I–I'm sorry," Lara said. "If I could *un*hear that, I would."

He sighed and then smiled at her. "It's not your fault. You weren't trying to eavesdrop." He slipped an arm around her waist and kissed her cheek.

"If it's any consolation," Lara said lightly, "I've already forgotten it." She swiped her hand over her head, as if erasing an imaginary slate.

Except that she couldn't stop thinking about what she'd heard. Trevor Johnson wanted representation? Why? Was he about to confess to murdering Evonda?

And even if that were true, why would he choose Gideon? Their accidental meeting at The Irish Stew several nights earlier hadn't exactly ended cordially.

Johnson's voice had sounded shaky, almost tearful. Was he in some sort of trouble?

Lara wanted to ask Gideon if he was going to return Johnson's call but stopped herself. It wouldn't be fair to put him on the spot. He was feeling bad enough about playing the message in front of her.

"Listen, I'm going to run," Lara said. "We both have lots to do."

Gideon hugged her. "Before you go, are you on board with my doing some grilling for you and Fran tonight?"

"Totally. What can I bring?"

"Other than your aunt, nothing. I've got steaks and burgers, salad fixings, and potato salad from Shop-Along's deli."

Lara snapped her fingers. "Corn."

"Hmmm. I didn't think of that."

"I'll pick up some ears this morning," she offered. "There's a farm stand over on Bedford Road."

"All right. You can do that, but nothing else, okay? Drive you home?"

"Nah. It's a nice morning, not too hot yet. I'll hoof it."

Gideon's office and apartment were housed in an older home only a short distance from Whisker Jog's town center. At the most it was a fifteen-minute walk back to Aunt Fran's. Lara needed the exercise. She'd been feeling like a slug over the past week. Time to get the blood pumping.

Plus, she could pop her head into the coffee shop and say hello to Sherry.

* * * *

"Hey, you're looking cheery this morning," Sherry said.

Lara slid onto her usual stool. "I'm not staying for breakfast. I was at Gideon's this morning, and he made French toast, bacon, and hash browns." She patted her stomach. "I'm stuffed."

"You were at Gideon's *this morning*?" Sherry said dryly. "With your overnight bag?"

"Well…you know." Feeling a blush creep up her neck, Lara waved a hand at her friend. "Anyway, I have a question to ask you. About that… *thing* you showed me."

Sherry looked alarmed. "Lara, you said you wouldn't talk about it!"

"I haven't talked about it," Lara said in a low voice. "I just want to know if I can take a pic of it with my phone. I promise not to show it to anyone. I only want to examine it a little more closely."

Sherry groaned. She looked around. "Mom's in the kitchen. I don't want her to know I kept it." She reached underneath the counter and whipped out the envelope. "Put it in your bag, quick," she said, shoving it at Lara.

Lara tucked it away. "I'll give it back. I promise."

"You don't have to," Sherry said. "Just don't show anyone!"

Lara's timing was perfect. Daisy pushed through the swinging door carrying a large tray laden with breakfast platters. She beamed a smile at Lara, then went over to a table where three men sat waiting for their meals to be delivered. When she was through, she came over and hugged Lara. "Hey," she said. "Seems like I keep missing you lately. How've you been?"

"Okay," Lara said. "Truth be told, Aunt Fran and I have both been going a little nuts. But it'll pass. It always does."

"I'm sorry you had to cancel your gig this afternoon," Daisy said kindly.

"Yeah, me too. But never fear—we'll still have the unveiling. As soon as things settle down."

Daisy hugged her again. "Love to Fran," she said, and toddled back into the kitchen.

"I should be heading home," Lara said. "Aunt Fran's been a little out of sorts. I want to be sure she's okay."

"I'm sorry to hear that," Sherry said. "Want some cookies to take with you?"

"Thanks, but not today. We still have some—"

"Hey, what are you doing here so early?" Sherry interrupted, grinning over Lara's head.

Lara turned to see a familiar, pleasing face coming toward them. Clad in a sky-blue, short-sleeved shirt and navy shorts, David Gregson looked at Sherry as if she'd single-handedly hung the stars. His smile stretching into a full-out grin, he leaned over the counter and kissed her. "I missed you," he said softly.

"Ditto," Sherry said.

A man at the far end of the counter made kissy noises at them.

"Knock it off," Sherry warned jovially, aiming a finger at him. The man laughed, then took a long swig of his coffee.

David slid onto the stool next to Lara. "Hey, Lara. I haven't seen you in a while. How are things going?" He lowered his voice. "I mean, you know, all things considered."

"Not bad," Lara said, "but it's great to see you. In fact, I was just talking about you yesterday. You and Sherry, that is."

"Uh-oh."

"Not to worry. It was all good."

Sherry poured David a mug of coffee. "So, don't keep us hanging. Why were you talking about us?"

"I was telling Kayla the story of how you two met, right here in the coffee shop."

"Kismet, right?" David winked at Sherry.

Sherry giggled, something she rarely did. "I still can't believe the way it happened. David wasn't even supposed to be working that day, but one of his coworkers had called in sick."

"That's right." David plunked sugar into his coffee. "My boss sent me in his place to meet with the owners of Plaid Brothers Landscaping, who were looking to buy new equipment. I was running early for my appointment and the highway was clogged with construction, so I decided to take the scenic route through Whisker Jog. When I saw this place, I figured I'd stop in and have breakfast. Not only did I land a big account that day but I met the most wonderful woman on the planet."

Lara smiled as if she was hearing the story for the first time. No matter how often Sherry told it, she never tired of listening to it.

"Anyway, why *are* you here so early?" Sherry asked David. "Not that I'm complaining."

"First of all, I wanted to let you know everything's all set for tonight. Reservations for seven thirty, signed and sealed."

Sherry did a fist pump. "Yes! Now will you please tell me where we're going?"

"No can do, my lady. It's a surprise, and you will just have to be patient. But I assure you, you're going to love it. Be ready at five, by the way. It's a bit of a ride."

"Now *I* want to know," Lara groused playfully.

"Sherry will tell you all about it tomorrow," he said. "So, tell me, how's Gideon these days?"

"He's great. Working hard, as always. I hope the four of us can have another date night soon."

About a month earlier, Lara and Gideon had joined Sherry and David for dinner at The Irish Stew. The evening had been fun and relaxing, and the men had gotten to know each other better.

"We will. Let's make it a plan," David said. He looked at his watch, then at Sherry. "Hey, hon, can I take my java to go? I don't want to be late for Kellie. She's the real reason I'm here so early." He stroked his light red beard.

"Wow. You're really getting spruced up for tonight, aren't you?" Sherry teased. "At least that better be why you're seeing Kellie."

David laughed. "Yep. Haircut and a beard trim. Gotta look my best for my one and only, right?"

A wave of emotion rose in Lara. Sherry and David were so perfect for each other. She loved seeing her friend so happy.

Sherry poured David's coffee into a takeout cup and snapped on a lid. He kissed Sherry again, said goodbye to Lara, and headed out of the coffee shop.

"He's so right for you," Lara said, feeling a bit choked up. "I wonder where's he's taking you this evening."

Sherry waved a hand at her. "You kidding? I already know."

"You do?"

"Of course. You think you're the only detective in town? He left printouts, including the menu, on the back seat of his car. I just *happened* to see them, sitting right there in plain sight underneath his day planner."

"In *plain* sight?" Lara said wryly.

"I know I shouldn't have snooped, but the secrecy was killing me." Sherry jiggled her fists. "Oh, Lara, I'm so excited. We're going to that restaurant at the top of the Prudential building in Boston!"

Lara squealed, then leaned over the counter and hugged her. "Oh, Sher, I know you're going to love it. I lived in Boston for years and never ate there! Take a few pics tonight, okay? And have a fabulous time."

Lara left the coffee shop feeling elated for Sherry, but a bit depressed about having canceled the reading room celebration originally planned for today. It couldn't be helped, and it was the right thing to do. Still, it felt like a blade to the heart.

Outside, the sun hovered in the eastern sky, peeking through wisps of fluffy clouds. The distant hills were a lush green that skimmed a cerulean sky. By noon, it would be a scorcher, but for now, the day felt comfortable.

At the kitchen table, Aunt Fran was enjoying a marmalade-coated English muffin with her orange-flavored tea. Dolce rested in her lap while she perused the morning paper.

"Hey, Aunt Fran," Lara said. She dropped her tote and her overnight bag onto a kitchen chair. Munster immediately trotted over and meowed up at her. Lara laughed and swept him into her arms. "Everything okay here?"

"Of course," her aunt said. "Things okay with you?"

"Good," Lara said carefully. "Very good. We've been invited to a cookout at Gideon's this evening. Steaks or burgers—our choice—on the grill."

Her aunt stiffened. "Just the three of us?"

"Just the three of us."

Uh-oh. What if Gideon invited Chief Whitley on the sly? He wouldn't, would he?

"I'll make sure of it, Aunt Fran," Lara promised.

"Then I accept." She tipped her head toward the large parlor. "Take a peek," she said with a cryptic smile.

Intrigued, Lara set Munster down and crept quietly into the parlor. The sight that greeted her made her gasp.

Smuggles and Snowball were curled up together on the sofa, their furry heads resting on each other. Lara brought her hands to her lips as her aunt came up beside her.

"Smuggles came downstairs?" Lara whispered.

"On his own," Aunt Fran confirmed. "I'm guessing he followed Snowball, but that's only a guess. He also ate from one of the bowls in the kitchen."

Lara felt her heart race. Smuggles was becoming part of the household.

She couldn't help wondering if he'd end up with them as a permanent resident.

It all depended on whether or not Brian Downing murdered Evonda.

Chapter Twenty-Four

As she promised, Lara drove over to the local farm stand to pick up corn for Gideon's cookout. In addition to six ears of fresh sweet corn, she bought three huge tomatoes, a pile of green beans, and a basket of strawberries. Gideon hadn't mentioned dessert, so she planned to surprise him with strawberry shortcake.

Lara stuffed her purchases into the cooler she'd brought along, then began heading home. When she reached the STOP sign at the corner of Bedford and Loudon, she paused.

Loudon Street.

Isn't that where the chief said Evonda lived?

She glanced in her rearview mirror. No one was behind her, but she flicked on her right-hand signal anyway and turned onto Loudon.

The street was lined with huge maples that shaded the well-maintained sidewalks. The homes were mostly Cape Cod–style, with a few bungalows mixed in. Save for a gray-haired woman planting impatiens around the base of her maple tree, no one seemed to be around. Didn't kids play outside anymore? When she was a kid, she'd be climbing trees or trying to spot salamanders along the creek behind Aunt Fran's vacant lot.

The woman planting the flowers looked up as Lara drove past. Lara smiled and waved, as if she belonged there, but the woman only stared at her with a stony expression. Had Evonda's murder set the entire neighborhood on edge? Made them wary of anyone they didn't recognize?

Lara realized that her slow cruising might be drawing attention. She didn't know Evonda's house number, but Loudon Street meandered on for quite a distance, so she kept driving. She was beginning to think her side expedition would turn up nothing when she spotted it.

It was a white Cape Cod with charcoal gray shutters, surrounded on three sides by carefully tended evergreen shrubs. A border of chipped stones edged in brick lined the front of the house. A set of wide wooden steps painted a muted gray and flanked by ornate, wrought-iron railings led to the front door, which was painted white. On the door was the massive image of a crow.

Lara pulled over, shoved her gearshift into Park, and gawked at the door. The crow was shown from a side view, its beak slightly open. From this distance, she couldn't tell if it was painted on or if it was some sort of Folk Art ornament. But it was definitely a crow, and a big one.

She had no doubt she'd found Evonda Fray's home.

In one of the downstairs windows, a curtain was suddenly thrust aside. A face appeared for a brief moment, then just as quickly disappeared.

Oh God, I've been caught spying, Lara thought, a wave of panic crashing over her. She threw the Saturn's gearshift into Drive and started to ease away when a man rushed out of the house and flagged her down.

Tim Fray.

Lara gave herself a mental bop on the head. Why had she come over here? How was she going to explain why she was checking out Evonda's house?

Another thought struck her. Could Tim have killed his mom? Had he gotten so fed up with her treatment of Jenny that he finally decided to eliminate her from their lives—permanently?

"Lara!" Timothy waved at her and strode toward the driver's side of the car.

Lara gave him a frozen smile that must have looked deranged. As he walked around the front of the car, he made a motion for her to power down the window.

She hesitated, then powered it down about halfway. "Hey, Tim."

"I saw you looking at the door," he said, peering at her over the top of the window. "Is that why you stopped?"

"I–I…yes. Well, sort of. I was over at the farm stand getting some veggies for supper, and on the way back, I noticed the sign to Loudon Street. I guess…I guess I was just being nosy."

Tim smiled. His eyes looked warm and kind behind his Buddy Holly specs. "You obviously noticed the crow. Everyone does. Want to come in? I don't have much to offer you, but Mom always kept cans of root beer in the fridge."

"Oh no, I don't want to bother you." *Or be alone with you.* "I'm sure you have enough to do."

"I've got plenty to do, but I'm ready for a break. I've been packing Mom's things in boxes, but so far, I've barely made a dent." He tapped the roof of the car. "Come on in for a few. I've got the AC cranked, so it's nice and cool inside."

An excuse flitted over the tip of Lara's tongue, but then she swallowed it back. This was an ideal opportunity to learn more about Evonda. The more she learned, the better armed she'd be to figure out who might have wanted her dead.

"Sure," she finally agreed. "Why not?"

She hoisted her tote onto her shoulder and slid out of the car. When Tim's back was turned, she pulled her phone from the tote and slipped it into the pocket of her shorts. She wanted it within easy reach, just in case...

Tim led her up the driveway, then around the side of the house to a screened-in porch at the rear. The yard was small, but the grass had been recently mown. A granite birdbath sat in the center of the lawn. In the far corner, adjacent to the wooden fence, was an apple tree loaded with tiny fruit.

Tim opened the door to the porch and escorted her inside. Lara was surprised at how homey it looked. She'd expected Evonda's tastes to run to hard lines and sharp corners to match her personality.

A round oak table graced by a centerpiece of dried hydrangeas surprised her, as did the two patio-style lawn chairs with their plump, colorful cushions. Several magazines were fanned out on the table—bird magazines, it appeared. It was a room where Lara could easily picture herself stretched out in one of the chairs, enjoying the summer breezes sifting through the screens.

"Let's go into the dining room," Tim said. "It's cooler in there. Can I grab a root beer for you first?"

"Oh, no, thanks. I'm good."

She followed Tim into the kitchen, which was tidy and immaculate. The stainless appliances shone, and the tile floor was spotless. Individual wooden shelves painted a distressed white dominated an entire wall. The shelves boasted a collection of miniature, vintage bird prints. If anyone had ever loved birds, it was Evonda.

Tim grabbed a can of root beer for himself and popped the cap. "This way," he said. They went down a short hallway and into the dining room.

Lara's eyes widened, and she had to stifle a gasp. Never before had she seen a room so...eclectic.

The wallpaper was a willowy green, emblazoned with crows of every shape and size. A mahogany sideboard was clustered with whimsical wooden crows. Shelves similar to the ones in the kitchen hung over the sideboard and on the adjacent well, but these shelves were highly polished and boasted a collection of porcelain crows.

I'd hate to have to dust this room, Lara thought. *It would take all day.*

Pictures of crows graced every wall. Some were old-style prints. Others were photos, gorgeously framed, that Lara suspected were Evonda's handiwork.

One print in particular caught Lara's eye. About eleven-by-fourteen and framed in ornate gold leaf, it was a side view of a crow with oddly human eyes. Garbed in black boots and a black cape, the crow seemed to be gazing at something in the distance. Lara thought she'd seen the print before, but she couldn't recall where. It was hauntingly beautiful and eerie at the same time. She loved it.

In the far corner of the room, three cardboard boxes were stacked atop one another. A wrought-iron chandelier hung over the antique dining-room table. The table was covered with photographs separated into piles.

"I've been sorting through Mom's photos," Tim explained, a catch in his voice. "Did you happen to see the display at the funeral home yesterday?"

"I did," Lara said. "Your mom was a talented photographer."

Tim shuffled some of the piles around. "These are some of the old pics I wanted to use in the display, but I had to pick and choose because there wasn't enough room." He pulled out a dining room chair. "Sit. Please." He slugged back a swig of his root beer.

Lara lowered herself onto the chair and rested her tote on the polished oak floor. She felt strange being there. She'd only met Tim a few days earlier, and not under the best of circumstances. Plus, technically, she was still a suspect in Evonda's murder.

As was he, she assumed. As far as she knew, the police hadn't ruled him out.

So why was he so anxious to show her around Evonda's home? Had he lured her inside with the idea of interrogating her? Lara also couldn't help wondering why Jenny wasn't there, helping him sort through his mother's belongings.

"Look at these," Tim said, pushing a small stack over to Lara. "Mom, when she was a kid." His face crumpled slightly.

He's like a little boy, Lara thought, *wanting desperately to paint his mom in a positive light.*

Lara went slowly through the stack, most of which were old, discolored Polaroids. As a young child, Evonda had looked happy and carefree. Pics of her as a teenager, which were few, showed a sad-faced girl with a distant gaze, as if the weight of the world rested on her shoulders.

Her heart jumped when she came across another one of Evonda with the white kitten. In this one, a sweet-faced Evonda was clutching the kitten to her chest, her chin resting on the kitten's head. Lara held up the photo to examine it more closely.

"I figured you'd like that one," Tim said quietly. "I know you run a cat shelter, and that Mom tried to say it was a cat café."

"Did she tell you that?" Lara set down the photo.

"Yeah, I stopped over to see her after work that day. She was superagitated over it. She got like that sometimes."

That surprised Lara. Evonda had seemed more triumphant than agitated the day she "inspected" the shelter. Had she had a change of heart?

No, that didn't make sense. The morning she was murdered, the cease-and-desist order was found on the front seat of her car. She'd obviously intended to file it with the court, and have it enforced.

Tim's eyes brimmed with tears. "That was the last time I ever saw her. Mom had a lot of enemies, Lara. I know that. But she wasn't the ogre some people made her out to be."

Lara felt her heart wrench. Whatever Evonda was, she was Tim's mom and he loved her.

"And for what it's worth," Tim continued, "I don't believe for a second that you had anything to do with her death."

"Well, thank you for that," Lara said with a nervous laugh. Did he have his own suspicions? With her forefinger, she touched the photo again. "When I look at this photo, it's hard for me to believe your mom really hated cats."

Tim shook his head grimly. "She didn't always hate cats. Not until that kitten destroyed her life."

For a moment, Lara was stunned silent. "Destroyed her life? I don't understand."

Tim sat down adjacent to Lara. "My mom was an only child. My grandparents had her later in life, and my grandmother absolutely doted on her." He swallowed hard. "When she was about seven, one of their neighbor's cats had kittens. Mom wanted one desperately. She begged her parents to let her have the only white one. My grandparents, especially my grandfather, weren't keen on having a cat in the house. But they finally relented and let her have the kitten. Mom named him Casper."

Lara felt a lump filling her throat. She sensed Tim's story was coming to a bad ending.

"They'd only had the kitten about three weeks when it happened. Mom was in school—first or second grade, I think. My grandmother had left the door to the cellar open. She was gathering up a pile of laundry to take down there to wash." Tim's eyes took on a haunted look.

"The kitten had apparently decided to explore the cellar, a place where he hadn't been allowed before. He was on the third stair down when my grandmother tripped over him. She was holding the laundry, so she didn't see him. She fell headlong down the stairs." Tim shook his head.

"Oh, Tim," Lara said.

"My grandfather witnessed the whole thing. He was in the cellar doing some woodworking when my grandmother started down the stairs. He saw the kitten, but by the time he called out to her, it was too late. She—" He swallowed again. "She couldn't be saved. She'd gotten a massive head injury when she hit the concrete floor."

Lara felt that same lump jamming her throat. "It wasn't anyone's fault. It was an accident."

"It was," Tim agreed. "But my grandfather blamed the kitten, which he never wanted in the first place. He lost the only woman he'd ever loved that day. For him, the world ended. For my mom, her childhood was shattered."

Lara brushed at a tear. "But...surely he didn't blame Evonda."

"Oh, but he did," Tim said, his voice raw now. "After that, he barely spoke to Mom. She was a little girl lost. Seven years old, with no mother to love her and a father who blamed her for the loss of his beloved wife. His rejection crushed her."

With that, Lara lost it. She burst into tears. Evonda had suffered so much, so needlessly. No child should have to endure that.

"Lara, I'm sorry. I didn't mean to upset you," Tim said kindly. He gathered up the Polaroids and pushed them to the far side of the table. "I told you that story only because I wanted you to understand. Mom was a good person. Circumstances made her crusty and surly, but that's not who she was deep down."

Lara felt foolish for blubbering in front of a near stranger. She reached down into her tote for a pack of tissues. She pulled one out and wiped her eyes. "It tells me so much about your mom, and how easy it is to misjudge people." She sniffled. "Tell me, what happened to the kitten?"

"My grandfather brought it back to the neighbor who'd given it to Mom. She was the one, in fact, who told me this story on the day of my grandfather's funeral. She said she never forgot the devastation in his eyes that day. He was a totally broken man. The memory of it had always haunted her."

"I'm surprised she'd tell you that at his funeral," Lara said. "It doesn't seem very...tactful."

His smile was somber. "No, it wasn't. But she wanted to get it off her chest. I think a part of her always felt responsible because she'd given Mom the kitten."

"Do you think your mom remembered much of that day?"

Tim shook his head. "She has vague recollections, but that's all. She remembers her dad marching over to the neighbor's with Casper in a cardboard box. For some reason, that stuck in her head. Mostly she remembers an unloving dad who pretty much ignored her after the accident. But Mom was smart, and plucky. She compensated by befriending the birds in their yard. Birds became an obsession that always stayed with her."

Lara's eyes started leaking again. "Tim, I've taken up enough of your time. I have one more question, and you can tell me to take a hike if you don't want to answer it."

"Fire away," he said with a cautious look.

"Who do you think killed your mom?"

"Oh. I don't think," Tim said fiercely. "I know."

"You do?" Lara said, hearing her voice rise.

He nodded. "In my opinion, the cops need to be focusing on one person, and one person only. Trevor Johnson."

Lara had been sure he was going to say Brian Downing. "Why do you think that?"

"Because of something the police confided in me. That morning, when Mom was killed, she'd started to write me a text. The police think she saw the killer approaching in her rearview mirror and tried to get a message to me. She was murdered before she could finish, but the text contained only three letters: K-R-A."

Lara was puzzled. "That's it? K-R-A? But—"

"Let me finish. I Googled Trevor Johnson and found out something *verrry* interesting. His mother's maiden name was Kramer. It's also Johnson's middle name."

"Why would your mom text you his middle name if she wanted to identify him?" Lara asked. "Isn't that kind of cryptic?"

"I thought of that," Tim said grimly. "My guess is that it was the first thing that popped into her head. She didn't exactly have time to spare, you know?"

"No, she didn't," Lara agreed, although she still doubted his supposition. Why would Evonda even know Johnson's middle name? Something about that didn't make sense. "Have you told this to the police?"

"I did, but it turns out they were on top of it all along." His eyes lit up behind his glasses. "Between you and me, they've been looking long and hard into Johnson's background. I wouldn't be surprised if they made an arrest very soon."

If that was true, it meant that Brian Downing had dropped to a lower number on the suspect list. If he was still a suspect at all.

Something else nagged at Lara. If Evonda saw the killer coming in her rearview mirror, why didn't she lock her car doors? Wouldn't that be the logical way to protect herself? She posed the question to Tim.

"Excellent point," Tim said. "The cops feel sure that Mom knew her killer, but that he somehow managed to put her at ease long enough for him to open the rear door of her car. Maybe he waved, said he just wanted to talk. Something like that. Once he was in the car, she was trapped."

It was a horrible scenario, if that's the way it actually went down. Poor Evonda. She was probably terrified, yet she kept her cool long enough to try texting her son.

"And no one saw anything?"

Tim shook his head. "It was too early for any of the neighbors to be up and about. Mom was an early riser, like all those birds she loved. She went to her office as early as five some mornings to catch up on paperwork. Whoever killed her knew that."

Paperwork? Whisker Jog was so small. How much paperwork could she have? How many places did she have to inspect? Did she have another job on the side?

Whoever killed her knew that.

Tim's words put another thought in Lara's head.

Jenny Fray. She'd been despised by her mother-in-law, treated like an outcast. Was the quiet young woman strong enough to have strangled Evonda? Had the police even considered Jenny a possible suspect?

If only she could talk to the chief about some of these things. Even though he tended to be tight-lipped about local murder cases, she usually managed to eke out a few tidbits from him. In the past, those tidbits had led her down the path to a twisted killer.

"How's Jenny doing through all this?" Lara asked. "It must be hard on her, too."

Tim averted his gaze. "She doesn't handle this kind of stress very well. She's been sort of quiet, sullen. My mom, like I told you, never liked Jenny. She didn't think she was good enough for me."

"But why? I don't understand."

"Well, first off, Jenny's mom struggled with addiction issues. When she was a kid, they moved around a lot, so Jenny didn't have much stability. Mom saw her as a bad match for me, but I wish she'd tried to understand her better. But like I said, Mom had her biases."

"I remember Jenny in school," Lara said. "She was only in my class one or two years, but she was such a sweet girl. She was kind of quiet, but the thing that sticks in my mind is the way she always looked out for other kids."

"That's my Jenny." Tim smiled, but he looked troubled. "I admit, we're different in a lot of ways. I like classical music, she likes country. I like romantic comedies, she likes horror. We eat totally different foods. I have sensory issues, so I despise anything slimy, like cooked spinach. Jenny, on the other hand, is a major veggie lover."

"But those aren't real differences," Lara said with a smile.

"I know. You're right." He let out a sigh. "Jenny'll be okay eventually. She's going back to work on Monday. Mom left a decent-sized estate, so I want to take her to Paris once this nightmare is over. Jenny's always dreamed of traveling there."

"That sounds…lovely." Lara felt her throat tightening again. "Where does Jenny work?"

Tim picked at a scab on his knuckle. "At the fitness center on the Moultonborough line. She's kind of a Jill-of-all-trades, I guess you'd say. Mostly she manages the check-in desk."

Does she also work out? Lara wished she could ask. *Could she have strangled a grown woman?*

No way could she pose those questions, though. Instead, she switched gears. "Tim, why did your mom love crows so much?"

He laughed. "Ah, I love this question. Crows are such clever birds. They have incredible memories. Did you know they can find food they hid six months earlier? That they can remember the exact location?"

"No, I didn't," Lara said.

"They'll even wait until they're sure no other crows are watching before they'll remove the food. They're also adept at using tools to get food. Crows will actually fashion a twig into a hook to extract insect larvae from trees."

Lara shuddered slightly in the frigid room. Tim must have set the AC on *North Pole*. "Amazing."

"Mom studied crows from the time she was young. Something about them gave her comfort during those lonely years growing up." Tim looked animated now. "Did you know she and her bird-loving buds called themselves the 'old crows'?"

A murder of crows…

"Actually, yes," Lara said with a grin. "I met them at the memorial service."

"They're quite the characters," Tim said. "Before my dad died, one of them, Letitia, used to flirt shamelessly with him. He was having none of it, though. He only had eyes for Mom."

"Did your mom know about it?"

"Oh, yeah. It was a big joke between them. No hard feelings on either side."

That surprised Lara. She'd have expected Evonda to be furious at her friend for making overtures toward her husband.

She pulled her phone from her pocket and checked the time. "Gosh, Tim, I've been bending your ear half the morning," she exaggerated. "I'd better get going."

Tim rose and walked her to the door. "Hey, Lara, before you go, would you mind if we exchanged cell numbers? That way, if I hear anything about an arrest, I can text you right away. And you…well, you can let me know if you hear anything, too."

"Um, sure," Lara said after a slight hesitation. No harm could come from him having her number, right?

They exchanged numbers, and then Tim's face reddened. "Lara, I have to confess something. After all this stuff happened with Mom, I'm afraid I couldn't resist Googling you. I read about how you helped the police in the past."

Oh, no. Not again.

"I didn't really help, Tim. You know that old saying, wrong place, wrong time? That's kind of how all that stuff happened." *Plus, I had a guardian cat dropping clues along the way. A cat who saved my skin more than once.*

"Well, anyway," he said, sticking out his hand, "I'm glad you came inside. I shared these things because I didn't want you thinking my mom was a monster."

Lara pumped his hand, which felt like a block of ice. "I understand," she said. *And I feel horrible for the things I said about her.*

She bade Tim goodbye and nearly ran to her car. The sudden blast of heat outside felt like blessed relief.

Chapter Twenty-Five

Lara was almost at the turnoff to High Cliff Road when she spotted a dark-colored sedan in her rearview mirror. Although her mind had been flitting in all directions, she sensed the car had been following her, a bit too closely, for at least the last few miles.

A coincidence, that was all, she told herself. This was a major road, heavily traveled, especially on a Saturday in the summer. She adjusted her sunglasses, then sent a furtive glance at her mirror. Between the angle of the sun and the tinted windows of the sedan, she couldn't tell if the driver was a man or a woman.

Lara kept driving, careful to stay just below the speed limit. She was almost home when the sedan escalated. It moved up swiftly until it was only inches from her rear bumper. Lara's pulse spiked. She no longer had any doubt—someone was trying to annoy her. Or scare her.

She tried once more to get a glimpse of the driver, but at that moment the sedan's high beams flashed on. Lara made a sharp turn onto High Cliff Road, leaving the sedan to peel away with a squeal of tires.

Her heart pounded all the way up the driveway. She'd just opened her car door when her cell pinged with a text. She dug it out of her pocket and opened it.

> *Lara, thank you for putting up with my sad tales*
> *today. It was good to have someone to talk to.*
> *Hope I didn't sound too gloomy. Tim.*

Wow. That was a surprise. It made her feel even sorrier for Tim.

He'd hadn't sounded gloomy, not really. He was in mourning. Lara understood that. After her dad died, Lara had been devastated for months afterward. She didn't think she'd ever get past it.

Tim's story about his mom and the white kitten had been heart-wrenching for sure. She understood, though, why he needed to tell it. Why he needed her to understand.

She debated whether or not to text him back but decided against it. Later, if she remembered, she'd flick him a quick response.

Munster greeted her at the door, meowing as if to chide her for being gone too long and jeopardizing his midday snack. She lifted him into her arms and hugged him to her chest.

Aunt Fran came out of the large parlor. "Lara, you look flushed. Is something wrong?"

Lara shook her head. "No, nothing. I'm fine. It's just really hot out." She grabbed a napkin from the holder on the counter and blotted the perspiration from her face.

"Are you sure that's all?"

Lara dropped onto a chair at the table. Once again, she didn't want to worry her aunt, but she didn't want to lie. She attempted to calm her nerves by taking several deep breaths.

"I went to the farm stand to get the veggies for tonight," she said, setting Munster in her lap, "and I ended up driving down the street where Evonda lived."

Aunt Fran sat down opposite her. "Go on," she said, as if she were back in her school-teaching days, urging a student to confess.

Lara related all the details of her visit with Tim, including the strangeness of Evonda's avian-themed décor.

"That story about the kitten breaks my heart," Aunt Fran said. "But it explains a lot, doesn't it?"

Lara nodded, a lump blossoming in her throat. "I said terrible things about her, Aunt Fran. I feel like such an awful person. What gave me the right? I didn't even know her!"

"You were reacting to her treatment of us, Lara," her aunt said sagely. "Perfectly understandable. We're all human. We get angry sometimes. That's the way it is."

Like the way you're mad at the chief?

Lara decided to skip the part about the sedan that had followed her home. For starters, she might have imagined it. Second, it might have been just an impatient driver who thought she'd been driving too slowly.

Aunt Fran leaned back to allow Dolce to leap into her lap. "Lara, I'm getting concerned," she said, her tone soft. "You're not out there, how shall I say this, asking too many questions, are you?"

Oh God, was she? Was she doing all the things that had gotten her into trouble in the past?

"I don't think so. It was a total coincidence that I spotted Loudon Street. I remembered the chief saying that was where Evonda lived. When I saw that crow on the door, I knew it had to be her house. I pulled over just to have a peek. I didn't expect Tim to come trotting out and lasso me in the way he did." She tried giving up a casual laugh, but it fell flat. Aunt Fran remained stone-faced.

"But why did you choose that particular farm stand?" her aunt said. "There's a closer one near the school."

"Honestly, I don't know." Lara groaned. "Oh, God, do you think my subconscious led me there?"

"I don't know, but I'm getting very worried." Aunt Fran rested a hand on Dolce's soft fur. "Lara, has…*she* visited you lately?"

Lara stared at her aunt. "She? You mean Blue? I…no, not since the day we were sitting here with Kayla. That was the last time I saw her."

Her aunt looked perplexed. "I was so hoping…"

Lara smiled. "It's not a magic trick, Aunt Fran. It's still a mystery that I can see her at all. We have to remember that. And believe me, there've been many times when I've doubted my sanity."

"All right. No more questions. You said you bought veggies. Where are they?"

"Ach. I left them in the car. They'll broil out there!"

Lara set Munster on her chair and dashed out to the car. She returned with the bags and set them on the counter. "I'll clean the corn before we head over to Gideon's. In the meantime, I'm going to make strawberry shortcake fixings."

"Ooh, that'll be a treat." Her aunt came over and inspected the veggies. "Can I make the biscuits for you?"

"That would be great. You wouldn't mind?"

"Not at all. Happy to do it." Aunt Fran sidled over to Lara. "You're sure it'll be only the three of us tonight, right?" she asked, sounding a tad suspicious.

"I'm sure," Lara said, but then realized she wasn't. Gideon hadn't really made that clear. "I'll call Gideon to make absolutely sure, okay?"

Aunt Fran kissed her on the cheek. "I'd appreciate that. Oh, I almost forgot. Kayla came by while you were gone. She brought over another box of books, courtesy of her gram's neighbor. It's on the floor in the reading room."

"I'm happy about the books, but I'm sorry I missed her. She's coming back later, right?"

"I'm afraid not," her aunt said with a look of concern. "One of her cousins is coming over with her new baby, and her grandmother insisted she hang around."

"Oh, well…that's okay, I guess."

In truth, Lara was disappointed. Over the past year, she'd gotten quite accustomed to having Kayla around the shelter. She wasn't only a part-time employee, she was also a good friend.

Lara hated seeing the mental gymnastics her grandmother sometimes put her through. She knew Kayla's gram loved her dearly and wanted only the best for her. But sometimes, in her zeal to maintain a close family unit, the woman failed to see her granddaughter's feelings getting lost in the shuffle.

Lara and her aunt threw together a quick lunch of watermelon slices and string cheese, washed down with minty iced tea. It was nearly one, the start of adoption hours.

Lara went into the meet-and-greet room and closed the door behind her. She wanted to spruce up the room without help from any feline volunteers, well-intended though they might be.

She began by wiping down the table, after which she set out a clean, cat-themed runner. She made sure the floor was spotless, and that the room smelled fresh. She finished by giving the windows a once-over with a few squirts of glass cleaner.

Next, she outfitted Twinkles, Dolce, and Munster with their "adoption day" collars. As Aunt Fran's original three cats, they wore the blue collars during adoption hours to signify that they weren't available for placement.

Glancing around the meet-and-greet room, Lara felt a swell of pride. This was their shelter—hers and Aunt Fran's. They'd created it from a spark of an idea—a flash of ingenuity that grew into something bright and special and wonderful. With help from Gideon on the legal end, they'd transformed Aunt Fran's Folk Victorian into a true feline refuge. A small one, yes, but still a shelter.

In the beginning, Lara and her aunt had both wondered if the shelter would be taken seriously. Would anyone actually adopt a cat from them? Or would people think they were just two crazy cat ladies, collecting strays and hoping someone might take a few off their hands?

Their concerns were short-lived. Over the past year and a half, and with Kayla's help, they'd rescued and adopted out more than twenty cats and kittens. And while they couldn't accommodate the number of cats a normal shelter could, the ones they'd taken in had each been given a fresh start in a loving home.

The door that connected the back porch with the new reading room hung slightly open. A sudden pang ripped through Lara, so painful it almost stopped her breath. Pushing herself forward, she stepped over the threshold.

The midday sun slanted through the windows, making the room even brighter and cozier than it already was. If it hadn't been for Evonda's murder, their closest friends would be there right now, celebrating the unveiling of the reading room. Despite the delays, and Charlie Backstrom's quirks, the project had been a huge success.

It killed Lara—metaphorically, of course—that they had been forced to cancel the weekend of events. Tomorrow, Sunday, would have been the first "read to a cat" day in the new addition. She'd had to call several people who'd already made appointments to give them the disappointing news.

The box Kayla had delivered sat in the center of the room. Lara dropped to her haunches and opened the flap. Colorful children's books were stacked neatly inside. They looked brand-new, as if the spines had never been cracked.

As Lara riffled through them, the selection amazed her. One title in particular made her smile—*Cary the Crow and the Hidden Spoon*. Was this a sign from Evonda that it was all going to work out? That her killer would soon be behind bars?

If only, Lara thought wryly. Evonda had wanted to shut down the shelter, not help them out.

Lara pulled the crow book out of the box so she could read it later.

It was exactly ten minutes past one when two smiling faces—a boy and a girl—peered through the glass-door pane. Behind them was a woman wearing cutoff jeans and an oversize gray T-shirt with a cat imprinted on the front. She waved and grinned at Lara.

"Hey there. Welcome to the High Cliff Shelter!" Lara greeted, ushering them all inside.

"I hope we're not too early," the woman said. She had a head full of unruly black curls and large, inquisitive eyes that made her look like a schoolgirl instead of a thirtysomething mom. "The twins, they've been bugging me all morning!" She placed a hand on each of their shoulders. "I'm Angie Duncan, by the way. These little monkeys are Archer and Anna."

The twins, who looked about five, had rust-colored hair, freckled faces, and mile-wide smiles. "Can we see your kittens?" Archer said eagerly. Lara assumed the boy was Archer.

"Have a seat and I'll tell you about the kittens. Can I get you some lemonade first?"

Three heads nodded vigorously, and Lara returned with four glasses of pink lemonade. She decided to wait before offering any cookies.

"We rescued a litter of four kittens a few days ago," Lara explained, setting down their drinks. "Right now, though, they're at the veterinarian's clinic. They're so young and tiny that they're going to need extra care for a few more days. Then we'll bring them back here, but it's going to be at least a few more weeks before they can be adopted. Maybe even a little longer."

Two freckled faces fell simultaneously. "Do you have any other kittens?" Anna asked.

"Not now, no. But we have a brother-sister pair of cats with great big paws who would love a great home."

"Do they have to go together?" Angie asked, looking dejected.

"We'd like them to, yes," Lara said. "They've never been apart, and they're quite attached to each other."

Angie took a long sip from her glass. "Man, that's delish," she said, setting down her glass. "The kids really want a kitten anyway, so I guess it doesn't matter."

Lara studied the woman. She needed to know much more about this family before offering any more suggestions. "Have you had cats in the past?" she asked.

"Yup," Archer piped in. "My grandma died last year, and we took in her old cat, Baby. Baby was nice, but she didn't play much. She wanted to sleep all the time."

"Baby, um, passed," Angie said quietly, making the sign of the cross. "The kids took it pretty hard."

"I'm sorry," Lara said.

A fluffy, cream-colored feline with stunning turquoise eyes suddenly leaped onto the table. Blue tucked herself between Archer and Anna, then gave Lara one of her trademark blinks.

Are you telling me they're okay?

Blue blinked again, then rested her head on her paws.

"How about this?" Lara said. "I can show you some pictures of the kittens. Next week, once we have them in the shelter, we'll call you and you can come over to see them. We'll have to keep them here until we know they're ready for a new family, though."

The kids looked at their mom, glee dancing in their eyes.

Angie bit her lip. "Okay, sure. That sounds good. The thing is, we'd like to get the new kitten settled into our household before school starts."

Lara did a quick calculation in her head. School wouldn't start for over a month. "I think the timing will work for you," she said. "Meanwhile, I'll give you an application and one of our adoption packets. There's even a printout full of tips on bringing a kitten into a home with younger children."

"Thanks, that'd be great," Angie said, winking at the twins. "We can be patient for a few more weeks, right?"

Archer and Anna nodded vigorously. "Yup!" they chirped in unison. "We wanna see the pictures!" Archer added.

Blue had already vanished. For the next ten minutes, the kids squealed over photos of the kittens while they finished slurping down their lemonade. They bickered over which kitten to adopt, but in the end agreed on the black-and-white fluffball Kayla had named Aden. That might change, of course, once the twins saw the actual kittens.

Lara sent them off with three of Daisy's sugar cookies, which added to their joy, along with a promise to call soon.

The remainder of the afternoon was quiet. Lara groomed each of the cats. Smuggles fixed his sleepy gaze on Snowball, his favorite new bud, while Lara brushed gobs of hair from the white kitty. The two had become so attached to each other that Lara was a bit concerned. What would happen when the time came for Brian to take Smuggles home?

Assuming he didn't get arrested for murder, she thought soberly.

It wouldn't help to fret about it now. She had enough things to worry about without adding more "possibles" to her ever-growing list.

Grateful for a bit of free time before they had to be at Gideon's, Lara went into her studio. She'd been itching to get back to Sherry's wedding invitations.

She'd just pulled out her colored pencils and her preliminary sketches when Aunt Fran popped in. Clasped between two pot holders was a small tray of warm biscuits fresh from the oven.

Lara took in a deep breath. "Mmm. They smell heavenly."

Aunt Fran smiled. "You had visitors," she said. "How were they?"

"Best I can tell, they're a nice family. I think they'll be a good fit for a kitten, but we'll definitely have to check their references."

Her aunt tried to peek at her sketches. "Working on something new?" she asked curiously.

"Kind of." Lara smiled. "I have to keep it a secret, though, so don't start pulling out the torture devices. My lips are sealed." She made an exaggerated motion of gluing her lips shut.

Her aunt laughed. "Okay, I hear you. Message received." She left Lara to work alone.

Lara spread her sketches over her worktable. The Renoir theme was taking hold in her mind. At this point, if Sherry didn't get engaged, Lara was going to be sorely disappointed.

Using her colored pencils, she spent the next hour or so toying with four separate designs. Each was a variation of the romantic theme depicted in Renoir's *Dance in the Country*.

Four designs. Between thirty and forty invitations. It was doable, Lara told herself. Unless Sherry decided to get married before the end of the summer. In that case, she'd have to think of an alternative to the hand-painted invitations.

Lara looked at her phone. It was nearly five. She still had to prepare the strawberries and whip the cream, then shower and get ready for the barbecue.

It tore at her to think about her aunt and the chief. Chief Whitley cared deeply for Aunt Fran, of that much Lara was positive. He was never going to be a cat lover, but he accepted that Aunt Fran was and admired her devotion. In turn, her aunt had been understanding about his mild aversion to cats. She knew the chief would never harm a cat, and that he'd fight to the death to protect one of hers. Even if he hadn't remembered Pearl's name.

Could they ever get back to where they were? Why did things have to be so complicated?

Lara was gathering her sketches into a folder when something fluttered to the floor near her chair. Startled, she snatched it up. It was the snapshot of her sixth-grade class that Aunt Fran had dug out from her old pictures.

She studied the photo again. Two rows of kids, standing in front of the blackboard. Some looking terribly serious, but most looking bored or distracted. One boy had made a goofy face just as the snapshot was taken.

Now, though, something about it bothered her. Had she missed something before?

Lara squirmed on her chair, then tucked one leg beneath her. She sensed a pair of eyes watching her and glanced up. Blue perched on the top bookshelf, staring at her. No blinking this time. Only an intense turquoise gaze.

You want me to examine the picture, don't you?

Still clutching the photo, Lara fished through one of her drawers. She shoved things aside until she found what she was looking for—her magnifying glass.

Holding the photo close to her face, she slowly moved the magnifier over the young faces. The first one that caught her eye was Jenny Fray—Jenny Cooper, then. Close up, Jenny looked even gloomier than she had at first glance.

Lara giggled at the images of Sherry and Gideon. As two of the taller kids, they'd been positioned in the back row—one grinning like a clown, the other pensive and serious.

She wrinkled her nose at her own image. Back then, she'd hated her hair. It was too curly and too red. She'd have given anything for Sherry's straight, raven-black locks. These days, she didn't mind her hair color so much, but she could do without all the curls.

Lara continued to scan the faces, back and forth with the magnifier until her eyes were nearly crossed. She rubbed her lids with her fingers, then went back to perusing the photo. When she got to the far-right side of the back row, she noticed something she'd missed before—the top portion of a crutch, propped against the blackboard. The lower portion was hidden by the boy standing in front of it. A painfully skinny boy with a choppy haircut, his mouth tightly closed, his hands clasped in front of him. No smile for this poor kid. Lara struggled to remember him, but her mind was a blank.

As for the other kids, she could recall a few of their names, but most had faded from her memory. She'd have probably remembered most of them if she'd gone to Whisker Jog High. Unfortunately, her folks had relocated to Massachusetts just in time for her to suffer through seventh grade with a class full of kids totally new to her. In retrospect, it hadn't been all that bad, but being without Sherry and removed from Aunt Fran had felt like a punishment she'd never deserved.

Maybe Gideon would remember some of the faces. He had an eye for detail and a great memory.

Lara set the photo on the corner of her desk, only to watch it fly off again. *Huh?*

She grabbed it off the floor, stymied. Something soft grazed her ankle—a slight brush of fur.

Instead of looking down, she peered again at the photo. One by one, she magnified each of the faces.

What am I supposed to see? Tell me truly, I implore.

Whoa. Where had that come from? Why did those words pop into her head?

In the next instant, she got it. It was a line from Poe's famous poem, "The Raven." She'd read it years ago in high school. It was quoted so often that she remembered some of the lines.

Ravens and blackbirds and crows…

…oh my.

Suddenly they were popping up everywhere.

Enough.

Lara put away her supplies and tidied up her studio. She snatched up the picture and brought it into the kitchen, where she shoved it into her tote.

She was glad to see that her aunt had fed the cats. Lara made short work of cutting and sweetening the strawberries and whipping the cream.

She was *not* going to dwell on murder this evening.

She was going to enjoy a peaceful evening with the two people she loved most in the world.

Chapter Twenty-Six

"How's your rib eye?" Gideon asked Lara. "Is it done enough?"

They sat at the picnic table behind Gideon's stately two-family home, where his office occupied half the first floor and his apartment was directly above it. An elderly woman, Mrs. Appleton, lived opposite him with her cat, Muffin. A financial consultant rented the other first-floor office, but she was never around on weekends.

Lara waited until she swallowed, then said, "Oh good gosh, it's perfect. A tiny bit pink in the middle and tender as a marshmallow."

"Thank goodness," he said, smiling over at her. "I have a tendency to overcook. I'm paranoid about raw meat."

Lara caught his gaze, and her heart pounded. He was so sweet, so thoughtful, so totally adorable. How did she ever get so lucky?

Aunt Fran had opted for a burger, claiming she could never eat a whole steak. "As for me, my burger is grilled exactly the way I like it. Well done plus."

They all laughed. "Come on, you guys. Have some more salad," Gideon urged. "Both potato and green. Otherwise I'll be eating the stuff all week."

Gideon had tossed together a colorful salad of romaine lettuce, Bermuda onions, and chunks of the fresh tomatoes Lara had brought over. Lara piled a little of everything on her plate. As they enjoyed their meal, she gave Gideon a condensed version of her "accidental" visit to Evonda's home that morning.

"Lara," Gideon said, after she'd told her tale, "didn't it occur to you, even for a second, that Tim Fray might have been dangerous?"

Lara winced. "I gotta admit, I kind of wondered if I was crazy to go inside that house with him. But other than Evonda's obsession with crows and other birds, the only intel I got out of the whole thing was that Tim is sure—I mean, *really positive*—that Trevor Johnson killed his mom."

Gideon nodded thoughtfully. "The police have Johnson in their sights, but that's about all I can say. They still haven't ruled out Brian Downing." Gideon speared a chunk of potato salad with his fork.

"Sounds like not much progress is being made," Lara commented.

"Not true. A lot of things are being kept under wraps right now."

Lara wondered how Gideon knew so much about it. Had Chief Whitley been confiding in him? Had the two been talking secretly?

"Well, I'm getting stuffed," Gideon said. "Better leave room for that corn."

"And the strawberry shortcake!" Lara reminded.

Gideon pushed himself off the picnic bench, then went over to the gas grill. Six ears of corn, coated in butter, had been wrapped in foil and set atop it. Using a pair of tongs, he turned them over. The foil tore, and the fake coals sizzled. Flames shot upward, and Lara heard Gideon curse.

Lara decided to let him deal with it. She wasn't very good with grills anyway. She gathered up their used paper plates and dumped them, along with the trash, into a brown grocery bag. She was setting out clean plates for the corn when she heard a car pull into Gideon's driveway.

Her stomach dropped. *Please tell me it's not the chief.*

She turned and glanced toward the driveway. A charcoal gray Hyundai with a bright yellow windshield decal idled there. Lara recognized the sticker. It matched the decal on the Saturn's windshield—a permit for the town's recycling station. She could just make out a driver and a passenger in the front seat.

At least it's not the chief, Lara thought with relief. She squinted for a better look, but she still couldn't see who it was.

"Um…Gid," Lara called out. "I think you have company."

Gideon didn't react, and she realized he hadn't heard her. She went over and stood beside him and had to stifle a giggle. One ear had toppled out of the foil and was stuck between the bars of the grill. "Someone just pulled into your driveway," she said. "Go ahead. I'll take care of the corn."

"Oh, thank the Lord." He handed her the tongs and kissed her on the cheek.

Lara watched him jog toward the driveway, then went back to her task. She managed to separate the foil and remove all six ears of corn with the tongs. Gideon had brought a platter outside, so she piled on the corn. The scent of the grilled, buttery kernels nearly made her swoon.

She was bringing them over to the picnic table when she noticed Gideon standing near the edge of the driveway. His arms were folded over his chest, his feet planted slightly apart. From his stance, she thought he was preparing to defend his home against raging marauders.

A man stood opposite Gideon, his head bent, his arms hanging at his side. Clad in a two-toned bowling shirt and tan chinos, he was shorter and stockier than Gideon. From the sharpness of Gideon's tone, she thought he was berating the man, but she couldn't make out the words.

Uh-oh. What was going on?

Her pulse racing, Lara went over to the picnic table and set down the corn. She looked at her aunt, who merely shrugged.

Lara sat on the bench facing the driveway. Should she go over and try to help?

The man shifted his weight and shot a glance toward Lara, and she caught a glimpse of his face.

"My God," she whispered to her aunt. "It's Trevor Johnson. What on earth is he doing here?"

Something Johnson said must have persuaded Gideon to relent. Johnson turned and lumbered toward his car, shut off the engine, and opened the passenger side door. A few moments later, an elderly woman wearing a pink blouse and flowered slacks emerged from the front seat. Johnson grabbed one arm and tugged, and Gideon gently took her other elbow. A pink purse dangled from the crook of Trevor's elbow as they helped the woman cross the lawn over to the picnic table.

"Lara, Fran," Gideon said, "this is Virginia Johnson, and this is her son, Trevor." He pulled over a plastic lawn chair for her.

Virginia puffed out a noisy breath as her son helped lower her onto the seat. The underarms of her blouse bore huge yellow stains, and her face was spotted with both perspiration and acne. She dropped down with a slight thud, a cloying scent wafting from her. It smelled like a disagreeable blend of sweat and rose water.

"You okay, Ma?" Trevor asked her, handing her the purse.

"Yes, dear," she said with a grunt, looking anything but okay. Her gray hair frizzed around her face in an unbecoming style, and her watery blue eyes looked tired and sad.

"Mrs. Johnson," Aunt Fran said kindly, "I'm Fran Clarkson. You're Daisy's friend, aren't you?"

Virginia's eyes brightened at being recognized. "Yes, I am," she said. "Oh, I know who you are now. Daisy talked about you all the time. She and I go way back. We used to play cards with a group at the church hall. Great bunch of ladies we had back then. 'Course, most of 'em are in the nursing home now. Or dead," she added flatly. She dug a crumpled tissue out of her handbag and swiped it over her face.

Gideon still looked annoyed at the unexpected drop-in, but he offered them both a glass of iced tea. Lara noticed he didn't offer Trevor a seat, probably because his mother occupied the only available chair.

"Uh, no, thanks," Trevor said, his face turning red. "Ma, you want iced tea?"

"Oh, that sounds hunky-dory," Virginia said, "but I can't risk the sugar. No, I'm fine, don't you bother about me." Still clutching the tissue, she opened her purse again. This time she pulled out a legal-size envelope. She gave it to her son and said, "Go ahead, dear, you tell 'em why we came here."

"Uh…" Trevor glanced around, and Lara realized he'd been expecting his mother to do the talking. Trapped now, he swallowed, cleared his throat, and said, "Mr. Halley, I, um, I called you yesterday, but you didn't call me back. Ma wanted me to wait till Monday to call you again. She said it wasn't polite to bother you on the weekend."

"You called after hours, Mr. Johnson."

"That's right," Virginia said with a brisk nod. "I told him he shouldn't have done that. I raised him to be a gentleman."

"But…my mom," Trevor pushed on, "she's feeling really bad about what happened to me now. And it wasn't her fault, not really. I…just got kind of stuck in the middle."

"Show 'em the picture." Virginia pointed at the envelope.

Picture? A weird feeling of déjà vu grabbed Lara by the throat.

Trevor opened the flap of the envelope and pulled out a photo. He gave it to Gideon, who studied it for a long moment. "All I see here is you and Daisy Bowker. One of you is handing the other an envelope."

Oh God, it was the same picture Sherry had given to Lara.

"It's Daisy, handing my son an envelope," Virginia verified. "Someone took that picture secretly and turned it into the town manager. She sent it anonymously, but I know darned well who it was—that awful Evonda Fray. She wanted to get Trevor in trouble so she could have his job!"

Lara's head spun.

Virginia barreled on. "But that's not what was in the envelope, was it, Trevvie? Go ahead, show 'em what it was Daisy gave you that day."

"Are you sure, Ma?"

"I don't want to keep it a secret anymore. Like Daisy said, it's nothing to be embarrassed about."

Trevor pulled out several sheets of paper and unfolded them. He gave them to Gideon.

"Before I read these, Mr. Johnson, I want to warn you that I am not your attorney. If there's anything incriminating here, I won't hesitate to report it."

Before Trevor could respond, his mother waved a hand at Gideon. "You go ahead and read it," she instructed. "Out loud, if you want to. You'll find out my boy did nothing wrong."

At that point, Lara couldn't even guess what was in the envelope.

Gideon's eyebrows dipped toward his nose as he perused the top sheet. "'Hyperhidrosis,'" he read, "'is a disorder that causes'"—he paused—"'excessive sweating, especially of the hands, feet, underarms, face, and head.'" His expression softer now, he looked at Virginia. "Mrs. Johnson, do you suffer from this?"

"I do. You can probably tell by looking at me that I've got something nasty going on." Her eyes grew weepy. "It's so embarrassing. Trevor used that Google thing and found out some stuff about it. Problem was, I was too embarrassed to talk about it, even with my own son. I told him to forget about it, I'd just live with it. My own doctor didn't have a clue. Just told me to bathe more often and be sure to use deodorant."

Lara guessed the rest. "You called your friend Daisy, didn't you, Mrs. Johnson?" she said gently. "You asked her for advice, and she looked it up. She printed out all that info on her computer and gave it to Trevor to give to you. You trusted her to get help for you."

"That's exactly right," Virginia said, her lower lip quivering. "My, you're a smart girl. Daisy did a lot more research than Trevor did. Plus, I knew I could talk to her, woman to woman. She hooked me up with a doctor that's gonna help me, I hope. It was a dermatologist I needed, but I didn't know that. Thanks to Daisy, I've got an appointment with a good one, but it's not for another three weeks."

Trevor blinked and put a hand on his mom's shoulder. "When we found out someone gave that stupid photo to the town manager, Mom told me she didn't care anymore about being embarrassed. She insisted I go to him and tell him what was really in that envelope. It wasn't a bribe at all. It was a personal communication from Daisy Bowker to my mom. I even showed it to him!"

"I'm guessing he didn't believe you," Gideon said.

"That's right. He said anyone could print out stuff like that after the fact."

"Did you ask Daisy to back up your story?" Gideon asked him.

"I did, and she's totally willing to talk to the town manager. But he doesn't want to hear it, Mr. Halley. He thinks I made all this up to save my butt and get my job back. He told me I was pathetic for dragging my own mother into my scheme."

Harsh, Lara thought, then something occurred to her.

"Trevor, if what was in that envelope really had been a bribe, that would've meant the coffee shop had some major health violations going on, right?"

"Exactly what I tried to tell him," Trevor said with a sigh. "But he claims my inspection just proves I'm lying. He thinks I checked off a few minor things on my report to make it look like I did my job. Said it was all a cover-up."

Talk about a rock and a hard place, Lara thought. One glance at the coffee shop's kitchen would tell anyone that it was as clean as a hospital.

"Who is the town manager anyway?" Lara asked. "I should know that, but I don't."

"Roger Bertrand," Gideon supplied. "Old-timer. Used to work for an insurance company before the town hired him as manager. He's not a bad guy, but he does everything by the book. Not much leeway with him."

"I know, and that's why I need your help, Mr. Halley. I didn't kill Evonda Fray, but it was her fault I lost my job. She'd been following me around for weeks, and I can give you proof. I just want you to hear my side of it. You have a reputation for honesty and fairness. The town manager will listen to you."

Gideon remained silent. Lara sensed he wasn't going to let Johnson off that easily.

"Look," Trevor said, sending Lara a sheepish look. "I–I know I came on too strong that night at The Irish Stew, and I'm really sorry. Sorrier than you know. But Mr. Halley, I'm begging you now to represent me. I want my job back, and I think I deserve to have it." His voice fell off and he rubbed his hands together. "I didn't do anything wrong, and I've never taken a bribe. Never."

Trevor looked at his mother as if to say: *Did I do okay, Ma?*

Lara didn't know what to say, or even think. She felt a twinge of pity for the man, even if something about him gave her a slight case of the willies. But if he really had been sabotaged by Evonda, he had every right to be angry.

Gideon appeared to be pondering the request, but Lara knew him better. He'd already made up his mind.

Looking defeated, her face beaded with sweat, Virginia tapped her son's arm. "Come on, Trevvie, help me up. We've bothered these nice folks long enough. I told you we shouldn't have barged in on their meal."

"Ma's right," Trevor said glumly. "We shouldn't have come here. We'll get out of your hair." He reached down to take his mother's arm.

"Johnson," Gideon said, "why don't you meet me in my office Monday morning at eight o'clock sharp? I'm not promising anything, but I'm willing to hear you out."

Trevor's eyes lit up. "Honest to God? Oh, thank you, Mr. Halley. All I'm asking is for a chance to tell my side of it."

"If you have any supporting documents or photos, bring them along."

Trevor promised to do so. After a round of clumsy goodbyes, the pair finally clumped across the lawn and drove off.

"Lara and Fran, I'm so sorry about that interruption," Gideon said, shaking his head. "I'm actually stunned at the nerve of the guy."

"I know, but it wasn't your fault." Lara squeezed his arm.

"Trevor does seem like somewhat of a dreary soul," Aunt Fran said. "But he cares about his mother. I'll give him credit for that."

"I have to confess," Lara said, "I felt a little sorry for him. Do you think he was telling the truth?"

Gideon scooped up the plate of corn. "My gut says he is, but I'll see what he has to say on Monday. I'll reheat these for us. Can't let this nice corn go to waste."

Lara wasn't sure if she was still in the mood for corn, but once Gideon reheated them and set the buttery ears on the table, they all dug in and powered through them like a trio of buzz saws.

"I feel like a glutton," Aunt Fran said, dabbing her lips with a napkin. "And we haven't even had dessert."

Lara had stored the shortcake fixings in a cooler next to the picnic table. She pulled everything out, grabbed a fresh set of paper plates, and gave everyone a generous serving.

"Oh, man, this is delish," Gideon said. "Did you add something to the cream?"

Lara grinned. "A touch of vanilla and a pinch of cinnamon. Makes all the difference, right?"

Gideon nodded and stuffed another forkful into his mouth. A dab of cream stuck to his top lip. Her heart twisted—he almost looked the way he had when he was twelve. She had a sudden urge to swipe it off with her finger, but she resisted.

Munching on a strawberry slice, she went back to thinking about the photo. The exact duplicate of the one Trevor had produced was on the desk in her studio. She'd kept her promise to Sherry and hadn't shared the story with anyone. Should she tell Gideon now? The cat, so to speak, was already out of the bag.

Lara pushed aside her empty plate. "Gideon, there's something I need to tell you—about that picture of Daisy and Trevor Johnson."

She related Sherry's story of finding the photo under her windshield wiper, and how Daisy had refused to discuss it and insisted it was nothing to worry about.

Gideon wiped his lips with a napkin and crumpled it over his plate. "Wow, you're even closer to the town grapevine than I am," he teased.

"You're not mad that I didn't tell you?"

"Of course I'm not mad. Sherry gave you that photo because you're her closest friend and she trusted you to keep it private. That's exactly what you did."

"Oh, whew! I was so afraid you'd think I was keeping secrets from you. That's not what I intended—not at all."

"Tell you one thing, though," Gideon added. "I wouldn't mind hearing Daisy's side of all this. Something tells me she might be the missing link. What do you think, Fran?"

Aunt Fran folded her hands in front of her plate and looked off into the distance. Some kids were playing in a neighbor's yard, and her gaze seemed focused on them. Lara knew better. From the moment they'd arrived there, her aunt had been way too quiet. She had a lot on her mind, and Lara suspected she knew the source.

"Aunt Fran? Are you okay?"

"Hmmm?" Her aunt blinked and looked at her through troubled eyes. "I'm sorry. My mind was lollygagging. I'm fine, only a bit tired." She patted Lara's hand. "Gideon, you've been a wonderful host and a superb chef. Lara, if you wouldn't mind running me home, I'll settle in for the night, and you two can enjoy the rest of the evening together."

Gideon trapped Lara's worried gaze with his own. Once again, she could read his mind.

"I'm not feeling too peppy myself," Lara said with a heavy sigh. "It's been a heck of a crazy day."

"You both need a good night's rest," Gideon said meaningfully. "You two go. I'll bat cleanup."

"You sure? I can help you carry—"

"Nope. I'm perfectly capable of carrying a few plates into the house and taking out the trash."

"Thank you, Gideon. For everything," Aunt Fran said. Tears glistened in her eyes. Though her aunt would never admit it, Lara knew she missed the chief.

"Everything's going to work out, Fran," Gideon said. "You and Lara head home, okay?"

He walked them both to the Saturn, then pulled Lara aside. "Honey, you're starting to worry me again," he said quietly. "You remember our code, don't you?"

The code. The secret signal that had saved her life last December. How could she ever forget it?

Oddly, they'd devised the code even before Gideon had learned about her guardian cat.

"I remember," Lara said. "Code Blue. But stop worrying. Tomorrow I'm going to work on some of my art projects. I'm not even going to think about Evonda Fray."

"Good."

Lara watched him wave as she backed out of his driveway. She loved him for understanding that she needed to spend time with Aunt Fran this evening. She also hated making him worry.

She'd gotten herself in fixes before that could've gone bad. Really bad. But sometimes things happened that were out of her control.

Unfortunately, Evonda's killer was still out there. Waiting? Plotting?

No way to tell.

But it wasn't her problem. Not anymore.

Nevermore...

The word from Poe's famous poem popped into her head. Appropriate, given Evonda's fondness for blackbirds of every sort. Lara was willing to bet "The Raven" had been Evonda's favorite poem, if she'd been into that sort of thing.

"Your mind is in a thousand places," her aunt said as they turned onto High Cliff Road.

"You know me too well," Lara said with a wry chuckle, but then she turned serious. "Aunt Fran, if you ever want to talk about anything...I mean, you know, about *anything*, I'm here for you."

Her aunt nodded. Dark creases hung beneath her green eyes, and her face was pale. "I know that, Lara. Right now, I'm so weary I can barely think. Maybe tomorrow we'll have a nice long chat."

"Let's plan on it," Lara said.

So much for keeping her aunt company this evening.

It was just as well. Neither of them was in a chatty mood.

It was enough to know that they were both home. Together.

Chapter Twenty-Seven

Once inside the house, Lara was restless. She finished her cat duties, then sat on the sofa with Snowball and Smuggles. She was amazed at how quickly the two cats had bonded. The sweet young female and the seasoned old gent. Almost inseparable now, the pair curled up in her lap in a furry ball.

Was it a sign? Lara wondered.

If Brian was the killer and was about to be arrested, then Smuggles would remain there as a permanent resident. She'd made that promise to him. Then what would happen if someone wanted to adopt Snowball? Lara and Aunt Fran might have a tough decision to make.

Snowball was still shedding. Her white fur clung to everything. "You need another good brushing," Lara told her, kissing her on the head. "I won't bug you now, but get ready for a big grooming day tomorrow."

Aunt Fran had gone to her room with a book and her usual cats—Dolce and Twinkles. The two were longtime best buds. Their favorite place to snooze was atop her aunt's bed.

Munster was MIA, which meant he was probably upstairs sprawled on Lara's bed. His habits tended to change with each addition to—or subtraction from—the household, but he was so easygoing that he just went with the flow. He'd have been adopted many times over if he'd been available. But he was one of Aunt Fran's three original cats, so the shelter was his forever home.

Orca and Pearl gazed at Lara from their favorite perches on the carpeted cat tree. Their tails twitched when she spoke to them. Lately, they'd been a bit subdued, not getting into too much trouble. Did the two rambunctious sibs sense the tension in the house over Evonda's murder? Lara giggled when she remembered how taken Gideon had been with Orca.

After checking out the TV lineup, Lara gave up. Nothing appealed to her, not even the programs on the mystery channels. They reminded her that their once-quiet little town had yet another unsolved murder of its own.

Lara gently set her lap cats on the sofa and went into her studio, closing the door behind her. She'd once made the mistake of leaving the door partway open. Not only had her art supplies been totally rearranged, but one of the cats had tried his—her?—paw at painting. The results had not been impressive.

She pulled out the designs she'd been working on for Sherry's wedding invitations. They were shaping up. The basics were there, but they still needed more work. Lara wanted the colors to be softer than in Renoir's *Dance in the Country*, yet vibrant enough to capture the beauty of the day.

And the love in Sherry and David's eyes.

A lump formed in Lara's throat. Would she ever be painting invitations to her own wedding, hers and Gideon's? Or was marriage a commitment that would never be the right fit for them?

Gideon had a daunting workload. He seemed to be getting more clients every week. Lara's life was tied to the shelter. It required physical work, but she also had a slew of administrative tasks that couldn't be ignored. It was the life she'd chosen, and she loved every moment of it. But a big question still hung over her—was it enough?

Aunt Fran and Kayla were wonderful, but the bulk of the shelter work still fell on Lara. She was grateful that Aunt Fran had had both knees replaced. The surgeries had replenished her spirit and given her life back to her. She talked about going back to teaching but hadn't made any firm plans.

So why was Lara so impatient? Why couldn't she be happy with the way things were right now?

Next March she'd be turning thirty. For a woman, it was a turning point—a time to think seriously about the future.

Tears pushed at her lids. She was tired, that was all. Overthinking everything. Making every anthill into a giant mountain.

Fatigue dragging her down, she put away the sketches and turned off the light. After ensuring that the door was closed all the way, she went into the new reading room.

She turned on the reading lamp, and a soft, cozy glow filled the room. The box of books Kayla had delivered still rested on the floor. Lara dropped down and sat cross-legged in front of the box. The more she fished through the books, the more she had a sneaking suspicion.

These books were brand-new.

Had Kayla's grandmother bought the books herself? If so, it was a kind and lovely way to honor Kayla's devotion to the shelter cats. Maybe her gram couldn't fully understand it, but she could respect Kayla's choice to work with animals.

Once again, the book she'd seen earlier made her smile. *Cary the Crow and the Hidden Spoon.* She pulled it out and flipped to the first page. The illustrations were charming, bursting with detail and color. She began to read and found herself enchanted by the story.

Cary the crow lived in a giant oak, high above the cottage where his favorite humans lived—a grandma, a little boy, and a baby girl. Whenever the humans left things where Cary could see them, he'd snitch them and hide them in his nest. His favorite object was silver and shiny, with a long handle. He could see his reflection in it! But soon he began to notice something. The humans didn't look happy anymore. Their mouths were turned upside down instead of right-side up. When the grandma cried that her best spoon was missing, Cary's feathers drooped with sadness. He knew what he had to do. One by one, he flew their possessions back to where he'd found them. The grandma was so glad that she hugged her spoon! When the humans saw what Cary had done, they began leaving little treats for him to hide—corn, berries, even bits of dried cheese—enough to feed him through the cold winter!

"Oh my gosh, that was such a cute story!" Lara blurted out. She started to close the book when a furry body leaped on it and held the pages down firmly.

Startled, Lara's heart jumped a little, but she remained very still. She stared down at Blue. The Ragdoll cat returned her gaze, her stunning turquoise eyes reflecting the light from the reading lamp.

She seems so real. How can it be that I can't touch her?

In the next instant, Blue faded.

Exhausted and overwhelmed, Lara burst into tears. It felt good to let out all her pain, all her frustrations. She cried until her head throbbed and her nose clogged.

Finally, her eyes achy and raw, she put all the books back into the box, closed it securely, and turned off the lamp.

But the crow nagged at her, pecked at her brain.

What are you trying to tell me, Blue? What's so important about a crow?

Chapter Twenty-Eight

On Sunday morning, Lara awoke early with a mild headache. Orca and Pearl had joined her in the night. Orca was half on and half off her pillow, his white whiskers tickling her ear. His sneaky sister was sprawled at the foot of the bed, chewing on what looked like the jersey T-shirt Lara had tossed into her laundry basket the night before.

"You monkey," she said, shoving her hair out of her eyes. She pulled Pearl closer and nuzzled her face, then eased her tee out of the cat's clutches.

She looked over at the big pillow in the corner of the room. The sight of Snowball curled up with Smuggles tore at her. The two cats looked as if they'd been best buds since birth.

Lara swallowed a few ibuprofen, then showered and dressed. She headed downstairs trailed by a gaggle of cats. After making quick work of her cat duties—fresh food and water, and litter scooping—she left her aunt a note and set out to the coffee shop.

She was almost at the downtown block that housed Bowker's Coffee Stop when a flurry of activity put her on instant alert. On the sidewalk, people stood around in small clusters, chattering and pointing toward the police station.

Oh God, something must have happened.

Lara threaded her way around a group of men having an animated discussion right in front of Bowker's. They nodded and moved away, and she rushed inside.

Sherry wasn't there, but Jill was serving heaping plates of eggs and bacon to the customers sitting at the counter. Luckily, Lara's usual stool was free. She claimed it before anyone else could come in and grab it.

Jill spotted her, waved, and trotted over. "God, it's like a zoo in here today." She rolled her eyes in the direction of her eyebrows, which today sported tiny barbells. She poured a mug of coffee for Lara and shoved a bowl of half-and-half packets at her. "Lemon poppy muffin?"

"Um, yeah, sure. What's all the commotion?" Lara asked her. "Did something happen?"

Coffeepot in hand, Jill gawked at her. "You didn't hear? The police arrested someone for that Fray woman's murder. A man. Brian something or other."

"Brian Downing?" The words almost snagged in Lara's throat.

Jill aimed a finger at her. "That's the one. Downing. Way I heard it, they found some evidence at his apartment that they'd missed before. Typical cops, right? Why didn't they find it in the first place?"

Lara was stunned. She knew Brian was a prime suspect, but she thought he'd eventually be cleared. Something about the man didn't scream "murderer."

"Does anyone know what the new evidence was?"

Jill shrugged. "Everyone says something different, so who knows? Except…well, I heard one of the staties talking about it this morning on his way out." She leaned closer to Lara. "I think they found something related to the murder weapon in Downing's car, or under his car, or something like that."

Murder weapon? Hadn't Evonda been strangled with a Polypropylene band? The police already had the weapon.

"I wish we knew more," Lara said.

"Yeah, me, too." Jill gave her a half salute. "Hey, I gotta split. I'll go fetch your muffin."

She toddled off, and Lara stirred her coffee. Jill returned a minute later with Lara's muffin, then went back into the kitchen.

Lara pulled out her phone and texted Gideon, asking if he'd heard the news. Three seconds later, her cell rang.

"Hi, honey. I can't talk, but I'm at the station now. What you heard is correct. Downing's been arrested."

"Did the chief call you?" Lara asked. She didn't understand why Gideon was suddenly in the inner circle of the police.

"Yes, but I can't talk now. Everything's hitting the fan, if you know what I mean. Downing's in a holding cell, squawking up a tornado. He claims he's been railroaded. Later today, they're going to transfer him to the Carroll County House of Corrections. Hey, I gotta run. Catch you later, okay? Love you."

"Love you, too," Lara said, but Gideon was already gone.

She slumped on her stool and stuck her cell in her tote. She was grateful for one thing. Smuggles was safe at the shelter. Brian had had the foresight to arrange for his cat's care, even before Evonda was murdered.

Wait a minute. Wait one nitpicking minute.

The truth struck Lara like a blow to the solar plexus.

Brian knew exactly what he'd planned to do, didn't he? That's why he took measures in advance to ensure his cat's care and well-being. Bringing Smuggles to the shelter, begging Lara to take in his cat while he supposedly looked for an apartment—it was all part of a carefully crafted scheme.

He was preparing to kill Evonda, so he went proactive, just in case the police figured it out.

Days ago, Brian had eagerly toured the shelter. He realized that if he left his beloved Smuggles there, his cat would be pampered and loved.

It would have been easy to collect a bit of cat hair from the resident cats during his visit. No shortage of that at the shelter. When Brian spotted the box in which the door had been shipped, he probably noticed the Polystyrene bands sticking out from it. He offered to do them a favor, to take it off their hands, and Lara had willingly agreed.

By using one of those bands to commit a horrible murder, Brian figured he could confuse the police, or at least throw them off his trail. Toss out a ball for them to chase. Leaving a bit of fur from Snowball and Pearl in Evonda's car was the perfect touch.

If Lara or Aunt Fran got nailed for the deadly deed, then he'd collect his cat and move on with his own life. He could sit at home with Smuggles and laugh while an innocent person or persons got carted off to prison.

If, however, the cops figured out that Brian was the killer, at least his cat was set for life.

For Brian, it was a win-win either way.

The thought made Lara sick. She'd totally misjudged Brian. She'd allowed his devotion to his cat to get under her skin and trick her.

Something about the scenario bugged her, though. Brian had to realize he'd be taking a huge gamble. Did he despise Evonda so thoroughly that he was willing to risk life in prison to do away with her?

Brian probably assumed that Evonda had a long list of enemies. Did he figure the police would bumble around for weeks, sorting through possible suspects? Evonda's role in getting Trevor Johnson fired was pretty much common knowledge. Johnson, with his sullen attitude and hangdog look, made the ideal "person of interest."

Jill hurried over to refill Lara's mug, but she put up a hand and stopped her. "Thanks, Jill, but I'm going to head home."

"You didn't even eat your muffin!"

"I know. I'll take it with me. Is Sherry around today?"

"Nope." She gave Lara a conspiratorial wink. "Between you, me, and the lamppost, I think something's cooking with those two. I can tell by the way Sherry's been avoiding all my questions. She and David went to some fancy-schmancy place last night, but she was acting all casual about it. Yeah, something's up. Mark my words."

Smiling, Lara snagged a napkin from the metal holder on the counter and wrapped it around her muffin. "Whatever it is, I hope it's good news."

"Aw, you can practically count on it."

Lara paid her tab and left a sizable tip. Before she could leave, she had to jostle her way through a throng of customers who were just entering the coffee shop.

Despite the climbing temperature, Lara was grateful to be outside. She was in a hurry now to get back, to see how Aunt Fran was doing.

It was shaping up to be one of those days—hot, steamy, and sticky. Tote on her shoulder, she started for home. It was almost eight thirty. Aunt Fran was probably already up and having her breakfast. Lara hoped she'd be in better spirits today. The night before, at Gideon's, she'd seemed weary and distracted.

Lara was more anxious than ever, now, to get home.

Chapter Twenty-Nine

Lara couldn't have been more surprised to see Chief Whitley's car parked in the driveway. She hurried inside, where he sat at the kitchen table. A mug rested in front of him, the tag of a tea bag dangling over the rim. Munster was sprawled over his knees like a lap shawl, purring up a drumroll Ringo Starr would've envied.

Lara stifled a giggle. The chief didn't look terribly comfortable, but he was enduring Munster's affections like a seasoned soldier.

On the stove, the teakettle shrilled. Aunt Fran pulled it off the burner and carried it over to the table.

Lara was relieved to see that her aunt's eyes were looking brighter this morning. Every hair was in place and a pink tinge colored her cheeks.

Aunt Fran smiled at her. "You're back already?" she said, her kettle poised to pour.

"Yeah, it was really getting crowded at the coffee shop, so I took my muffin to go." She removed it from her tote and set it on the counter. "Morning, Chief," she said to Whitley.

Her aunt poured boiling water into the chief's mug.

"Good morning, Lara," the chief said. "I suspect you already heard the news." He squeezed the water out of the tea bag with his spoon. Lara noticed he was careful to keep the scalding water away from the feline plopped in his lap.

"About Brian Downing? I did," she said, slinging her tote over a chair. "I'm still having trouble wrapping my head around it. I totally misjudged the guy. I just didn't think he had enough motive. Not to kill anyway."

Aunt Fran took her seat opposite the chief. The remains of an English muffin and a fresh mug of tea sat in front of her on the table. "I agree with

Lara. And that's not just because Brian's a cat lover." She fixed a hard look at the chief, but a slight twinkle escaped.

A flush creeping up his neck, the chief stared down at his mug. "I'm going to be honest with both of you. Motive wise, I didn't see it either. Not at first. But the investigators went back to Downing's apartment house yesterday. They found a twin to the Polypropylene strap Evonda Fray was strangled with. It was lying right there in the parking area, about a yard or so from Downing's SUV."

Something about that bothered Lara. Hadn't the crime scene techs already searched that entire locale? Or had they skipped over it because it wasn't the actual crime scene?

Whitley took a tiny sip from his mug, wincing at the hot liquid. "But there's also the matter of the cat hair," he added a tad more quietly. "Lara, you told the investigator that you gave Downing a brief tour of the shelter. They're going on the assumption that either Pearl"—he shot a glance at Aunt Fran—"or Snowball's fur clung to his shoe. Somehow it got transferred to Evonda's car when he was strangling her."

"Chief, the investigator—that Cutler guy—told me that the cat hair analysis was inconclusive."

"He didn't tell you all of it. It wasn't one hundred percent conclusive, but there's a ninety-one percent chance that the cat hair found at the crime scene came from this shelter."

"He was being evasive on purpose, then." Lara felt her blood boiling. How dare the guy fudge the truth?

"What the state police believe," the chief calmly went on, "is that Downing grabbed all the straps from that box he took to the recycling station, and maybe stuck them in his pocket or tossed them into his SUV. The one they found yesterday was probably a stray that fell out of his vehicle. Or out of his pocket. Either way, it ties him directly to the murder. I came here to let both of you know before you heard it somewhere else. I should've guessed that the grapevine had already reached you, Lara."

"Yeah, well, the coffee shop is a great source of gossip. True gossip, in this case," she added.

She thought about mentioning Gideon, but then nixed the idea. This was about Evonda, and her murderer.

"Chief, does Tim Fray know about the arrest?" Lara asked.

"He does. He was informed early this morning. He seemed shocked by the news. He'd been sure the killer was someone else."

Lara knew that, but she didn't want to let it slip to the chief. He'd think she'd been asking questions again. Poking her nose where it didn't belong.

"I'm not trying to shift the blame," Lara said, "but have the investigators looked hard enough into Trevor Johnson? He wasn't exactly president of Evonda's fan club."

"The former health inspector? Oh, you bet they have. They've looked at him every which way but loose, to coin a phrase." He shook his head. "Time wise, it doesn't fly. Johnson had driven his mother to her sister's house in Cummington, Mass, two days earlier. They didn't get back until late Tuesday, long after Evonda was found in her car."

"Where's Cummington, Mass?" Lara asked him.

"The Berkshires. Maybe an hour and a half from Albany."

"Witnesses?"

"Loads," the chief confirmed. "It's a dead end, Lara. Johnson wasn't involved." He looked at her, and she saw the empathy in his eyes. "I know this is a hard pill to swallow about Downing. But there's a lot more you don't know. The investigators spoke at length to several of his coworkers. Bottom line—he wasn't the most popular guy, and that's putting it mildly. A couple of them went so far as to say they're happy he was arrested so they'd never have to work with him again."

Lara's stomach sank. "Did he harass people? I mean, you know—"

"No," the chief said. "Nothing like that. He's apparently one of those guys who's always right. Never sees anyone else's side of things. One fellow said that in their weekly meetings, Downing never agreed with anyone about anything. He always had a better way of doing things. It drove everyone nuts. Only one woman defended him."

Lara nodded. "It was probably the woman who told him he should adopt a cat."

"Actually, I think it was." The chief attempted a smile.

Lara remembered what Brian had said about his wife leaving him, how she'd torn his world in two. She now suspected that he suffered from post-traumatic stress. Maybe if he'd gotten help sooner—

"Hey, look, I have to run," the chief said, casting a glance at his knees. The furry rug was still there, purring up a thunderstorm.

"Jerry, I have some of those fig cookies you like," Aunt Fran said, a slight lilt in her tone. "Would you like to take some with you?"

The chief's face brightened. *With hope?* Lara wondered.

"Thanks, Fran, but I'm good." He patted his abdomen. "I had a big breakfast this morning. Gotta be ready for the thundering hordes today. It won't be long before the TV vans'll be blocking the street in front of the station." He reached down with one of his large hands and tickled the fur between Munster's ears.

Lara exchanged glances with her aunt, who was trying desperately not to react.

Dolce strolled into the kitchen and claimed Aunt Fran's lap. The other cats, except for Twinkles, were probably in the large parlor. Twinkles was either on her aunt's bed or sunning himself in her bedroom window seat. He was aging, slowing down, and napped a lot more these days.

Things were normalizing in the household, except that now Smuggles was a permanent resident. Once Brian was convicted and sent to prison, he'd never see his cat again. The thought weighed on Lara's heart like an anchor.

The chief finished up his tea in a few big gulps, then stuck his hat on his head. "Fran, thank you for the hospitality. Lara, good to see you again."

"Same here, Chief."

He shook his head and gave a slight laugh. "I'm grateful for one thing," he added, his gaze aimed at Lara. "You won't have to go around looking for murderers this time. This one's a done deal."

Lara wasn't sure she appreciated his phrasing. "Chief, I never actually *looked* for murderers. You know that, right?"

Whitley held up a hand. "I hear you," he said. "But you sure were on a roll there for a while. I'm glad this one's wrapped up. Now all we have to do is tie it with a bow." He gave Munster a slight nudge. "Sorry, big guy, but I gotta go back to work."

The cat took the hint and went off toward the feeding station to check out the offerings.

"Thanks for stopping by, Chief," Lara said. "I'm happy that Evonda's murder's been solved, but I'm sad it turned out this way."

"You liked Brian, didn't you?"

"I did."

"As did I," Aunt Fran said with a sigh. "I'm still having trouble believing it."

"The truth hurts," Lara added bitterly.

Aunt Fran rose and set the black kitty on her chair. "I'll walk you out, Jerry."

Lara watched the two of them stroll outside. The sight of them speaking again eased the dull ache in her stomach.

Unfortunately, the ache came roaring back when she thought about Brian Downing.

He'd used them, taken advantage of their trust.

Lara wasn't going to get over it for a very long time.

Chapter Thirty

Despite her battling emotions, Lara realized she was hungry. She removed a jar of marmalade from the cupboard and brought it over to the table, along with her lemon muffin. She was spreading a thick layer over half the muffin when her aunt came back inside. Aunt Fran's smooth cheeks had turned slightly pink.

"You're looking much more chipper today," Lara told her. "Did… anything in particular happen?"

Her aunt sat down. "What happened is that I stopped acting like a buffoon."

"You never acted like a buffoon." Lara slid a corner of the muffin into her mouth.

"Don't defend me," her aunt said crisply. "That day, when Jerry forgot Pearl's name, I was so incensed I couldn't think straight. I snubbed him and made him suffer for days, all because I was being a silly snit. When I saw him pull into the driveway this morning, I knew I had to set things right."

Lara smiled. It was good to see her aunt behaving like her old self. "Aunt Fran, the last thing I would ever call you is a silly snit."

"Well, then, I acted like a teenager. Last night, at Gideon's, it was eating at me—the way I treated Jerry. I felt as if I dampened that lovely barbecue for both of you."

"You absolutely did not," Lara said. "It was Trevor Johnson who dampened the evening, if anyone did. I still can't believe the nerve of him!"

"It was pushy, to say the least," her aunt said. "But Johnson's mother is a nice woman. I felt so bad when she told us about her medical problem. I can't even imagine how mortifying it was for her to talk about it in front of us."

"I know. That was heartbreaking, wasn't it?" Lara wrinkled her nose. "I still say Johnson would've made a perfect suspect."

Aunt Fran shook her head. "Not really, when you think about it. In my opinion, he'd have had to get permission from his mom before he did anything that rash. But since he has an airtight alibi, it's all moot."

"Moot. What a weird word." Lara groaned. "I know you're right about Johnson. I'm just so seriously bummed about Brian. Gideon told me he's been raising a huge ruckus in his holding cell. They're going to transfer him to the county jail later today."

"It saddens me, as well," Aunt Fran said. "But we can't say that we really knew Brian, can we?" She gave Lara a meaningful look. "Let's not forget how people have surprised us in the past when their true intentions were revealed."

Lara didn't need to be reminded. Memories of murderers past were never far from her thoughts.

"I guess what bugs me most is that the whole thing was so premeditated. He risked everything for sheer revenge. If he'd killed her in a fit of rage, that would be one thing. But this—" Lara shook her head.

Aunt Fran replaced the cover of the marmalade jar. "I suspect there's a lot that we still don't know. In the meantime, we have a new member of the household."

"Smuggles." Lara smiled. "He's such a sweet guy, and Snowball adores him. At least Brian brought him to the right place."

Aunt Fran reached over and squeezed Lara's hand. "That's right. That's the unexpected blessing, isn't it? Speaking of blessings, are you going to church with me later?"

On Sundays, Lara and her aunt usually attended the weekly service at Saint Lucy's. Lara preferred the noon service, because it gave her the entire morning to wind down from all the activities of the week.

The idea of sitting in an unair-conditioned church for an hour didn't especially appeal on a day like this. But she'd go for her aunt's sake. She could think of plenty of people who could use a prayer or two.

"Sure," Lara said. "We'll leave about twenty-five of?"

"It's a date."

Lara swallowed the last of her muffin. She wiped her hands, then rose and collected the dishes from the table.

Today she wanted to go back to her wedding invitation project. It was starting to become an obsession. She was almost certain Sherry would be making an announcement soon. When that day came, Lara wanted to have her preliminary sketches ready to surprise her friend.

After rinsing the dishes, Lara went into her studio. First things first: She turned on the floor fan. It didn't give much relief, but it was better than nothing.

The morning sun was slanting through the room's sole window. Lara normally loved working with natural light, but today the shadows were distracting. She pulled down the shade and flicked on the overhead light.

Perfect.

She pulled out the sketches again and spread them over her worktable. This time she wanted to work with Renoir's *Dance in the Country* directly in front of her. She wanted to glean what Renoir felt when he was creating the spectacular painting.

Lara booted up her iPad and propped it on its stand. She went to one of her favorite art Web sites. It had links to the works of artists from many different periods. She tapped on the link to Renoir. Images of his works came up immediately.

Renoir had always been one of Lara's favorites. She loved his use of bold, bright colors, his masterful depiction of facial expressions. She tapped a few keys and pulled up the image of *Dance in the Country*. She sharpened her pencils and began to sketch.

She'd been working only a few minutes when her cell rang. She snatched it up when she saw that it was from Glindell Veterinary Clinic.

"Lara?" came a warm, familiar voice.

"Yes. Amy. Is something wrong? Are the kittens okay?"

The veterinarian laughed. "Oh my gosh, yes. The kittens are fine. That's actually why I'm calling. We have an emergency situation going on this morning. Six Yorkie pups found in an abandoned shack. Barely four weeks old."

"Oh, no. The poor little darlings—"

"It's under control," Amy assured her. "They're all being cared for now. What would help tremendously is if you could pick up the kittens this morning. It would free up some space, but mostly our resources, so we can focus on the pups."

"The kittens are okay to leave?" Lara fretted.

"Perfectly. No need for us to keep them till tomorrow. That little gold one that had us so worried has made incredible progress!"

Lara smiled. "That's Fritter. He's a boy, right?"

"Nope. A little girl," Amy corrected.

"I should have known. I'm so bad at telling boy kittens from girl kittens."

Lara looked at her cell. It was already quarter to eleven. She'd been working on her sketches longer than she realized.

"Can we swing by a little after one?" she asked the vet.

"Mmm...it sure would help if you could pick them up now." Amy sounded stressed. "You already know the drill for young kittens—feeding, litter, all the fun stuff. I'll wash your car and bake you a batch of coconut cookies if you pick them up now," she kidded.

Lara chuckled. "Not necessary, although I might take you up on those cookies. I'll be there in a jiff."

She put away her supplies and closed the door to her studio. She found Aunt Fran upstairs, vacuuming her bedroom. Lara gave her a time-out signal, and her aunt clicked off the vacuum. Lara explained the urgency with the kittens.

Aunt Fran gave her a gleeful smile. The idea of having four new kittens in the household lit up her world.

"I'll go with you," she said, rubbing her hands together. "Oh, I can't wait to see the little angels."

"You're okay with skipping church?"

"I'm fine with it. Think of how many animals we're helping, not to mention Amy."

'Nuff said, Lara thought.

Lara went into the isolation room and took one last look around. Anticipating the kittens' arrival, she'd already scrubbed everything and set out a fresh, shallow box of clay litter. The babies would be spending the next several days in this room, getting acclimated to their new digs.

She'd also thrown a set of clean sheets and a lightweight blanket over the cot she kept in the room. With kittens this young, middle-of-the-night feedings were crucial to their survival. She'd be spending several nights in there with them, if not the next few weeks.

Lara tingled with excitement. This is what they were meant to do. The reason she and Aunt Fran created this haven for cats.

Within five minutes, she and her aunt were buckled into the Saturn and on their way to the animal clinic. Lara flicked on the AC to try to cool down the car, which already felt like the inside of a pizza oven.

Soon they'd have their hands full of fluffy, adorable, *needy* kittens.

Lara wiped her mental slate clean of bad thoughts.

Today was all about their new charges—four little darlings who depended on them for their very survival.

Chapter Thirty-One

Lara cupped the golden furball to her chest. "Oh, you are so sweet," she cooed. "How did you get so adorable?"

Aunt Fran smiled over at her, her hands wrapped gently around the kitten Kayla had named Aden. "This baby's trying to purr, but I don't think he's quite there yet." She held him up to her face and nuzzled his nose.

"I talked to Kayla," Lara said. "She's bummed that she couldn't be here to welcome the kittens."

"I'm sure she feels bad," her aunt said. "But she'll see them tomorrow."

After Kayla's grandmother learned that the first "read to a cat" Sunday in the new addition was canceled, she'd commandeered Kayla into helping out with yet another family gathering. Kayla felt locked in—she'd agreed to help. She didn't want to disappoint her gram by bailing on her at the last minute.

Amy had guessed that the kittens were about five weeks old, which meant they were ready to be introduced to wet kitten food. Lara had set out a large plate and lined it with the high-quality brand they used. The kittens nibbled away at it, slowly at first and then with a bit more gusto. Two of them stepped directly into the platter and ate from there. Laughing, Lara eased them back in front of the plate to give each of the tiny felines an equal chance.

Once the kittens had stuffed themselves, used the litter box, and were curled up in their cozy bed, Lara and her aunt backed quietly out of the room. They'd left the kittens with fresh water and a freshly scooped litter box. Lara would be checking on them often, socializing them and encouraging them to get accustomed to humans.

Curious noses poked into the doorway, but Lara gently pushed them away.

"You'll get to meet the babies soon," she told Pearl, who was itching to get in there to check out the new arrivals.

Orca attempted an end run from Lara's other side, but she caught the trickster in time. "That goes for you, too," she said, scooping him into her arms. The cat reached up with one massive paw and touched her cheek. "Never mind trying to bribe me," Lara said, kissing his whiskers. "You'll have plenty of time to meet the newbies." *Unless you get adopted first.*

Downstairs, Aunt Fran poured each of them a glass of iced tea, then spread out the Sunday paper on the kitchen table.

Lara took her glass into her studio. She set it down on her coaster and closed the door, determined to get back to her wedding invitation sketches.

The moment she tapped her iPad, it sprang to life. The image of *Dance in the Country* was still there. Her sketches were right where she'd left them.

For a while, she toyed with the details of the groom's face. David's features were pleasingly even, his eyes the color of a young fox. With his neatly trimmed hair and beard, he actually resembled the man in the painting, although David's hair was more of a ginger color.

Lara couldn't begin to guess how Sherry would style her hair on her special day. The once-prominent railroad spikes that had made up her former coif had softened after she met David. These days, her friend sported a straight bob that framed her face beautifully.

The sketches were preliminary anyway, not etched in stone. The final invitations would be done in watercolors. Lara couldn't wait to present her ideas to Sherry. If Jill had been right, her friend was already cooking up a way to make the happy announcement.

She switched gears and began drawing the wedding gown. Should it be straight or flowing? White or ivory? Lacy or plain?

Lara's pencil had barely touched the paper when her iPad flew off the table. The sudden shift in the room's energy made her heart jump.

There wasn't so much as a breeze coming in. She hadn't even turned on her floor fan. The room's sole window was closed against the summer heat.

Lara looked down. She wasn't totally surprised to see the furry face of a cream-colored Ragdoll cat. Blue stared up at her, her chocolate-tipped paws resting on the tablet. She blinked at Lara once, then once again.

Lara's heartbeat quickened. Blue was obviously trying to tell her something. Why did her clues always have to be so cryptic?

She bent and retrieved her iPad, setting it back on her worktable. "Ach," she muttered to herself. "Where's my painting?"

Renoir's *Dance in the Country* had vanished. In its place was a very different image.

This one was a painting of a crow. A crow with strangely human features, wearing a cape and black boots.

Lara glanced down at the spot where the tablet had fallen. Blue was gone.

And suddenly she remembered. This was the painting of the boot-clad crow with the oddly human eyes. The same print Lara had seen in Evonda Fray's crow-infested dining room.

Lara pulled the iPad closer. The simple caption beneath the image read Krahe.

Krahe.

The word began with the letters K-R-A.

Heart thumping, Lara rubbed her forehead with her fingers. Her head swam. A surge of heat crept up her neck, making her face feel flushed. She slugged back a gulp of iced tea, then carefully set down her glass.

On her cell, she Googled the word "krahe." It took only seconds for its meaning to pop up.

It was the German word for "crow."

K-R-A. Those were the exact three letters Evonda had texted—or attempted to text—to her son right before she was murdered.

Lara took in a deep breath. She had to let Tim Fray know what she'd stumbled on. It probably meant nothing, but at least he could check it out. Maybe his mom had left him a letter, or a will, or a list of her final wishes. Something she didn't want him to read until after she was gone.

She was glad, now, that he'd asked to exchange contact info with her. Lara pulled up the text he'd sent her yesterday, in which he'd thanked her for being a sounding board. She'd never gotten around to responding, but now she tapped out a message. As briefly as she could, she told Tim what she'd discovered.

Disappointed when he didn't return her text right away, Lara took another sip of her iced tea. After a quick bathroom break, she returned to her studio.

A text from Tim was on her cell.

Wow. Thx for this info! Can U meet me @ Mom's in 30 so we can chk it out?

Lara groaned. Did she really want to get involved? Evonda's killer was in custody—that was the important thing.

Besides, she had too much to do today. She had kittens to care for. She was also hoping to connect with Gideon later, if he could snag a few free moments.

Lara started to text Tim an excuse why she couldn't meet him when Blue suddenly leaped onto her worktable. The cat sat calmly, gazing at her, her turquoise eyes as serene as a cool lake.

Her cell pinged with another text.

I kno I'm imposing but I trust yr judgt.

Lara stared at the message for at least a full minute. Then she texted:
Okay. See you there.

She shoved her cell into her pocket and left her studio. She closed the
door quietly and went into the kitchen.

Aunt Fran was reading the editorials, her reading glasses slanted on
her nose. From the frown on her face, Lara suspected she was reading an
opinion with which she didn't agree.

"Hey, Aunt Fran. I'm going to go out for a few. My eyes are crossed
from sketching. Can you check on the kittens if I'm not back in an hour?"

"Of course I can. Are you sure you're okay? Your face is a bit flushed."

"I know." She pushed her hair back with her hand. "I think I need some
air. That room gets hot."

Her aunt raised her eyebrows. "It's broiling outside," she pointed out.

"Yeah, but at least it's real air. Not stuffy, indoor air."

"You don't need to worry about the kittens," her aunt said. "Did you
forget that I'm the original cat lady?" She flashed a smile at Lara.

"Oh, I could never forget that." Lara plunked a kiss on her aunt's cheek,
inhaling her light, floral scent.

Heart in her throat, she hopped inside the Saturn and headed in the
direction of Loudon Street. This time she knew exactly where to go.

Chapter Thirty-Two

Less than ten minutes later, Lara pulled up in front of Evonda's Cape Cod–style home. It really was a lovely residence. Aside from the massive crow on the front door, it looked like any other well-kept house. Evonda had kept her place in pristine form, from the neatly trimmed lawn to the graceful front entrance. The light gray steps with their white risers looked freshly painted. If Tim decided to sell, he wouldn't have any problem finding a buyer.

Except for the fact that a murder had been committed in the driveway.

Grateful for the swatch of shade in which she'd parked, she shut off the Saturn's engine. Something nagged at her, some silly thing she should have remembered. She squeezed her eyes shut and tried to lasso it into her memory. But whatever it was, it had already flitted away.

The driveway was empty, so she was the first one here. If Tim didn't arrive soon, she'd have to start her car and run the AC. On a day like this, the car would stay cool only for a short time, even in the shade.

From the depths of her tote, her cell pinged with a text. Lara fished it out. It was from Tim.

Got held up. Key undr frog. Go inside. I'll B there in 10.

Lara blew out a sigh. *Really?* she thought. She was tempted to drive away, to let Tim know that she didn't have time for this today.

She glanced at the house again. Curiosity tugged at her.

"Under the frog," she mumbled, shaking her head. What kind of a security system was that?

Sliding her cell into her pocket, she grabbed her tote, locked the car, and went up the front walk. Sure enough, a concrete frog crouched on the bottom step. Had it been there yesterday? She couldn't remember.

Lara lifted the frog and saw a brass key. *Unbelievable*. She scooped the key into her hand and climbed the stairs.

What if a neighbor sees me? she suddenly wondered. *What if someone calls the police?*

She quickly turned the key in the lock. The door opened smoothly, as if it had recently been oiled. Cool air instantly caressed her face. She was glad Tim had left the AC on, although it seemed like a waste of energy in an unoccupied house.

Lara closed the door but left it unlocked. She found herself in the foyer adjacent to the dining room. A faux mahogany coatrack rested in the corner, a black umbrella dangling from one of the pegs.

It's too quiet in here, she thought with a shiver. If Tim didn't arrive soon, she was going to text him that she couldn't wait any longer and bail on him.

But first she wanted a peek at the crow. Or the "krahe," as it was called.

Careful not to disturb anything, she went into the dining room. The photos Tim had been sorting the day before were gone. Had he packed them all up?

Against one wall, several more boxes sat atop one another. Tim had obviously done more packing after she'd left yesterday. From the sideboard, the wooden crows seemed to be watching her every move.

Shaking off the notion, Lara looped her tote over the back of a chair and gazed around. The print was still there on the wall—"Krahe."

She wanted so badly to remove it from the wall. She wanted to study it more closely.

Something about the painting drew her to it, like a moth to an open flame.

The crow itself fascinated her, with its feathers drawn up around its neck like a cape, its feet clad in a pair of witchy-looking boots. Most haunting was the crow's wide-eyed, almost mesmerizing stare—the small eyes that seemed to blaze into the depths of the human soul.

Okay. She couldn't stand it anymore. Tim had texted that he wanted her help, right? That he trusted her judgment?

Lara reached up and with both hands removed the print from the wall. The ornate gold frame gave it some weight, so she carried it carefully. She pulled out a dining-room chair, sat down, and rested the painting on her knees.

Oh, if only I could paint like this, she thought with a twinge of envy.

Lara reminded herself why she was there. In the moments before Evonda was murdered, she'd texted three letters to her son: K-R-A.

If Lara was right, there was something special about this print. Something that Evonda wanted Tim to figure out. What was it?

Then it struck her. The children's story—*Cary the Crow and the Hidden Spoon*. In the book, the crow had used his nest as a hiding place for his treasures. Had Evonda done the same with her favorite crow? Used it as a hiding place?

On a hunch, Lara ran her hand along the back. Her fingers slid under the wire hanger, and she felt something crackle.

She flipped over the print and rested it facedown in her lap. A pocket made from brown wrapping paper had been affixed to the back. Bulging slightly, it was held in place by masking tape on all four sides.

Heart thumping, Lara slowly peeled back the top strip. With two fingers, she reached into the gap and pulled out the contents. She found herself staring at a small stack of professional-quality photos.

The first snapshot was of a low, rectangular building with a flat roof. Beneath each of its two windows were wooden boxes, painted white, dotted with newly planted petunia plants. A sign flashing from its roof identified the building as The Roundup Tavern.

In the next pic, Jenny Fray was emerging from the driver's seat of a dark-gray sedan. The photo had been taken in a parking lot, presumably behind The Roundup.

The next photo captured the image of a man standing beside a pickup, the door of which was half-closed. In the next shot, the man was approaching Jenny, a grin stretched across his features. The pictures were crisp and clear, taken from a distance with a zoom lens.

No. Please. It can't be…

One by one, Lara flipped through the pics, her stomach growing sicker with each image.

The next several photos were of Jenny and her lover, locked in various stages of an intimate embrace. The pictures had been taken in the daytime, so there was no mistaking their identities.

"Oh!" A noise from the back porch made Lara jump. Was that the door closing?

"Lara?" a man's voice called out.

Her heart weighted with sadness, she cleared her throat and said, "In here, Tim." She shoved the photos back inside the makeshift hiding place. No way she could hide them now. Like it or not, she'd have to show them to Tim.

His footsteps grew closer as he came through the kitchen. Hands on his hips, he grinned at Lara from the doorway to the dining room. "Hey, you got here pretty quick. Did you find what you were looking for?"

Lara felt her face drain of color. "Ch–Charlie. What are you doing here?"

Charlie Backstrom's brown eyes hardened. "I'm here to see you, Lara. I have a feeling you found the secret treasure."

Chapter Thirty-Three

Lara forced a smile. She wiped her hand discreetly over her pocket to be sure her cell was still there. "What do you mean? There's no treasure here. How did you even get in?"

Charlie pulled out a dining-room chair, straddled a corner, and sat down hard. The legs creaked under his weight. Ignoring Lara's question, he circled his gaze all around the dining room. "Man, that woman was batcrap crazy, wasn't she? First time I ever walked in here and saw all these freakin' crows, I thought, *cripes, I'm in a Hitchcock movie.* You know the one I mean, right?"

Lara nodded, afraid to take her eyes off him.

"I should've known you'd unlock the secret code," he said with a wink. "In school, you were one of the smart ones. Not *the* smartest, but you were up there."

School?

"What are you talking about, Charlie? We were never in school together."

He shook his head, disgust flaring in his eyes—eyes she couldn't believe she'd once found attractive. "That day, when I first showed up at your place to go over the construction specs, I figured you'd say, 'Hey, Chuck L., I remember you from middle school! How ya doing?' But you didn't."

Lara shook her head, but then, slowly, it all came back.

In middle school, there were two Chucks in her class—Chuck L. and Chuck M. That was how the teachers kept their names straight.

She thought back to the photo, the one her aunt had found of Lara's sixth-grade class.

Oh God...

Chuck L. The skinny, closed-mouth boy standing in front of the blackboard, a crutch propped up behind him. He'd broken his leg and it hadn't healed properly. Jenny Fray—Jenny Cooper, then—felt sorry for him and insisted on helping him to class. Small and shy, she carried his books for him, every day, for weeks. The two became almost inseparable.

"Come on, Charlie," Lara said, again forcing a smile, "you don't look anything like you did then. Look at you now! Handsome, strong—"

"Stop the bullcrap, Lara. Whatever you were trying to hide before I came in, hand it over."

Lara looked down at the print, still resting on her knees. She pulled the photos out of the hidden pocket and gave them to Charlie.

He flipped through them quickly, his face reddening with anger. "Evonda showed me these, but then she hid them. I never had a chance to look for them. She was always hovering over me, ragging on me, telling me I was doing everything wrong. Jenny looked for them, too, but she never found them. And all this time, they were right there. If only I'd known."

It wouldn't have mattered, Lara knew. Evonda had been a photographer. She could have made new prints.

Glaring at her, Charlie shoved the photos into his shirt pocket and looked around at the walls. "I built all these shelves, you know. I painted them three different times before that witch was satisfied. And those front steps? Did you notice them?" He lifted his chin toward the front entrance.

"I did," Lara said. "They're beautiful."

"Should've been a one-day job. Took me three before the evil queen was satisfied."

"Well, they—" Lara stopped short, choking on her own words, and in the next instant she got it. "Evonda was blackmailing you, wasn't she, Charlie? She found out you and Jenny were having a fling. She took pictures and threatened to expose both of you."

"Blackmail?" Charlie's laugh was harsh. "Yeah, I guess you could call it that. Evonda had a different term for it. She called it an 'exchange of services.'" He put air quotes around the words. "Said it was purely a business deal."

"And her service was keeping her mouth shut."

It was all starting to make sense, now. That day when Nina said she couldn't locate Charlie. He was at Evonda's—doing work for her under the threat of her exposing his affair with Jenny.

"Who paid for the materials, Charlie?"

"She did. No way I could, not with Nina watching the books like a hawk. I'd pick them up at the supply store real early in the morning, then drive them to her house and unload them. I told her I couldn't risk my truck being seen there all day, so she'd follow me back to the supply store and I'd park my pickup in the corner of the lot. After she decided I'd done enough work for the day, she'd drive me back to my truck." He swallowed, and Lara saw the shame in his eyes. "Nina knew something was up, but she didn't know what. I had to lie and tell her I was doing charity work for people."

Lara shook her head. "Evonda used you, Charlie. What I don't understand is why. Why you had a fling with Jenny when you have a wonderful wife who adores you."

His eyes turned glassy. "*Used* to adore me. Things started to change between us. Her family never accepted me. After a while, Nina started to wonder if they were right. I could see her drifting away from me."

"I don't believe that," Lara said, trying to sound soothing. "I've seen you two together."

"What you saw was a lie," he said. "Funny thing is, for a smart gal, you were one of the easiest ones to fool."

"Where did you first run into Jenny?" Lara asked him. "At the Roundup?"

His eyes flashed, then his body slumped. "I started going there more and more, drinking with my buddies. Then this one night, Jenny came in with a girlfriend of hers. It was unreal. Even after all those years, she recognized me." He hung his head. "We sort of...got reacquainted. We started to rendezvous there during the daytime. That was Jenny's favorite word—rendezvous. She said I've always been her hero, that she's loved me since we were kids."

Outside, in the driveway, a car door slammed.

Tim. Thank God.

"Charlie," Lara said, light suddenly dawning, "how did you know I was coming here?"

He laughed and shook his head. "You texted Tim, right? Well, a little bird intercepted the text while her hubby was in the shower. Lucky thing, huh? I guess that's why they say timing is everything."

The sound of light footsteps drifted from the kitchen. Then a pale, unsmiling face appeared in the doorway. Dressed in short shorts and a frilly halter top, she looked almost too young to drive.

"Hi, Lara," Jenny Fray said. "By the way, Tim won't be getting your text. I deleted it from his phone. I also let the air out of both his front tires, so he won't be stopping by any time soon."

Lara felt every cell in her body morph into pudding.

That's it. That's what was bugging her.

Tim's text yesterday was written in full sentences. But his responses today were in textspeak. Lara should have caught it sooner.

His unflinching gaze still fixed on Lara, Charlie pulled the photos out of his pocket and handed them over his shoulder to Jenny. "She found them."

With each photo she viewed, Jenny's white face turned grayer. "My God," she said. "These are close-ups." Her eyes flitted to the *Krahe* print resting on Lara's knees. "So all this time, they were right there…" She moved closer to Charlie and laid a hand on his shoulder.

He shook her off. "Get away from me. I told you, it's over. It ends now, today."

Jenny shook her head. Tears blossomed in her eyes. "No! You don't mean that, Charlie. We were meant to be together—"

"No, we were not," he spat out. "I love Nina. You were there for me when I was hurting, but I'm past that now. I want things to be the way they were with my wife, before you ever walked into that place. I want my life back!"

Jenny sobbed and shook her head. "Don't say that. You don't mean it."

"You let the air out of my tires. Out of both our tires!"

"I–I was only trying to get your attention," Jenny blubbered. "I hadn't heard from you in a couple of weeks. You were ignoring me!"

He shook his head. "Geezum, you still don't get it, do you?"

"And yesterday," Lara said, "you tailed me. Didn't you, Jenny?"

Jenny pouted. "I came over here to see how Tim was doing—I was afraid he might stumble on those photos while he was packing—and I saw your car pull away. I wasn't sure who it was, so I followed you. Big deal."

A knot formed in Lara's abdomen. Tiny, jagged pieces of a murderous puzzle began falling into place.

Nina holding Pearl, then petting Snowball.

Charlie picking lint off Nina's pink jersey.

No, not lint. Cat hair.

Lara pulled the *Krahe* print closer to her waist and then slipped her hand inside her pocket. She took in a quiet breath. "But you can't get your life back, can you, Charlie? Because you took the straps from the box our door came in, and you used one of them to kill Evonda."

Jenny's eyes widened in horror. She backed up against the sideboard, jostling it with such force that the wooden crows rocked. "You're insane. Charlie wouldn't kill anyone."

Charlie's face went slack, and he spoke in a monotone. "I heard that witch's voice that day, that awful cackle, coming from your living room. She didn't know I was there because we'd taken Nina's car, remember, Lara?"

Lara nodded. It all came back.

His eyes glazed over. "It hit me then, how I could get rid of her and plant phony evidence. While you were still talking to her, I took those bands from the box, rolled them up, and stuck them in my pocket. Nina didn't even notice. She thought I was setting the box outside to get it out of your way."

"And when you were leaving, you picked a wad of stray cat hairs off Nina's jersey. You must've stuck that in your pocket, too, didn't you, Charlie? It was the perfect way to throw off the cops—leaving the cat hair in Evonda's car. Making me and my aunt look guilty."

He laughed, a demented sound that chilled Lara's veins. "Know what the best part was? Stuffing that ugly sneaker in her mouth. Shutting her up for good. I had work gloves on, so I didn't leave prints."

Lara's fingers curled around her cell phone. "Right now, an innocent man is sitting in jail, Charlie, taking the heat for your crime. What did you do? Go over to Downing's apartment and drop one of those plastic bands next to his SUV?"

Charlie shrugged. "It worked, didn't it? It wasn't hard to figure out who the cops were homing in on, and where he lived. Small-town gossip—you know how it is. After I planted that plastic band near his car, I called in an anonymous tip and sent the cops chasing another wild goose. Don't worry. All he needs is a good lawyer and he'll beat the rap."

Releasing a high-pitched squeal that nearly pierced Lara's ears, Jenny slid to the floor and collapsed. She curled into a ball, burying her face in her hands. Harsh sobs racked her small frame.

Lara knew her time was running out. She slid her cell out of her pocket, then located Gideon's most recent text and tapped the response box. She managed to tap out Code BL before Charlie tore it out of her grasp.

"Hey, what do you think you're doing?" He stared at the phone, panic filling his eyes. He jabbed frantically at it with his finger. "How do you turn this thing off?"

Charlie cursed violently, then threw Lara's phone across the room. It bounced off the wall and clunked to the floor.

Lara flung the *Krahe* print off her lap and flew off her chair, making a desperate dash for the front door. Charlie tackled her, knocking her to her knees with a thud. She cried out, and Charlie grabbed her hair.

"Let go of me, Charlie!" She reached behind her and raked his hand, but it was like clawing hardened steel.

In the next instant, there was a loud crash and the sound of shattering glass. Startled, Charlie swung around, momentarily releasing his grip.

Lara turned toward the sound. Above the sideboard, a flash of cream-colored fur careened across the top shelf, sending porcelain crows of every size sailing off the edge. The lower shelf had already been decimated.

Blue wasn't finished. From floor level, she leaped onto the shelf on the adjacent wall, batting every crow off the edge as if she were enjoying a pleasant game of ping-pong.

Only Lara could see Blue, which elevated Charlie's horror. He stared at the carnage, his face whiter than salt. He dropped to his knees and started to cry, just as Jenny went deathly still. "Go away, Evonda! Leave me alone," he wept, rolling onto his side.

Lara left him whimpering on the floor and raced outside toward her car. Her tote and her phone were still in the house. The Saturn was locked.

She looked around frantically. Save for the buzz of a lawn mower, the neighborhood was as silent as a cemetery.

Across the street and down a short distance, a man wearing headphones was mowing his lawn. Lara ran over and waved her arms at him. "Please! I need help."

The man, his belly straining his white T-shirt over a pair of plaid shorts, paused the mower and lifted the headphone off his right ear. "Sorry?"

"Please call the police," Lara said, raising her voice over the mower's engine. "The man who killed Evonda Fray is in her home right now."

The words had no sooner left her mouth when the screech of tires tore her attention back to Evonda's. Charlie Backstrom was backing his truck out of the driveway at approximately the speed of sound. He roared off, leaving a trail of gray exhaust spewing behind him. Lara prayed to God he hadn't hurt Jenny.

The man shut off his engine. He jerked a cell phone out of the pocket of his shorts and called 9-1-1.

"Thank you," Lara said, her voice shaking hard. "I have to go back to be sure Jenny's okay."

"Not alone, you're not."

They both dashed across the street and hurried inside Evonda's. Jenny was sitting up, leaning against the wall, tears streaming down her face. One thin ankle rested on a shard of black porcelain, a stream of blood oozing from it.

Lara gasped out a breath of relief and dropped to the floor beside her. Shards of porcelain crunched under her legs, while Jenny sobbed into her shoulder. "Oh, God, how could he do that?" she choked out. "I loved him. How could he kill someone?"

The neighbor ran into the kitchen and returned with a heap of dish towels. His hands shaking, he gently lifted Jenny's ankles and rested her legs on the towels. "I–I'm sorry," he stuttered out. "I'm not so good with blood."

Blue lights flashed outside. Within seconds, a pair of uniformed responders were inside the house, checking both women to be sure they were okay. "Ambulance is on its way," one of them said.

"Jenny needs one, but I'm okay," Lara told him.

"Let's wait and see," he said, humoring her.

The next face she saw was Aunt Fran's, striding toward her with outstretched arms. Lara ran to her aunt and squeezed her hard, tears squashing against both their cheeks.

After a few minutes, her aunt still clutching her arm, she was led by the younger of the two officers into a different room—a parlor. Bright and sunny compared to the dining room, it was amazingly bird-free. He steered her over to a flowered sofa and tucked a fluffy lilac pillow under her arm.

"Stay here for a while, miss," the officer instructed kindly. "We'll need to take a statement from you. Can I get you anything? Some water?"

Lara sniffled hard. "No, I'm fine, but you need to find Charlie Backstrom. He killed Evonda Fray and he's getting away."

The officer's jaw hardened. "Believe me, we're on it. He won't get far." He went off to join the others.

"Aunt Fran, how…why, I mean—"

"That text you sent to Gideon. He was just pulling into our driveway when he got it. He'd come over to update us on Brian's arrest, but when he read your text, he ran into the house, wanting to know where you'd gone."

"But you didn't know!"

Aunt Fran fixed her with a mock stern look. "That's right, because you didn't tell me. I had to do a little detective work. I went into your studio and saw your iPad sitting on your table. You must have looked up Evonda's address, because the directions were staring right up at me."

But I didn't look up Evonda's address. I knew exactly where she lived.

"Um…"

"Gideon called the police, and then I jumped into his car and we raced over here. Lara, did I hear you say Charlie Backstrom killed Evonda?"

"He did, but it's a very long story. I'll catch you up on everything later. Where is Gideon, by the way?"

"The police detained him outside. He must be ready to—"

"Lara!"

Gideon covered the distance in one long stride and dropped onto the sofa beside her. He pulled her into his arms and hugged her close. "My God, Lara, are you okay? What on earth happened?"

She gave him a quick summary with a promise to fill in the details later.

Red lights flashed in the window. Lara glanced over and saw the tail end of an ambulance pulling away from the house. She looked down at her hands. "Someone should call her husband."

Gideon nodded. "They will. Don't worry."

A face appeared in the doorway, one Lara had hoped never to see again. She felt her muscles tense.

Wearing khaki Dockers and a green golf shirt, Lieutenant Cutler said, "I'm sorry, but I'm going to need to take Ms. Caphart's statement."

"We'll be waiting right outside," Gideon said, and then left with Aunt Fran.

Cutler sat down in an armchair next to Lara. "I hear you've had quite the afternoon," he said quietly, the kindness in his eyes surprising her.

She took in a shaky breath. "You're right. I have." She looked him directly in the eye. "I don't even know where to begin."

He leaned back in the chair and crossed one leg over the other. "Why don't you start at the beginning?" he suggested. "And we'll go on from there."

Chapter Thirty-Four

The following morning, they sat around Aunt Fran's kitchen table, Lara cupping Fritter to her chest. With one hand, she slid the photo of their sixth-grade class over to Gideon. "Now look at this picture," she challenged, "and see if you can find Charlie Backstrom."

Gideon, clutching Aden to his shirt for dear life, pulled the photo closer. He studied it for at least a full minute, then shook his head. "Nope. I can't pick him out. I do, however, see an adorable girl with curly red hair, freckles on her nose, and an impish smile. Now *that* girl I remember." He faked a puzzled look. "I wonder whatever happened to her."

"Hmmm. Last I heard, she was helping her aunt run a cat shelter. Not to mention driving a local lawyer crazy."

Gideon laughed, and Aunt Fran smiled at their exchange. "So, all this time, Charlie Backstrom was Chuck L. from your class."

"Chuck Larrabee," Gideon confirmed. "I have a pretty good memory, but even I didn't remember that. We never saw him again after sixth grade. He moved to Vermont with his mom and her third husband and took the stepfather's name. It was a transformation for him. Chuck L. becomes Charlie Backstrom. New dad, new school, new friends."

"I know one person who never forgot him," Lara said.

Aunt Fran nodded. "Jenny Fray. Née Cooper."

Two hours after Charlie had tried to escape, the state police pulled him over near the entrance ramp to Route 93. He was arrested without incident, according to Sunday evening's news report.

Lara picked up Fritter with both hands and tucked her gently under her chin. The kitten's tiny mewling sounds clutched at her heart.

She couldn't imagine how Tim Fray was feeling right now. It had to be devastating, learning that his wife had been having an affair with the man who ended up killing his mom.

And then there was Nina. Lara felt terrible for her. Would she stand by Charlie at his trial? Or would she completely wash her hands of him? Either way, their marriage was shattered. Lara had no doubt that Nina's family would welcome her back to the fold—so long as she lived the rest of her life sans Charlie.

There were still a few things about yesterday's nightmare that baffled Lara. Aunt Fran had found her iPad open to the directions to Evonda's house. But Lara was sure she hadn't looked them up. When she'd left to meet Tim yesterday, she knew exactly how to find her way there.

No, something else had been afoot. Or on four feet, to be exact. A guardian cat with powerful protective instincts who'd once again intervened.

There was something else Lara remembered, something that clinched her earlier suspicion. During the chat she'd had with Nina at the clam shack a few nights ago, Nina had mentioned that Charlie still used a flip phone. He was totally helpless with a smartphone.

Lara had never sent her text to Gideon yesterday because she'd never gotten the chance. Unwittingly, Charlie had sent it himself when he was stabbing at her phone, trying to turn it off.

"By the way," Gideon said, "I canceled my appointment with Trevor Johnson this morning. We've rescheduled for Thursday morning."

"He's willing to wait that long?" Aunt Fran reached over and gently took Fritter from Lara.

"Not really, but I didn't give him a choice. He's a strange guy. He's more concerned about getting his job back than he was about being a murder suspect. Talk about single-minded."

A strange guy indeed, Lara thought. *But at least he's not a murderer.*

Gideon and Aunt Fran exchanged glances. "Um, Lara," Gideon said. "Do you know how those figurines ended up smashed all over Evonda's dining-room floor? Jenny Fray insists she had nothing to do with it. When the police pressed her on it, she looked almost frightened."

A flush heated Lara's cheeks. "Jenny never went near those figurines. That much I can confirm." She sent him a meaningful look. "Sometimes things happen out of the blue that we can't explain, right?"

Like the painting of the crow that popped up on her tablet in place of the Renoir.

Gideon gave up a tiny smile. "Message received. Of course, that's not exactly an answer I can take to the state police."

Once again, Lara wondered why Gideon was privy to all the police goings-on. Was there something he wasn't telling her?

Luckily, Cutler had believed her when she gave him her hazy account of how the *Krahe* painting appeared on her tablet. One minute she was looking at *Dance in the Country* and the next a different painting appeared. *Who can make sense of these Web sites?* she'd asked him with an innocent shrug.

Aunt Fran stared at her. "Lara, are you saying that Blue was there yesterday? At Evonda's?"

"She was. She distracted Charlie by knocking all those crows to the floor. He thought it was Evonda's ghost, coming after him from the grave."

"Is that when you ran outside?"

"Exactly. All I knew was, I had to get out of there." She frowned when something else occurred to her. "Gideon, do you think Jenny will be charged with anything?"

"No, I don't think so. She made a bad choice, having an affair with Charlie, but she didn't have anything to do with killing her mother-in-law, or with covering it up."

"Another thing I meant to ask you. Do they know the name of the neighbor who helped me yesterday? I'd like to thank him personally."

"I'll find out for you," Gideon said. "He gave his statement to the police."

"Hey." A tap at the screen door.

Aunt Fran's face brightened. "Brian. Come in, please."

Garbed in cargo shorts and a wrinkled tee, Brian Downing stepped into the kitchen. His face drooped with fatigue, but his eyes shone with the relief of being freed from a murder charge.

"Brian, good to see you," Gideon said. "You're looking much better today."

"Yeah, no kidding. Yesterday I was looking at murder one and today I'm a free man. You helped me a lot, man. Thank you."

"My pleasure." Gideon rose off his chair and transferred Aden to Lara. "Hey, I've absolutely got to run. Today's going to be a little crazy." With a promise to see the women later, he kissed Lara on the temple and waved goodbye to everyone.

Brian smiled and rubbed his hands together. "That's a supergood guy you got there, Lara. Better hold on to him." His smile faded, and his gaze drifted sideways. Was he thinking of his ex-wife?

"Aw, geez, you guys have kittens now?"

"Yep." Lara grinned. "Four new little angels. Hey, can I get you a drink? We were just having some lemonade."

"Nah. Thanks anyway. You guys have done enough. I've been nothing but a big pain in the posterior. I just came to get my dude. And pay you for taking care of him."

The sound of Brian's voice attracted a crowd. A crowd of two, that is. Smuggles lumbered into the kitchen and sauntered over to his dad. Snowball followed close behind, unwilling to let her newly acquired BFF out of her sight.

Brian crouched down and held out his arms. "Hey, big guy, did you miss me?" He swept the gray cat into his arms and hugged him fiercely.

Snowball looked up and meowed. Gazing down at his bestie, Smuggles squirmed in Brian's clutches. "Hey, what's wrong, Smugs? Don't you remember me?"

Lara looked at her aunt, whose brow furrowed in dismay. She knew they were thinking the same thing.

"Brian, isn't this the day you were supposed to move?" Lara asked him.

"That's off the table," he said. "I'm going to work something out with Tim Fray to keep my apartment."

Lara was surprised. "Did you call him?"

"Nope. He called me." Brian distracted Smuggles with a tickle under the chin. "Said it didn't make sense for him to let go of a good tenant. The apartment house is his now, so he can do what he wants."

"Well, that's good news," Aunt Fran said. She looked pointedly at Lara. "Brian, can you spare a few minutes to chat with us?"

His face fell. "Uh-oh. I knew it. Something's wrong, isn't it?"

"No," Lara assured him. "Nothing's wrong. But something's changed. Sit for a few, okay?"

Brian set his cat gently on the floor, then pulled out a chair and sat. Smuggles immediately went over and joined Snowball, who rubbed her chin against his ears.

"You can probably guess," Lara began, "that Smuggles has gotten very attached to one of our shelter kitties." She explained how Smuggles and Snowball had bonded over the past several days. How the two were nearly inseparable.

"Wow. Of all the things you could've said, I never expected that." He drummed his fingers on the table and looked at the pair. They'd flopped together on the kitchen floor like a pair of mismatched rugs. "But now that you say that," Brian went on, "I noticed the change in Smuggles the second he walked into the kitchen. It's almost like…like he got younger while he was here instead of older. I can see it in his eyes."

Lara smiled. "That often happens when a younger cat is introduced to a senior one." She glanced over at the fluffy Ragdoll cat who'd leaped onto the chair next to Brian. Blue gazed up at Brian with heartfelt approval.

A grin split Brian's face. "Well, I think there's an easy solution."

"We think so, too," Aunt Fran said. "But...you'd have to fill out an application, and we'll need to approve it. That means checking references."

Brian's grin slipped away. His face reddened. "Listen, I know the cops talked to some of my coworkers, and I know most of them didn't exactly sing my praises. I get it. I'm not the easiest guy to work with."

"But I'm guessing you weren't always that way," Lara said.

"You're right. My divorce did a number on me. I should've gotten counseling then, but I didn't. I got Smuggles instead." He offered a crooked smile.

"And that was a wonderful thing," Aunt Fran said. "But sometimes it helps to talk to someone, too. There's a lot of good that can come from it."

"I know. When I was sitting in that holding cell yesterday, I got to thinking about stuff like that. I'm definitely going for counseling, as soon as my cats are settled in." Eyebrows raised, he flashed them both a hopeful smile.

"I have a suggestion," Lara said. "Why don't you leave both cats here for a few more days. It'll give you time to work things out with Tim and get ready for a new member of the household."

Brian's smile widened. "Now that's the best idea I've heard all morning. You got yourself a deal."

Chapter Thirty-Five

Lara gazed around the new reading room, unable to stop grinning.

Floor-to-ceiling bookshelves painted sky blue, stocked with children's books, lined two of the walls. Sunlight streamed through the insulated windows that faced the backyard. Large floor cushions and comfy kitty beds nestled among low, child-size chairs.

"I've got goodies," Kayla announced from the doorway. Balancing a tray covered with plastic wrap on one shoulder, she pushed her glasses higher on her nose with the other. She stepped inside and closed the door.

"Oh, they look yummy!" Lara said, taking the tray from her. She set it down on the long table they'd brought into the reading room.

An eye-popping selection of appetizers covered the tray—cherry tomatoes stuffed with goat cheese, antipasto skewers, and other delights. Tucked among them were seedless grapes and rose-shaped radishes. The deli department at the Shop-Along had outdone itself.

"There's another tray in my car," Kayla said. "I'll stash it in the fridge until we're ready for it."

Kayla looked especially nice today. Her lips shone with gloss, and she'd swiped a bit of color over her cheekbones. She wore a loose-fitting pink top over black capris, with espadrilles on her feet.

"Kayla, you look terrific," Lara told her.

"I do?" Kayla blushed shyly at the compliment. "Um, gee...thanks, Lara." She retrieved the second tray and delivered it to the fridge.

With Kayla's help, Lara put together the champagne punch she'd been itching to make. Fruity, golden, and bubbly, it looked like the nectar of the gods in Aunt Fran's cut-glass punch bowl.

Speaking of whom, where was Aunt Fran?

Lara knew her aunt had spent half the morning hollowing out half a watermelon and filling it with melon balls, pineapple chunks, strawberries, and blueberries. Shaped like a basket, it rested on one corner of the table. The other corner boasted a tray heaping with Daisy's cat-shaped sugar cookies.

Kayla glanced through the doorway. "Oh my gosh, Brooke's here already!"

The Westons were one of Lara's favorite families. Brooke Weston was an occasional volunteer at the shelter, when she wasn't off on a babysitting job. Her mom, Heather, and brother, Darryl, strode in holding a wrapped package.

Heather hugged Lara. "Nothing special. Just a few new books," she said, presenting the gift.

"Much appreciated," Lara said. She set it on the floor under the table.

"I can't wait to read to a cat!" Darryl said.

Lara thought back to the day she first met Darryl. In a way, all of this had started with him. He'd struggled to read aloud until a certain Ragdoll cat sat beside him, after which he began zooming through books. It was a while before Lara understood what she'd witnessed that day—the guardian cat no one else could see, who'd been with her since she was a child.

Guests and gifts kept arriving. Brian Downing had declined their invitation, but he'd sent them a generous check. Three days earlier, he'd taken both cats to his apartment. He'd already sent Lara and Aunt Fran about a thousand pictures. Lara missed Snowball horribly, but the sweet white kitty had found her forever home and given Smuggles a fresh outlook on life.

Lara went into the kitchen for some extra napkins just as her aunt came downstairs.

"People are here already?" Aunt Fran said. "I'll have to give myself a tardy check mark."

Her aunt looked radiant in a cabbage-colored silk blouse, white slacks, and emerald-green sandals. Her dark hair, threaded with gray, fanned away from her face in soft waves.

Lara laughed. "No tardy check marks for you, Aunt Fran. You're entitled to a little extra time to gussy up. You look beautiful."

As if the timing had been planned, Chief Whitley poked his head into the kitchen. "Am I too early?"

"Just on time," Aunt Fran trilled with a slight flutter of her hand.

Resisting an eye roll, Lara said, "Come on in, Chief. Whatcha got there?"

He came into the kitchen holding a gift bag the size of a small car. He held it up and looked at Aunt Fran. "If I may…" he asked hesitantly.

Her aunt nodded, and the chief reached into the bag. He extracted several smaller, bright-colored gift bags, tissue poking out of each one. One by one, he set them on the kitchen table. Each one was different, and each had a tag.

Lara read the tags. "Munster, Twinkles, Orca, Pearl…" she said, and looked at him. "There's one for every cat in the house!"

Aunt Fran's green eyes misted. "Oh…" she said and swallowed.

"And one for each of the kittens," Lara added, choked up now herself. She peeked into one of the bags. Each one was stuffed with feline toys and treats.

He shrugged and gave Aunt Fran a sheepish look. "I'm sorry, Fran. I knew you had new kittens, but I didn't know their names."

Aunt Fran laughed and hugged him, and Lara scooted from the room. No way she wanted to intrude on that.

She headed for the reading room, where the noise was amping up. They'd left the connecting door open to the meet-and-greet room to make extra space, but the cats had been banished to the house for the celebration. It wouldn't do to have inquisitive feline noses and paws checking out the food trays and sampling the hors d'oeuvres.

Where was Gideon? He still hadn't arrived. A combination of worry and ire shot through her.

Mary and Chris Newman were there, chatting with Brooke. They'd just returned from vacation and had missed all the craziness with the murder. Mary was grateful, but Chris was disappointed. As a reporter for the local paper, he was sorry he'd missed out on the story of the week. Lara greeted them warmly, and they handed her a gift. At this rate, the shelter would have enough books to fill the Boston Public Library.

Sherry, David, and Daisy arrived holding a gift bag. Inwardly, Lara groaned. Where would they put all the books? After a round of hugs, Lara peeked inside the bag. An antique print of a little girl reading to a black-and-white cat was tucked inside. "Oh, I love it," Lara said. She squeezed her friend hard.

"I can only stay a few minutes," Daisy said, hugging Lara. "Duty calls. The masses must be fed."

"I know how it is," Lara said. "But I'm so glad you made it."

"Lots to tell you," Sherry said, her face bright with joy. "In a little while, okay?"

Lara nodded.

Aunt Fran came in with the chief, and everyone began mingling.

At last, a familiar face came in by way of the meet-and-greet room. Gideon smiled and wrapped Lara in a hug. "Hi, honey. Sorry to be so late. Stuff…happened. Plus, I had to park down the street. It's getting busy here!"

Lara's stomach dropped. "What stuff? Bad stuff?"

"Heck no. It's all good. I'll tell you about it later. But speaking of good—you look fantastic!"

"Well, thank you, kind sir. And for that I'll fetch you a glass of champagne punch."

Secretly, Lara was more than thrilled at the compliment. She'd abandoned her usual casual attire for the sea-blue, jersey knit dress she'd splurged on. A wispy chiffon overlay with a tulip-style hem gave it a touch of elegance, as did her matching tassel earrings. A cat-shaped pendant made from tiny sapphires hung from her neck on a white-gold chain. Gideon had given it to Lara last Christmas, and she treasured it.

Now, of course, she was itching to hear Gideon's news. She knew she'd have to wait till they were alone, but the suspense was killing her.

Munching on a cookie, Lara peeked through the screen door just as another familiar face came up the walkway. Her heart dropped.

Tim Fray.

He stood on the path and glanced around the yard, as if he was debating whether or not to come in. Lara excused herself and went outside.

"Hi, Tim," she said quietly.

"Hey, Lara." He started to take her hand, but then changed his mind and gave her a light hug. "I didn't mean to crash your party, but I just wanted to thank you. For everything." He blinked behind his dark-framed glasses.

"I'm not sure I helped, but I'm glad to see you. How are things going?"

He shrugged. "Okay. I'm wrapping up Mom's affairs. There's a lot more to it than I thought." He gave her a sad smile. "What you really want to know is how things are with Jenny, right?"

Lara felt a guilty flush creep up her neck. "I guess that's part of it."

"I'm sorry to say, we're splitting up. Our marriage is too broken to be repaired."

"I wish none of it had to happen, Tim."

Tim took in a long breath. "Jenny never got over her schoolgirl crush on Backstrom. I guess when she saw him that night at the tavern, it all came rushing back."

And Charlie, whose own marriage was stumbling, gave in to temptation.

"I keep thinking about those photos," Tim said. "I keep asking myself why my mom hid them behind that print. All I can think of is that she must've been saving them for her ace in the hole."

"I'm not sure what you mean," Lara said.

"She'd been trying to talk me into leaving Jenny. Kept saying she was all wrong for me. Mom was biased from the beginning, but at some point, she apparently started following her. Got herself an eyeful when she caught Jenny meeting Backstrom behind that tavern," he added grimly.

"So she took pictures of them and developed them," Lara said, "hoping she'd never have to show them to you. If she could persuade you to divorce Jenny, she could keep them from you forever."

"It sounds crazy, I know," Tim said. "But in a way, it was quintessential Mom, especially the way she hid those pics behind her favorite wall hanging." He shook his head. "Funny thing is, I'd never have remembered the name of that print. You're the one who figured out what K-R-A meant."

And sometimes I wish I hadn't, Lara thought glumly.

But if she hadn't, Charlie might have gotten away with murder.

"Backstrom destroyed most of Mom's treasured figurines," Tim said bitterly. "He must have done it after you ran outside for help. Jenny claims she doesn't remember."

Lara felt her cheeks turning berry red. "Everything happened so fast, Tim—"

"I know. Don't give it another thought." He reached out and touched her arm, then looked toward the house. The celebration was in full swing. "Hey, look, I've intruded long enough. Go back to your party. I just want to say: You're an amazing woman."

"Lara?" Kayla stepped outside and came over to Lara. She handed her a full glass of champagne punch. "I wondered where you'd gone off to. You left yours on the table, so I got you a fresh one."

"Thanks, Kayla." Lara took a sip. "Tim, this is my good friend and our extraordinary shelter assistant, Kayla. Kayla, this is Tim."

Tim stared at her, and Kayla pushed up her glasses. "Very pleased to meet you," he said.

"I...uh...I'm pleased to meet you, too."

Lara quickly intervened. "Unless you're in a hurry, Tim, we'd love it if you joined us. There's plenty of food. Right now, I need to find Gideon, who seems to have vanished. Kayla, would you mind showing Tim around?"

Kayla swallowed. "Oh...gosh, yes. I mean, no, I wouldn't mind." A smile crept across her face.

Lara left the two strolling into the reading room together and went around the house to the kitchen entrance. She tiptoed quietly into the large parlor. Gideon was standing in front of the carpeted cat tree, murmuring in a singsong tone to Orca.

"You're being very mysterious today," she said, coming up behind him. "First you disappear, and now I catch you sneaking in here to play with cats."

Gideon laughed. "Sorry. I'm being rude to your guests, aren't it? I took a fast break and then I noticed Orca staring at me from his perch. I couldn't resist coming in here and playing with him. Remember I told you he can high five? Okay, watch this. Orca," he said, holding up his palm. "High five."

After a few seconds, Orca held up one massive paw. Gideon touched it and said, "High five!"

Lara rolled her eyes and giggled. "Very impressive, but you do realize Orca has six toes?"

"Even better!" Gideon laughed and grabbed her hand. "Come over here," he said, leading her over to the sofa. "I know I've been a bit secretive lately, but I'm ready to tell you my news. Does the name Marvin Dobson sound familiar?"

"Uh, no. Not really," Lara said. "Is he your news?"

"In a way," Gideon teased. "Okay, I won't keep you in suspense any longer. Marvin's been the town's attorney for the past…oh, four or five hundred years, I'd say. Great guy, but way past retirement age. He's finally giving it up and moving to Florida. So…the town needed a new attorney, and they've asked me if I'd accept the job."

"Gideon!" Lara threw her arms around him. "That's great. Such an honor!"

"In this little town, it's only a part-time position," he cautioned, "and my regular workload won't go away. I'm thinking of taking on an assistant, but that remains to be seen." He looked over at the cat tree. "Not to change the subject, but…do you think Orca would be happy living with me?"

"What?" Lara gaped at him. "You want to adopt him?"

"Yeah, I do. Him and Pearl both. They're a package deal, right?"

At that moment, Lara's heart melted. "Gideon Halley, you never stop surprising me." She kissed him soundly.

"Speaking of surprises," he said, "I have more news. This time it's about Trevor Johnson. The town manager reweighed the facts, and he also met with Daisy. He concluded that Johnson hadn't violated any regulations. If the select board concurs, Johnson will be getting his job back."

Lara was stunned. "That's good news, I guess. It'll make his mom happy anyway."

The front door flew open, and Sherry stormed in like a gust of wind, tugging David behind her. "There you two are! I wondered where you disappeared to. We have news to share, and we're not going to wait a minute longer." She looked at David and smiled. "Go ahead, sweetie."

Lara's pulse raced. *This is it.*

David cleared his throat. "Okay, here goes. I have asked Sherry if she would do me the honor of becoming my wife, and she—"

"Accepted!" Sherry thrust out her left hand and squealed.

Lara gasped. A gorgeous oval diamond glittered from Sherry's ring finger. Lara grabbed her friend and hugged her, then did the same with David.

"Wow. Fantastic news," Gideon said, embracing them both. "Congrats to both of you."

"Guys, can I chat with Sherry privately?" Lara said. "It'll only take a minute."

The men nodded, and Lara dragged Sherry into her studio.

"Did this happen last week in Boston?" Lara asked her.

"Yes, but with everything else that was going on, we wanted to wait for the right time to tell you."

Lara pulled out the sketches she'd completed. "In anticipation of this announcement," she said slyly, "I took the liberty of creating four different designs for your wedding invitations. These are pencil sketches, but the real ones will be hand-painted, in watercolor, by yours truly."

Sherry stared at them, covered her mouth, and burst into tears.

"It's okay!" Lara said, "I can change them. We don't have to—"

Sherry threw her arms around Lara, almost knocking her over. "You're the best friend in the whole world, do you know that?"

Lara laughed and cried, and they all went back to the reading room to join the other guests.

It was nearly five when the last guest trickled out. Tomorrow would be the first "read to a cat" day in the new addition. Seven children had already reserved times throughout the afternoon.

To Lara's surprise, Tim Fray was still there. He'd been chatting almost nonstop with Kayla and was apparently in no hurry to leave.

Kayla came over to Lara. "Lara, do you think it would be okay if we brought the kittens in here? Just for a few minutes?"

Grinning, Lara excused herself, and they both dashed upstairs, returning a few minutes later with a large box. Four adorable, furry faces poked their noses in the air.

Everyone gushed over the kittens, and Tim asked if he could hold one.

"This one's Aden," Kayla said, lifting the one kitten she'd named. "After my grandfather."

Tim cupped Aden to his chest. "Gosh, he's a sweetheart. That's a great name, too—very distinguished. It suits him." He looked around bashfully at everyone, then returned the kitten to Kayla. "I have a feeling I'll be coming back here, very soon."

Gideon squeezed Lara's hand.

"Hey, is that what I think it is?" Tim reached up to one of the bookshelves and pulled out a volume. "Yes! This is *Cary the Crow and the Hidden Spoon*. This is a classic. When I was a little kid, Mom read this to me all the time."

Why am I not surprised? Lara thought.

Her gaze traveled over the room. The kittens were nestled in their box. The people she cherished most in the world were all here.

"Okay, find a seat everyone," she said, taking the book from Tim.

Sherry glanced around. "Uh, Lara, these seats are all for kids."

"That's okay. Try to squeeze into them. Either that or stand."

Gideon and the chief opted to stand, while the women dropped onto low chairs. Hands in his pockets, Tim stood beside Lara, his expression soft with remembrance.

Lara opened to the first page. "'Cary the crow,'" she began, "'lived in a giant oak, high above the stone cottage where his favorite humans lived...'"

Acknowledgments

To my editor, Martin Biro, and my agent, Jessica Faust, all I can say is… you both rock! Without you, the Cat Lady Mysteries would have remained a distant dream.

I'm grateful for the entire team at Kensington for their hard work in making the series sparkle in the eyes of readers. From the artwork, to the genius marketing, to the help with social media, thank you all a million times over.

A huge "thank you" to Elizabeth Butcher for naming the golden kitten "Fritter," and a big shout-out to Elise Barrette for contributing the name of her cat, "Aden," to one of the black-and-white kittens.

To my husband, my family, and my wonderful friends, I couldn't have done any of this without you.

Most of all, I thank my readers for embracing the series and for loving cats. It has made all the difference.

If you enjoyed *Claws of Action*, be sure not to miss all of Linda Reilly's Cat Lady Mystery series, including

Feline deadly this Christmas...

Whisker Jog, New Hampshire, celebrates all things Christmas, and few things are more beloved than the town's annual holiday cookie competition. Lara Caphart, who runs the High Cliff Shelter for Cats with her Aunt Fran, is waiting for the green light for a brand-new category: pet-friendly cookies. But when the woman filling in as a last-minute judge dies after sampling someone's Santa-themed treat, Lara's recipe for healthy cat snacks will have to be put on the back burner.

The victim, Gladys Plouffe, was the town's roundly despised former home economics teacher. The chief suspect is the mother of Lara's best friend, who was hell-bent on walking away with the bake-off's cash prize. Cryptic clues from beyond the grave only deepen the mystery, pointing to a cat with striking blue eyes—a cat who bears an uncanny resemblance to Lara's mysterious Ragdoll. As Lara begins a dangerous game of cat and mouse, not even her significant other may be able to stop a perfectly clawful killer from getting away with the purr-fect crime...

Turn the page for a special excerpt!

A Lyrical Underground e-book on sale now.

Chapter 1

"Lara, I need your help," Sherry Bowker said. "I think my mom is about to commit murder. Someone has to stop her, and I've decided that someone is you. You're the one who's had experience with this murder gig. You're the perfect gal for the job."

"What? Me!" Lara Caphart huffed out a breath. "I beg to differ, Ms. Bowker. What you call experience was more like bad luck. *Really* bad luck."

Over the past year Lara had encountered two different murderers. She'd come out of it with her life intact but had no intention of performing any encores.

"Yeah, you *say* that," Sherry said darkly. "But there's something about you. You have a knack for latching on to killers. I don't want my mom to be one of them. Think of it as murder in reverse."

Lara groaned. "I do *not* latch on to killers. Not intentionally, anyway." She went back to the task at hand, namely, untangling a lump of matted fur from Purrcival's silky neck. The sweet-tempered cat with the kaleidoscope markings had a knot that just wouldn't quit.

They sat cross-legged on the floor in the large parlor of the Folk Victorian home in Whisker Jog, New Hampshire, owned by Lara's Aunt Fran. Eleven months earlier, the house had officially become the High Cliff Shelter for Cats. Lara and her aunt had already rescued several cats and placed them in loving homes. The shelter's current feline community consisted of Aunt Fran's own three furbabies, a feral male, and four kitties that were rescued over the summer.

"First of all," Lara said, smiling at what she hoped was her friend's grand exaggeration, "I can't picture Daisy Bowker killing anyone, let alone killing David's mom. Second of all—"

"But that's just it! She's been doing things *so* out of character lately. Even David has noticed it." A slight flush tinged Sherry's cheeks. "He's worried that *his* mom is becoming a bee in *my* mom's bonnet. He doesn't know how to stop his own mom without hurting her feelings."

Sherry had been seeing David Gregson for about five months now and still wore the glow of having found the so-called perfect man. Lara thought it was way too early in the relationship to make that assumption. Still, she was happy for Sherry's newly minted romance. She hadn't seen such joy in her friend's eyes for a very long time.

Lara liberated the furry knot from the soft-bristled brush and wrapped it in a paper towel. She kissed Purrcival's head and released him from her grip. He rubbed his face on her chin, then padded away to score some extra love from Sherry. Sherry took the cat in her lap and stroked his mat-free fur.

Sherry groaned. "It's all about the cookies, Lara. Mom and Loretta each got an email three days ago. They're both finalists in the Whisker Jog Annual Cookie Challenge. I'm so bummed. I was praying Loretta wouldn't make the cut."

"Okay, well, that doesn't sound so bad," Lara said. Except she knew that Daisy was putting all her hopes on winning the contest this year. She'd placed second three years in a row. This year she had her heart set on winning the thousand-dollar prize from the sponsor, The Bakers Thryce Flour Company. As for Loretta, Lara wasn't so sure about her intentions. She didn't really know the woman.

Sherry sank her fingers into Purrcy's soft fur. The cat closed his eyes and purred. "You don't get it, Lara. Lately, Loretta's been copying everything Mom does. Last week she got a new hairstyle that looks suspiciously like Mom's. Short in the back, longish on the sides, with a single blond streak. She's like, you know, almost stalkerish!"

"That only means she admires Daisy," Lara pointed out, though the image of a woman in her fifties copying another woman's hairdo gave her a slight chill. "You should be happy."

"I should be, but I'm not. It means she's competing with Mom. I'm not sure *what* she's competing for, but she's in the flippin' cookie contest. I didn't even know she'd entered, and now she's one of the thirty finalists!" Sherry pulled a strand of her raven-black hair into her mouth and chewed the ends. Lara hadn't seen her do that since grade school.

"I hear you, Sher. And I'm not trying to dismiss your feelings. But trust me, Daisy won't do anything crazy, even if David's mom is driving *her* crazy."

"Maybe not," Sherry said grimly. "But you'd better be there. Just in case." Her shoulders sagged. "Unfortunately, there's one more thing that will *not* make Mom happy."

"Uh-oh."

"Yeah. Uh-oh. I just found out this morning that Gladys Plouffe, my old home ec teacher, is going to be one of the two judges. She's a last-minute sub for the music teacher, who fell down the stairs two days ago and broke both her ankles."

"You mean...the Plouffeinator?"

"You remembered," Sherry said dismally. "And you never even met her!"

"I remember you telling me about the abominable Miss Plouffe," Lara said. "Among other lovely names, you called her a witch of a...well, you know."

"She tormented me in school, Lara," Sherry said. "Gave me Ds for no reason except that I couldn't, *to save my life,* thread that stupid sewing machine. Back in the day, Mom had more than a few screaming matches with her. I'm dreading Mom finding out that she's a judge."

"Does the...does Miss Plouffe still teach home ec?"

"She did until a year ago. Finally, *finally* the witch retired. But she had clout in that school, Lara. No one's really sure why." Sherry's eyes took on a glazed, faraway look. "I can still see her, sitting alone in her room chomping on a ham sandwich. She never ate lunch in the teachers' lounge, probably because none of them could stand her. I can't think of one friend she ever had in that school."

"Maybe she has dirt on someone," Lara joked.

Sherry didn't smile. "Has to be something. Anyway, you have to be at that competition next Saturday to keep a close eye on Mom."

"Sher, I think you're overthinking it, but I'll definitely be there. I mean, who loves cookies more than I do?"

Sherry gave up a tiny smile. "Probably only Santa Claus."

* * * *

Lara hadn't told anyone, but she'd tried entering the contest herself. Not with people cookies, but with cat cookies.

Cookies for cats, that is.

The yearly cookie event was sponsored by The Bakers Thryce, a privately owned flour company founded at the end of World War II by one of Whisker Jog's most beloved entrepreneurs—Holland Thryce. The business flourished until Holland's sons, Tate and Holland, Jr., joined the company. It wasn't long before all three had a falling out. Tate left with a bitter taste in his mouth, while Holland and his elder son continued with the business. Not long after Holland Jr.'s son, Todd, was born, he and his wife died in a boating accident, leaving the child in the care of his grandparents.

As for Holland, who'd long since rolled out his last mound of cookie dough, his legacy thrived. His grandson, Todd Thryce, had carried the company into the twenty-first century by stubbornly refusing to go public. He'd also moved the company's offices to a prestigious New York address.

None of which meant anything to Lara. It was the cookies and the contest she cared about.

She bit her lip and frowned. The letter she'd received ten days ago from the company was signed by Thryce's personal assistant, Alice Gentry. Lara's suggestion that a pet-friendly cookie category be added to the lineup was soundly, if politely, denied. "You may enter cookies that *look* like cats," Ms. Gentry had crisply stated in the letter, "but not cookies that are *for* cats."

The letter went on to say that if such a category were added, there would be no fair way to judge the entries. They couldn't exactly ask the judges to taste cookies made from tuna, pumpkin, and boiled chicken livers.

Lara had to admit, they had a point. But that got her brain cells fired up. She came up with a way the cat cookies could be judged...and encourage cat adoptions at the same time. She only wished she'd thought of it before she sent off her letter to the company.

There was one more thing she could do, she decided. The contest was held each year in the gymnasium at Whisker Jog High School. In the opposite wing of the school, in the cafeteria, those who didn't make the cut could offer their cookies for sale. The proceeds went to the local food bank.

She sat at the kitchen table and booted up her tablet, the scent of cloves and cinnamon wafting around her. Aunt Fran had made a pot of mulled cider. It simmered on the stove, making the room smell heavenly.

For some reason, the internet connection took forever. After what seemed like several minutes, Lara tried to pull up the Web site for the cookie competition. Another long wait. When the site finally came up, she smiled.

"You look intense," Aunt Fran said, coming up behind her.

"Ach!" Lara jumped. "I didn't even hear you. You're quieter than a cat sometimes, you know that?"

Her aunt winked at her. "The easier to spy on you, my dear," she said in a mock evil voice. On her shoulder, a small white cat with one blue eye and one green eye perched contentedly. The cat peered around the kitchen, her pink nose lifting at the scent.

Lara smiled and held out her arms to the cat. Snowball leaped softly onto her lap and rubbed against her snowman-themed sweater. Lara bent and kissed the little feline's soft white head.

"What do you think about this?" Lara asked her aunt. "What if I make my cookies for cats and sell them at one of the tables in the school cafeteria? According to the Web site, there are three tables left, and they're up for grabs. It'll only set me back ten bucks for the day."

"Go for it," Aunt Fran said. She pulled two Santa-shaped mugs out of her cupboard and set them on the counter. "You might start a whole new trend."

Lara tapped at her tablet. The connection was slow, deathly slow. It took a few minutes to get to the page where she was able to reserve a table.

Aunt Fran set a mug of spicy warm cider on the table, behind Lara's tablet. "Thanks," Lara said distractedly. "Now I'm having trouble getting onto Google. The Wi-Fi's acting wonky. It has been all day."

Her aunt sat down adjacent to her. She wrapped her hands around her own mug and then took a slow sip.

"What are you trying to find?" Aunt Fran asked.

Lara grinned. "Cookies for cats. I want to find a recipe that I can tweak and make into my own. It'll be so much fun to experiment."

"You've only got another week," her aunt warned.

"Don't remind me," Lara said wryly. After Thanksgiving was over, the days leading up to Christmas seemed to fly by on speedy little reindeer hooves.

"Darn." Lara scowled and swiped at her tablet. The Wi-Fi was definitely acting up. Finally, she set aside her tablet and pulled her mug closer. The moment her lips touched the warm cider, she felt a smile creep across her face. "Yum," she said, after taking her first sip. This is positively scrumptious."

"Thank you." Aunt Fran looked pleased.

"You know what? I think I'll go to the library. I'll bet they have a book or two on pet-friendly recipes. Plus, I'll get to see that adorable Santa scene they set up every year."

"Sounds like a plan," Aunt Fran said. "When you were a kid, you loved that display. I used to have to drag you out of there before we got locked inside the library."

Munster chose that moment to stroll into the kitchen. An orange-striped cat with big gold eyes, he was one of the original feline residents before Aunt Fran began taking in rescues. A lovable darling, he looked miffed at the sight of Snowball nestled atop Lara's flannel-lined jeans. He promptly turned up his nose at her and plopped onto Aunt Fran's lap.

Lara laughed. She drank the rest of her cider, then said, "And I have to let you go, Snowball, so I can pop over to the library." She gave the white cat one more kiss and set her gently on the floor.

Across the table, a sudden movement caught Lara's eye. A fluffy, cream-colored cat with chocolate brown ears sat gazing at her. Her eyes were the bluest Lara had ever seen on a cat. The Ragdoll cat blinked once, then rested her chin on the table. A sure sign that Lara was on the right path.

You want me to make those cat cookies, don't you? Lara asked silently.

The Ragdoll—Blue—blinked again. In the next instant she was gone.

About the Author

Photo by Harper Point Photography

Raised in a sleepy town in the Berkshires, Linda Reilly has spent the bulk of her career in the field of real estate closings and title examination. It wasn't until 1995 that her first short mystery, "Out of Luck," was accepted for publication by *Woman's World Magazine*. Since then she's had more than forty short stories published, including a sprinkling of romances. She is also the author of *Some Enchanted Murder*, and the Deep Fried Mystery series, featuring fry cook Talia Marby. Linda lives in New Hampshire with her husband, who affectionately calls her "Nose-in-a-book." Visit her on the web at lindasreilly.com.

The meow of death . . .

Whisker Jog, New Hampshire, is a long way from Hollywood, but it's the place legendary actress Deanna Daltry wants to call home. Taking up residence in a stone mansion off Cemetery Hill, the retired, yet still glamorous, septuagenarian has adopted two kittens from Lara Caphart's High Cliff Shelter for Cats. With help from her Aunt Fran, Lara makes sure the kitties settle in safely with their new celebrity mom.

But not everyone in town is a fan of the fading star. Deanna was in Whisker Jog when she was younger, earning a reputation for pussyfooting around, and someone is using that knowledge against her. After being frightened by some nasty pranks, Deanna finds herself the prime murder suspect when the body of a local teacher is found on her property. Now, it's up to Lara, Aunt Fran, and the blue-eyed Ragdoll mystery cat Lara recently encountered to collar a killer before another victim is pounced upon . . .

Here, killer, killer, killer . . .

For the first time in sixteen years, Lara Caphart has returned to her hometown of Whisker Jog, New Hampshire. She wants to reconnect with her estranged Aunt Fran, who's having some difficulty looking after herself—and her eleven cats. Taking care of a clowder of kitties is easy, but keeping Fran from being harassed by local bully Theo Barnes is hard. The wealthy builder has his sights set on Fran's property, and is determined to make her an offer she doesn't dare refuse.

Then Lara spots a blue-eyed ragdoll cat that she swears is the reincarnation of her beloved Blue, her childhood pet. Pursuing the feline to the edge of Fran's yard, she stumbles upon the body of Theo Barnes, clearly a victim of foul play. To get her and Fran off the suspect list, Lara finds herself following the cat's clues in search of a killer. Is Blue's ghost really trying to help her solve a murder, or has Lara inhaled too much catnip?

Printed in the United States
by Baker & Taylor Publisher Services